Allee Richards' short fiction has been published widely in Australian literary magazines and anthologies, including *Kill Your Darlings*, *The Best Australian Stories*, *New Australian Fiction*, *Best Summer Stories*, *The Lifted Brow*, *Voiceworks* and *Australian Book Review*. *Small Joys of Real Life* is her first novel. It was shortlisted for the 2019 Richell Prize for Emerging Writers and the 2020 Victorian Premier's Literary Award for an Unpublished Manuscript. She lives in Melbourne and works as a theatre lighting technician.

Small Joys of Real Life

Allee Richards

hachette
AUSTRALIA

For Mum

The author acknowledges the following quoted material: *p. 91*: William Shakespeare, *Much Ado About Nothing* in *The Complete Works*, Michael O'Mara Books Limited, London, 1988; *p. 227*: Zadie Smith, *Swing Time*, Penguin Random House UK, London, 2017.

hachette
AUSTRALIA

Published in Australia and New Zealand in 2021
by Hachette Australia
(an imprint of Hachette Australia Pty Limited)
Level 17, 207 Kent Street, Sydney NSW 2000
www.hachette.com.au

Copyright © Allee Richards 2021

A catalogue record for this book is available from the National Library of Australia

ISBN: 978 0 7336 4547 1 (paperback)

Cover design by Alissa Dinallo
Cover image courtesy of Shutterstock
Author photograph courtesy of Karin Locke
Text design by Bookhouse, Sydney
Typeset in 12/17.7pt Simoncini Garamond by Bookhouse, Sydney
Printed and bound in Australia by McPherson's Printing Group

MIX
Paper from
responsible sources
FSC
www.fsc.org   FSC® C001695

The paper this book is printed on is certified against the Forest Stewardship Council® Standards. McPherson's Printing Group holds FSC® chain of custody certification SA-COC-005379. FSC® promotes environmentally responsible, socially beneficial and economically viable management of the world's forests.

THE FIRST TIME I MET you was unremarkable. We were at the Clarke Street house, this June just gone. All my friends were there, plus Travis, as he and Renee had started dating. You'd come with Travis. It wasn't a party, just a gathering of us. The nights had become utterly bitter and we'd decided to rechristen the chimenea for another winter. I arrived at eleven, after a show. I was in the dregs of a season and had reached that particular state of delirium where I was sick of playing for even the weirdest laughs. Midway through a show lines that were never meant to be funny – *Pass the milk, Johnny* – are played and played and played, and afterwards the cast laughs about how easy it is to make an audience lose it to anything if you ham it up enough. But I was past that; all that was keeping me going was the knowledge that each act only went for an hour and I could count the number of times I had to do the show again on two hands. I didn't know then that it would be my final show.

You were the first person I saw that night. Standing in the doorway to the kitchen, on the outer of my friends. I passed you on the way to the fridge, where I placed the beers I'd brought. Whatever conversation had been happening moments before was interrupted with the cheer of my name and someone asked me about work. I quoted a line from the script, exaggerated, like a character in a play acting that they're in a play. My friends in the kitchen laughed and I left to go stand by the fire outside. I passed you in the doorway again and you introduced yourself. I shook your hand but didn't bother saying my name as everyone had yelled 'Eva!' when I'd arrived. I found Annie and Sarah in the backyard and I don't remember anything else about that night. Not because I got blackout drunk, which I occasionally did back then – it was just an unremarkable evening.

THE SECOND TIME we met was two weeks later. Gareth Liddiard was playing in the front bar at The Tote. You were there with Travis and Renee and I was with Sarah and James. No Annie, as she wouldn't drink the night before a big week. It was a 'secret show' – one they don't advertise or sell tickets to, but tell people to tell people. The place was steaming with the smell of bodies and beer. We were stuffed from door to door, beanies and coats in hand. A line of people pressed right up against the bar looked like they were standing guard, armed with their pints. This was why when Sarah, James and I saw you three we didn't try to move towards you but just smiled from across the room. Each time the crowd loosened slightly we would shuffle a little closer, and you to us, and eventually I was standing between you and Sarah. I remember Gareth Liddiard saying, 'This is a song about divorce. You've all been divorced, yeah? You're ugly enough to be, anyway.' We all laughed, Sarah the loudest. We were in the middle of the crowd and kept being pushed closer to the stage. People trying to move through the room would get stuck. Beers were held aloft to save them being spilled. More than once, I ended up with a person paused near me, their beer held uncomfortably close to my face. At one point a girl standing in front of us spotted a friend who was standing behind us. This girl reached her hand back between you and me, grabbed her friend and pulled her close. She kissed one cheek, then, when her friend had already started moving away, she pulled her back and kissed the other. 'I just got back from Europe,' she said. You and I widened our eyes at each other, shared a silent laugh. Gareth Liddiard started a new track and at the end of that, while we were clapping lightly, we looked at each other again, exchanged knowing smiles.

The group of us sat in the courtyard that night drinking pints. Beanies and coats back on, shoulders hunched for warmth. There were three smokers, which counted you but not me. Travis announced that you had just started up again and you replied, 'Back with a vengeance.' You were unashamed, rolling new cigarettes with one still smouldering between your fingers. We didn't talk that night, not one on one, but our eyes met often and we nodded at one another's contributions to the conversation. I remember Travis told us about his band. You described their style as 'dreamy metal', which I found hard to imagine, although the fact Travis was in a band was unsurprising – he almost always spoke like he was at a mic. We also talked about the fact that there's a Nicholson Street in Brunswick East so close to a Nicholson Street in Coburg. You said it was because the street once stretched the entire way, until houses were built between the two parts. Otherwise two streets so close together wouldn't be given the same name. I nodded, staring at you. I never know basic, interestingly uninteresting facts like this and I always wonder how other people do.

THE LAST TIME I saw you was mid-July. I was at a party with Sarah. I don't know whose party; Sarah had been invited through someone at work. I hadn't expected to see anyone we knew, but you were there with Travis. He was high, eyes like a possum's, telling everyone how much he loved Renee. The lethal combination of two kinds of ecstasy – the synthetic kind and that of the newly in love. 'She's, like, the coolest girl in Melbourne,' he told me. She broke up with him the following weekend, the poor bastard. But as she would say later, thank God she did it when she did. If she'd waited just two more weeks, she would've been stuck. Nobody wants to dump the bereaved.

I remember asking you, 'Does Travis realise he only ever talks about himself?'

You laughed with your eyes closed, silent. Nodded your head. 'I think he does realise.' There was so much affection in your voice. You shook your empty beer, like rattling a change tin. I drained the rest of mine and followed you to the bathroom. I got fresh beers from my bag and you cut lines on the vanity. That was when I told you how much I hated acting. How when I was younger I'd wanted to be a dancer, but I wasn't flexible enough and everyone told me I had the face and the body for acting. I started to feel the MDMA hot in my arms and face and my sentences were rolling, rambling. 'That doesn't even mean anything, because if you don't have the body for acting you can just not eat or work out or whatever.' I told you how I got my first TV role straight out of school and how ironic it was that most people I went to drama school with were failing auditions while I got all the jobs and I didn't even think I was any good.

'Isn't that exactly why you get them?' you asked.

'It is, it is!'

I tried to steer the conversation to you, but you deflected. At most you offered me one or two comments before you'd shift back to me. I was high so I didn't notice at the time; I just kept talking.

We held hands in the back seat of the Uber on the way to my house, not having kissed yet. We giggled as we walked up my driveway. Sneaked through the house to my room, even though we knew we weren't going to disturb Sarah because we'd left her at the party. We didn't actually kiss until we landed on my bed. Our sex was like our conversation. You went down on me for a long time and when I tried to return the favour you stopped me. 'Just relax,' you said. We sobered up as we did it and afterwards kept talking. Silvery light was peeking in around the edges of my curtains and you told me I needed to quit my job. 'You can't live your life saying you'll get around to doing something you know will make you happy.' You were lying on your back in my bed. Your hands were laced together on the centre of your chest and your eyes were closed. I traced a finger through your pale chest hairs. 'You just have to do it,' you finished.

September

I WAKE TO THE SOUND of the shower running. One and then the other, but almost simultaneously – apples being tipped from a bag – I remember what day it is, what I have to do today, all the facts of my life right now. It's Saturday. I don't have work today. Don't know when I'll have work again. I remember what I do have to do today and I think about the fact that the shower is running. There's only one reason Sarah would be up and ready to go earlier than we have to on this Saturday – because she hasn't slept. I'm still tired. My doona is comforting like the arms of a bad man, warm. I know I have to get up because of where we're going this morning, and also because sleeping more won't help this tiredness.

I think about walking in on Sarah in the bathroom, but I'm sure I'll vomit after I pee, so I go to the backyard and squat. I hitch my oversized t-shirt to my belly – it's white and says *Nobody really cares if you don't go to the party* in large print – and watch as my urine disappears into the grass and then eventually begins to pool there. I've just finished pissing when I begin to gag. I manage to repress it, but then I gag again and vomit. A small bit of bile, maybe half a cup, splatters on top of the foaming piss.

Back inside I put the kettle on then lean against the kitchen sink, head tilted down, looking at my phone in my hand. Sarah opens the sliding door to the kitchen, one hand across her chest holding her bath towel.

'What's wrong?' she asks.

I lift my head and look at her. Realising I'm not upset, just looking down, she turns to leave then almost immediately turns back and says, 'Hi, by the way,' before going to her room and closing the door. She looks pissed off and terrified. She definitely hasn't slept.

I brew coffee and the smell almost gets me. I turn quickly and hang my head over the sink. Small pieces of waterlogged onion and flat-leaf parsley crowd the plughole. I manage not to spew this time. I make Sarah a cup of coffee, very weak. I leave it outside her bedroom door and then I shower myself.

WHEN WE LEAVE for the appointment, it takes ages just to back out of the driveway. It's Saturday and people are going places, like to Bunnings, and whoever designed Thornbury was entirely short-sighted about how many people would eventually live here and how many of us would drive cars. Finally, there's a break in traffic and we get going. I'm driving, because Sarah had amphetamines last night.

'I'm such an idiot.'

'You're human: we're all idiots.'

'Is that a line from a play? You always say it now.'

I don't always say it now, but I did say it once recently when Sarah told me she was sleeping with her ex. And it is especially stupid for her to end up in this state today. A throwback to two years ago, when we were all on the fresher side of twenty-five and Sarah's Facebook name was 'Sissa' and she took antidepressants and ecstasy on alternating days and cried to me and Annie about it a lot. I don't say any of this, though.

'I was only planning on getting really drunk, and then this girl in the toilet offered me a pinga and she was pretty so I just took it. Do you have any water?'

I reach over with my left arm and flick open the glove box. There's a plastic bottle, half full. It's probably very old, most likely given to me on a set.

Sarah has a sip then exhales. She looks sweaty and tired, like she's run a marathon. She looks like shit.

'She probably would've hooked up with me,' she continues, 'but then she was telling me about her shithead boss and then I was helping her draft an email to him and then we sent the email.'

I've often wondered in the past year, since Sarah cleaned herself up somewhat, how I used to manage this. Annie and I would tell each other we were such good people, such selfless friends, to deal with her cycle of going on a bender, crying about her life, showering, repeat. And now I remember it – the joy of this version of her. She'll cry herself to sleep tonight. I'll have to soothe her, lie about it not being that bad, how it's understandable . . . whatever she wants to hear. But Sarah is the only person I know who would get high and help draft a stranger's email to their boss. Laughing now, I'm reminded that I'm not a big person, and that I love her.

'I feel awful.' She pulls her denim jacket over her head and slides down in her seat.

'Look, your baby probably had a sick one last night, getting high, and now it's coming down and it wants to kill itself. You're, like, the best mum ever.'

I turn the radio up and we spend the rest of the drive trying to find a station that plays good music this early on a Saturday. Sarah says, 'I hate this song,' and I change the station. And again, and again. Eventually we arrive without having found one.

We get a park on the street directly in front of the building. In most circumstances this would feel lucky, but luck in this situation feels ominous.

'I can't be bothered.' Instead of unbuckling her seatbelt, Sarah slides even further down in her seat, as though she's trying to slip out of view of anyone in the building.

I switch the engine off and turn to face her. 'You're going to go in there and then it'll be over and we'll go home.'

I skip the part where her uterus is vacuumed.

THERE'S NOBODY HERE. We stand on one side of a glass door, through which I can see a standard waiting room. Padded chairs and ugly patterned carpet. No children's play area, like in other doctors' surgeries. There's a desk, but no woman with a name badge behind it, and a single closed door, which I assume leads to the appointment rooms. I hit the doorbell on the intercom again and again, but nothing happens.

'What the fuck is this?' says Sarah. 'Let's leave.'

'What? And you'll just have a baby?'

Immediately I put my arm around her, regretting my bluntness.

Eventually a receptionist appears. I see her notice that Sarah is crying.

'Is everything okay?' she asks as she unlocks the glass door to let us in.

'Yeah.' I don't know what else to say. *Don't worry, she just had pingas last night and she hasn't slept. The tears aren't about the abortion – we're pro-choice.* 'Sarah Burns.'

We take a seat in the waiting area as the woman goes behind the reception desk and begins typing. Eventually she prints something out and leaves again. I realise she's dressed like a nurse.

'She's on reception and she's a nurse,' I say.

'Maybe the receptionist is hungover and called in sick.' Sarah has her eyes closed, her head leaning back against the wall. It looks like she's steeling herself.

'Maybe the receptionist is the woman from the toilets last night. Maybe it's the boss here you emailed.'

Sarah scrunches her face – a bit of a laugh, a bit of a cry.

When the nurse–receptionist reappears and says, 'Miss Burns?', Sarah looks at me. Any resolve she'd felt moments ago has disappeared; she looks as confident as a guinea pig.

'After this, we get to go home,' I tell her. I'm talking to her like she's a child, but she doesn't object.

She sighs, stands. I reach for her hand, squeeze it. 'Let me know if you need me.' We both know she won't be able to.

This is the first time I've ever been to an abortion clinic and yet when Sarah told me weeks ago that she was pregnant I was surprised at the knowledge I had somehow acquired without ever needing it. I knew abortions were four hundred bucks, but eight hundred if you want to go under. I knew that you should definitely go under. I knew there were two places in Melbourne to get them. And now I'm sitting here and Sarah is getting an abortion and suddenly I realise I have no idea how long this will take. An hour? Two? Five or ten minutes? I think about looking it up but don't, because I don't want to freak out when it takes way longer or shorter than it's meant to. I wait and try really hard not to think about the time I played a swimmer who had to get a backyard abortion in order to compete in the 1956 Melbourne Olympics. I remember stripping down to my undies side-stage so the costume department could scrub fake blood from my legs in the quick-change. There was fake blood down to my ankles. I don't think about this at all.

SARAH SLEEPS AND I promise her I will stay home in case anything happens. I vow to myself I'll have the house cleaned and dinner cooked when she wakes, but we only have bread and corn and I can't go out to get more food without leaving her and I can't do any real cleaning without making a lot of noise. I wipe dust from the leaves of our houseplants and scrub a dark green ink stain of wilted spring onion from the bottom of the vegetable crisper. My phone tells me it's twenty-six degrees today, hotter than it's been in ages. It feels too hot for early spring. I don't actually remember the temperature of this time last year, but I know that if it was this warm a year ago we'd be in the park. I can picture what Edinburgh Gardens must be like right now – a throng of male and female mullets, bikes, eskies, dogs.

I close all the blinds and turn off the lights, keeping the house dark and cool, like we do in the middle of summer. I lie on the couch and wait until I'm needed for something, I don't know what.

Eventually I wake to the sound of the shower, just like I did this morning. I sit up on the couch, uncomfortable, unused to sleeping on my back. I reach for my phone on the windowsill and see it's 7 p.m. I boil the kettle then take two cups of tea to Sarah's room and place them either side of her bed. Before I get in, I lift the doona to check there's no blood on the sheets, which there isn't. When she returns, I'm horrified for a few seconds at how bad she looks, before I remember she didn't sleep last night and she looks about the same as she usually does after a bender – like she's aged ten years overnight. Sarah is one of the most beautiful people I know, except when she's hungover. She has pale skin that looks like porcelain when she powders it but translucent when she hasn't slept. Her red hair is long and thick, but it knots quickly if left unbrushed. Her dark eyebrows are striking when she's made-up but look drawn on, caricatured, when she's not. Her countenance is much like her moods – ugly–beautiful, hot–cold.

I ask her how she's feeling.

'Really shit.'

'Well, that's to be expected.'

She drops her towel and pulls on a t-shirt. For the few seconds her naked body is exposed, I stare at her abdomen, expecting maybe to see a scar, even though I know that's not how it's done.

'Yeah, but it's hard to know what's to be expected because I had an abortion and what's to be expected because I went out last night.'

'Was it fun at least? Who was there?'

'I don't know,' she says at first. 'Renee. Ginnie. Matthew. Travis.'

I feel sick when she says his name even though I'd asked wanting to hear it.

'I can't believe Travis was there, actually.' Sarah leans in close to her mirror, runs her fingers over her face. 'He was all mopey.'

'Understandably.'

'Yeah, I know – so maybe stay home if you're sad your mate died.'

I cross my hands over my abdomen.

When Sarah finishes at the mirror, she turns to me. 'What are you doing?' She's looking at me holding my stomach.

'I'm starving.' This isn't a lie.

'Me too.'

There's a KFC at the end of our street. I don't go there because I'm a vegetarian and actors aren't meant to have fast food pimples. Sarah isn't vego, but maintains she doesn't go because I make her feel bad about it, though I don't remember ever telling her it was disgusting and neither does she. But about twice a year, if there's an emergency situation, we go there together. We call it the emergency department. I offer to go alone this time, but Sarah says she'll come too.

'Maybe a walk will help me.'

I think this is probably true for the comedown, probably not true for the vacuum.

My sense of smell has become so acute that sometimes I think I can smell the fat from the ED when I'm in our backyard. We're only halfway down the street when I first think I might spew. I decide to fill up on chips, reasoning that I should be able to stomach those.

On the walk back, a hot plastic bag in my arms, I'm almost quivering with nausea.

We sit cross-legged on Sarah's bed. She's eating chicken and I'm washing down chips, one at a time, with a sip of water. A record plays softly below our conversation and we don't talk about the abortion. We talk about Sarah's ex who 'did this to her', and we talk about a campaign she's working on that requires her to run an Instagram account for a houseplant. I update Sarah on the situation with my agent. 'She says I'm too famous to sell insurance, not famous enough to sell face cream.'

'I never saw it,' Sarah says. 'Why everyone thought you were a good actor.' She pauses, sucking grease from her fingers. 'Your stage face reminded me of someone looking bored during sex.'

I feel vindicated and offended at once.

Sarah hasn't noticed that I haven't been drinking for the past two weeks, or that I've been vomiting at least once a day and sleeping in the afternoons. She never seems to notice me much, in fact. Only when she berates me for not being home on a night when she wanted company. Mostly friendships aren't like relationships, where you check in and evaluate and worry yourself sick if it's not working. A lot of the time friendships probably aren't working – not in the sense of being toxic and full of screaming (although occasionally they are), but in the sense that they're not doing anything, have been put to rest like a bicycle on a rack. You exist alongside one another, separately. Then one day something happens, like one of you has an abortion or maybe you just get high and you have a conversation where you talk about yourselves, and you realise that all that time spent existing alongside one another, seemingly not caring, allowed some kind of understanding to seep between you. Suddenly you're having this conversation and you realise your friend understands things about you that you didn't and they're presenting you and your life to you in ways you hadn't seen before and you're falling in love with your friend the way you only fall in love at the beginning of a relationship. And it's because of this love, its surprising appearance and depth, that I get swept up in our friendship for a moment and I tell Sarah I'm pregnant.

'Are you kidding?' She gags on her chicken. Wipes her mouth with her palm and then wipes her hands on her sheets.

'No. I'm having a baby.'

'And you're telling me now?'

I was planning on waiting until Annie got back from Japan for this. I was planning on telling Annie first.

'I've been dying,' I say. 'I've been vomiting in the shower with the water running so you wouldn't hear me.'

'I heard you; I just thought you were hungover.'

Even though I haven't had a drink in weeks. I feel a twinge of annoyance, despite all the love I felt moments ago. I listen to the record filling the silence and realise that from now on Jen Cloher will probably always remind me of this day with Sarah.

'Well, I can't lie to you,' she says eventually. 'It fucking sucks. I swear it felt like my cervix was being stabbed with a knitting needle. It was horrid. I'm sorry, but it's your fault for telling me you're pregnant when I'm coming down.'

She went under, so she shouldn't have felt anything. Unless maybe you can still feel something. Or maybe she decided to save four hundred bucks and not go under. I want to ask, but I decide against it for now.

'I'm having a baby, Sarah.' I stare at her eating chips. I keep staring until she stops eating.

'Why?'

'I want to.'

'No, you don't.'

I continue staring at her and I can see the moment she realises what I'm saying. She peers at me, like she's reading fine print on my face. She doesn't say anything, just watches me. I feel sick, maybe because of all the salt or maybe the admission or maybe the foetus. It starts to rain outside, slow and heavy drops. I can hear cars driving fast, and that makes me feel sick too. Sarah takes a breath, about to speak, but then I see another thought cross her face. 'Wait,' she says, although neither of us was speaking. 'Who's the father?'

'It's Pat.'

I'm surprised and a little relieved when I start to cry. I thought women got weepy when they're pregnant, but this is the first time in weeks that I've cried, the last time being five weeks ago, when I suggested to Pat that we see each other again and he said no. Since then, when I cried because I thought he didn't see me as girlfriend material, I haven't cried. Not when I found out he was dead; not when I was told it was suicide; and not after that, when I found out I was pregnant with his baby. I dry my eyes with my palms because my fingers are salty.

'I think the salt is giving me anxiety.'

'Have you told Travis?'

'I'm not going to tell anyone who the father is. Only you and Annie.'

I'd planned to tell Sarah and Annie what I told my mum – that the father was a tourist visiting from overseas – but the lie wilted in my mouth the second Sarah asked me.

If Sarah feels sorry for me, or happy, she doesn't show it. She stands up from the bed.

'Look, maybe I'll tell Travis eventually,' I say. 'I just can't right now.' This isn't true. I know that this is not true at all.

'I'm going to sleep. Move.' She takes the cardboard box of chicken with two hands and places it on the floor. She gets back into her bed and wraps her doona tightly around herself. Clenched in the sheets, her face is hidden, but I can see her forehead is furrowed.

'I thought I'd sleep here with you tonight,' I say, although I'm already getting up.

'The doctor said I might bleed in the night. I don't want to spill my abortion all over you.' She's loud and harsh, her words clear even from under the doona. I'm not sure if it's true about the blood.

When I curl up in my own bed I want to cry again but I'm too pissed at Sarah, so I play the same Jen Cloher album and I stare at the stains on my bedroom ceiling, misshapen circles of damp. When I'd imagined telling my friends I'd pictured them squealing like girls on television, even though we don't often do that.

I channel my frustration into masturbating, give it a good shot for a couple of minutes, but I can't get it going. I haven't been able to do that in weeks either. I haven't cried. I haven't wanked. All I do is feel sick. I refocus my anger on Sarah and eventually, somehow, I feel myself starting to slide into sleep. Pregnancy will do that to you. No matter how angry or worried or busy you are, you're always twice as tired.

I DON'T KNOW IF SARAH disapproves of what I'm doing or if she's mad I stole the attention from her own crisis. I don't know what the rules are for having a dead man's baby and while it feels as though we're all meant to treat abortions like root canals now, I don't know if maybe that's insensitive too. It's easier for me to put up with her being momentarily mad and let it pass than it is to sift through these feelings, so that's what I do. I suspect this is what she's doing too, and that she knows she can only get away with being angry at me for a short while, so she'll make it count.

For a week we live like actors in a play that's been canned by the critics. We hate ourselves and we hate each other and we don't talk about the fact that I'm pregnant, not directly. Sarah complains the toilet smells like vomit so I go outside to throw up. She cooks salmon for dinner every night, which she wouldn't usually do.

'You know there's going to be more plastic in the ocean than fish by 2050,' she tells me, cooking the dinner I can't eat.

I told her this recently.

'The world is fucked,' she finishes.

The fish smells strong and I try hard not to gag.

'Your plant is dead,' she says one night, a response to my asking how her day was. She points to the fern in our lounge. Leaves browning at the edges or speckled with yellow and greying in their centres. She looks me in the eye. 'You killed it.'

I walk in the kitchen and see her reading my copy of *What to Expect When You're Expecting*. She puts it down as soon as she sees me. 'You need vitamin D,' she says.

'I've been sitting outside every morning.' I smile at her.

'Then why are you still so pale?' She goes back to reading my book. The house is quiet. The days are long.

I'm heavy and clogged, haven't shat for days. I google 'taking laxatives pregnant'. I don't even need to open any of the search results to learn that I am constipated because I am pregnant. That's not a side effect they put in a lot of movies. Knowing the cause doesn't put me at ease. I feel twisted up, physically and emotionally. I'm grumpy because I'm constipated. I'm pissed at Sarah for being pissed with me. Sarah is angry with me because I'm pregnant. I'm constipated because I'm pregnant. If I tried to map out the cause and effect of it all I'd end up with mess on a page.

On Friday night Sarah and I mount our bikes in the driveway to ride to Clarke Street in Northcote.

'Ready to go?' I say.

She eyes me critically. 'You're not going to be able to do this soon. You won't be able to balance once you get really fat.'

She rides fast ahead of me, even up the hill on Westbourne Grove that usually we would walk together, bent over, pushing our bikes like prams. Now she stands on her pedals, her arse stuck out behind her, moving side to side. I take my time, arrive long enough after her that our friends might think we've come from different places. I'm afraid of them realising she's mad at me. As though if they realise that they might guess why.

Later, sitting around the fire pit, someone asks why I'm not drinking. I say I have a role as a marathon runner coming up and no more questions are asked. It's amazing how easily people believe you are going about your life being you.

'You better lose some weight then,' Sarah shoots at me across the circle. None of our other friends comment on her comment.

'It's okay,' I whisper to myself back at home, under my doona. 'Annie will be back soon.'

IN THE MORNING I MADE coffees that went cold while we had sex again. We used a condom that time. I remember walking across my room to the dresser to get it and being conscious of you looking at my arse. Conscious in a good way, as it was taut then; I was still working out. It's amazing how quickly I've changed. I'm softer now, whether because I'm pregnant or because I stopped exercising as soon as I quit acting I'm not sure, as both happened at pretty much the same time.

I should've thought then about not having used a condom the night before, and that afternoon I should've gone to get the morning-after pill for the second time in my life. But it wasn't until the next day that I realised. I got the used condom from our morning sex from my paper basket and moved it into the kitchen rubbish that I was about to throw out. I didn't want the pasty, foggy smell of semen to accumulate in my room. There was one condom, not two.

But it was too soon after my period to be ovulating, surely.

I'd had unprotected sex a handful of times before and never got pregnant.

This, I assume, is what I thought. I don't actually remember thinking about it that much. What I did think about was lying against your body, tracing my finger through your sparse chest hair and kissing your neck, my nose burrowed in behind your ear. I thought about the conversations we'd had that morning. We'd talked about climate change, about how the international climate council had estimated the human race had twelve years to change course before we reached the point of no return. How many years are we at now – eleven or ten? We'd actually talked about children, which sounds like fiction, but we did. I said I thought it was morally irresponsible to have a child – twelve years! You said, 'The solution to climate change isn't to stop having children.' A simple sentence, uttered with more surety than anything I'd said. Which was why, when I realised I was pregnant, I dismissed climate change as a reason not to go through with it. And I think that was why I took your advice about acting to heart, too. Why I told my agent I didn't want any more work. You seemed more certain than me. You were definitely more confident, I'd thought.

'You can't live your life saying you'll get around to doing something you know will make you happy,' you said. 'You just have to do it.'

ANNIE LOOKS TANNED AND SOMEHOW older, as if her holiday gave her new wrinkles under her eyes. She has big brown freckles on her face that I don't remember. Her dark, boxy haircut looks fresh, despite her having only arrived home two days ago. It suits her and confirms a suspicion I've always had – that Annie will age much better than Sarah and me. We talk about her trip for all of two minutes. I tell her I've left my agent, sort of. She tells me she knows I'm pregnant.

'Are you happy?'

It's one of those spring days that is warm and cold in patches, changing whenever a cloud passes over the sun. I'm seated on the edge of a large planter box in her garden in Collingwood. She's in there on her hands and knees, still wearing her netball uniform from a game this morning. I'm drinking a glass of water she had poured for me when I arrived. I can hear the trams on Smith Street behind us. I am pregnant. These are things that I know.

'I'm doing it.'

'Good. Then I'm happy for you.'

She tugs at a stubborn weed that's grown in the tight space between the planter box and the fence. She grunts as she pulls it out.

'Can you talk to Sissa?'

Annie and I sometimes refer to Sarah by her old Facebook name when she's acting like a brat. I know she's already spoken to Sarah – that's how she knows I'm pregnant; what I'm really asking is for her to tell me what Sarah said. Annie doesn't answer, doesn't look at me. She drops the weed on the ground then picks a pea from the vine and eats it, shell and all.

'Have you been to the doctor?'

'Yes.' I answer impatiently, a little offended she thinks I wouldn't do this.

'What did they say?'

The appointment basically consisted of another pregnancy test, a referral to the hospital, where I don't have to go for a while, and where to book in a scan, which I haven't followed up on.

'She said I'm doing great so far.'

'Are you going to contact Pat's family?' She hands me a pea, a casual gesture to offset the heavy question. This must be what she and Sarah talked about. I open the shell and run my finger along the tiny blips of vegetable inside. I regret being testy with my first response. I don't look at her when I speak.

'Can we just park that one for now?'

'How are you going to afford it if you're not acting?'

A born lawyer, her questions are pointed and specific.

'I have savings from that miniseries in New Zealand last year.'

I can't help but say this with resentment. When I went to Centrelink, hoping to get unemployment benefits, I found out I have too much money to qualify for government support. I told the woman I was pregnant – one of the first people I told, and one of the least interested. She explained that I would be eligible for money once the baby is born, but not now. I remind myself this is a good thing. Other people need taxpayer dollars more than me.

'Will you ever act again?' Annie asks.

'I don't know.' I eat my pea.

I quit my agency before I found out I was pregnant. I ignored calls from my agent, Kate, for a week until she gave up ringing me. When I found out, I rang her back, and with no reference to her ignored calls, asked her if I could do commercials but not actual roles. Kate asked if I was having a meltdown. I said no, but I didn't tell her about the baby. Sometimes I think that if I miscarry I might just go back to acting, which doesn't really make sense, because I quit before I knew. I decide if the collection of cells survives this hardest part, I'll take it as a sign that I'm on the right path. Already I am shifting responsibility.

'It's amazing.' Annie flicks a small piece of uneaten stalk into the garden.

'What?'

'That you're actually going do it.'

She pulls off her gardening gloves and comes to sit beside me on the edge of the planter box. She drinks from my glass of water, then refills it with the garden hose and hands it back to me. Together we do the sums, calculating how long I can survive on the savings I have, minus my rent and the money I need for food and bills. We look over her backyard and talk about how I'll pay the rent and not about how the father of my child killed himself. I'm aware that Annie's equanimity is potentially as insincere as my own – in my heart I am screaming – but I appreciate its reliability.

When we eventually go inside, Annie's boyfriend James has started dinner. 'Is Sarah coming over?' he asks.

'Yes,' says Annie, looking to me, not James. I smile at her, but she doesn't smile back. Her look is mildly disapproving. I want to argue – *These are extreme circumstances; it's not like Sarah and I are so immature we can't remain civil for a few weeks without you* – but I know that raising that point would also disprove it.

When Sarah arrives, she comes straight for me.

'Hello, friend that I love.' She gives me a hug and pats me gently on the back. When she pulls away, she puts her hands on my cheeks and looks me in the eye. 'It's a good thing there's going to be more of you.'

We smile at one another. She throws her backpack on Annie's kitchen table and pulls out two bottles of wine. James lines up four glasses and Sarah places her hand over the top of one. She rubs my stomach, friendly this time, not like when she told me I'd be too fat to ride a bike. James looks between us, wearing an expression I often see on him – one of not being in on a joke.

SARAH AND ANNIE and I met in primary school on the Sunshine Coast. Sarah and I were friends from year one; Annie didn't arrive until year four. She was a sweet, obedient girl whom Sarah and I used to dominate. Annie always had two biscuits in her lunchbox – Iced VoVos or Monte Carlos – that she would hand over to each of us. If we ever had to pair up, for schoolwork or a bus seat, it was always Sarah and me together, Annie left behind. And in four square, Annie was forever in the dunce position despite being much better than both Sarah and me at P.E. I shudder when I think of these things now. None of us ever mention it.

When we moved to high school the bullying stopped completely. I'd love to say it's because we'd matured but I think we were intimidated. There were more students in our year level alone than there had been in our entire primary school. We shuffled close together for comfort. The three of us weren't popular, but we weren't unpopular either. Annie was excellent academically and Sarah and I were good enough. Same with our behaviour. Sarah and I occasionally got detention – for talking in class or being late, never anything serious – but Annie not once. At some point, around year eleven, we started dreaming about moving to Melbourne. It was possibly after the first presentation we had about going to uni and what courses we could do. Or maybe it was that the bands we thought were cool on Triple J were mostly from Melbourne. Or both. I don't remember much about school from then on. A part of me had mentally clocked that we were leaving and I didn't need anyone but the friends I was leaving with. Other people from school did move here eventually, a couple of years after us. Annie would catch up with them and tell us about it, but neither Sarah nor I bothered introducing them to the city. Sarah called them 'followers'. I was self-aware enough to know that sounded arrogant, but I agreed with her. When I'd dreamed of Melbourne at school, I pictured wearing denim jackets and berets on campus and drinking pints of beer, even though I didn't like the taste at the time. I'd break up with lots of boyfriends, smoke joints and amble down corridors between classes. Drama school was basically exactly what I'd envisaged but what's happened after is completely different. I thought once I started working, I'd have a big open-plan apartment with a record player, vintage furniture and a hot boyfriend I'd drink wine with. I'd envisaged having money and also nice things. A good career but also lots of spare time. At least this dream mostly came true for Annie, who probably doesn't begrudge occasionally feeling on the outer of Sarah's and my bullshit now.

I SIT ACROSS from James at the kitchen bench as he cooks. He's making a salad, one that requires two pans and the oven on the go. Annie is behind us in the dining room, choosing records. Sarah speaks to us from the back door, pausing after statements to blow long, thin streams of smoke outside. Everyone but me is drinking wine. It's dark now and the kitchen is filled with warm light, soft music and familiar, contented voices. I've told both my friends now. Sarah is no longer mad at me. I should feel relieved, but instead I feel hyper attentive. Like when you've just taken drugs and your senses are alert, waiting for what's next to kick in.

Sarah is quizzing James about his masculinity and buying habits. She tells us she's working on a project to sell a line of alcopops to boys. When Sarah started working in advertising, she was going to transfer her skills into positive behavioural change, try to make people use green bags or waste less food. I haven't heard her talk about that plan in over a year now.

James is talking about a spreadsheet he has for his purchases and Annie and Sarah are laughing. I go to the bathroom frequently. I'm still constipated but I also need to pee constantly. I thought that only happened when the baby was squashing your bladder. Apparently it's the size of a grape, but somehow already I'm always on the toilet.

I'm quiet over dinner, only picking at my food.

'I thought pregnant women were always hungry?' says Sarah.

'They're also always nauseous,' says Annie.

James chokes on his wine.

THERE'S A HOUSE party in Coburg. I say I'm not going. Then Sarah says Travis will be there so I say I'll go. For an hour, two at most. We leave the dishes for Annie and James tomorrow and call an Uber.

I regret my decision even before the car has arrived. It's not like I'm going to tell Travis that I'm pregnant to his dead friend at a party. I'm not planning on telling him at all. It's not like I'm going to ask him if he knows why his friend killed himself. I'm not even sure what I want him to say. That Pat left a message for me before he died? I know this won't be true. I sometimes draft messages to Travis, limp apologies and generic offers of support. I don't send them. I only met Travis a few months ago. He wouldn't want my condolences and he wouldn't understand why I want his. There are so many things that, if true, I don't want to know – that Pat said nothing about me after we slept together; that he mentioned I'd asked him out and he said no; that he was so depressed he hardly spared a thought for me – and yet I want to be near Travis, to hear from him. As though I'm holding out hope he might actually have something nice to say. Something that would make me feel better, whatever that might be. It's like the unhinged feeling of lusting after someone I know is unavailable.

Travis has no idea that I'm obsessing over him like this or what I'm hiding from him. At least I think he has no idea. The fact that I don't know heightens my obsession.

'Drive carefully, she's pregnant,' Sarah tells the driver from the back seat.

'There's lots of drunk people out tonight,' the driver says to James, who's in the front.

The Coburg house is huge and, even full of people, it feels open. The kitchen has a high peaked roof. Large square windows with dark wooden frames make up most of a rear wall facing the big backyard. It's a stunning place that nobody we know will be able to afford even to rent in ten years. Maybe five. I follow Sarah to the laundry when we arrive. She collects two beers from the trough and hands me one.

'Are you serious?'

'I can't hold them both – it'll look like I'm stealing.'

She takes another beer and puts it in her handbag. I crack the tin and take one small sip, which I'm relieved to find tastes like shit. Maybe because I'm pregnant or maybe because it's a cheap beer, bitter and watery.

'Cheapskates.' Sarah shuffles the beers and ice around looking for something better.

For the first hour of the party I'm unbearably anxious. I give my beer to Annie and then regret it. Without something in my hand, I keep touching my face. A disco album is playing. Long tracks, some over ten minutes. No more than four bars looped again and again: the musical equivalent of a dog turning on the spot, chasing its tail. I see Travis early and avoid him. Like I'm trying to play it cool, not wanting him to realise my fixation. Or maybe I'm just nervous. He's sitting by a fire at the back of the garden. Occasionally he goes inside and each time he does I keep my eyes on the back of the house, waiting for him to return. I notice a guy with floppy auburn hair and a beard staring at me as he stands in line to use the outdoor toilet. I stare back for a few seconds then turn away. When I look over again he's still watching me. The door of the outhouse opens and he smiles my way before he turns around and steps inside. He must be doing a shit, I think. Otherwise he'd just pee along the side of the house.

Annie and I have lots of half-conversations with other guests, some we've met before and some we don't know. Engineers and web designers and one doctor. All people with degrees, supposedly smart people. Someone asks me what I do and I reply that I'm unemployed. I say it proudly; I don't say that I'm between jobs or freelancing. Someone else says, 'You're an actor, aren't you?'

'No.' I smile at Annie.

The most painful thing about acting is that people mistake it for being interesting. Acting in theatre is as repetitive as working in the same cafe every day except worse, because you serve everyone the exact same meal at the exact time. In this analogy, television work is the equivalent of someone ordering something and then sending it back so that you have to repeat the entire process, beginning with hello, anywhere from twenty to sixty times.

I've always known how to act. The secret is not to learn. Go: I snap my fingers and I act. I never understood colleagues who, before a performance, would do yoga or stutter their way through the alphabet. An actor I once worked with would walk up and down the rows of the auditorium, occasionally stopping at a particular seat to say an ex-boyfriend's name. D25 was Derrick and B17 was Robert. She walked every row like this in a fabricated ritual.

I studied classical ballet when I was growing up. That demands preparation. It's learned in excruciating increments and is absurdly precise. It's actually grotesque what the dancers do with their bodies, but it looks beautiful. Almost nobody is good enough to do it professionally. I wasn't. When I failed my first audition to study dance, they told me I should audition for the acting stream. I never wanted to act, but I wanted a reason to stay in Melbourne with my friends, so I auditioned and I got in and now that's the story of my life so far, the one I'd told Pat when I first met him. I've got almost every role I've applied for since. Auditions are like dates – if you reek of desperation it's over before it begins. The same as walking on stage. Just act! Now. Do it. Newspapers loved to call Eva McMillan the one actor who kept the drowning ship afloat. I saved the show. I made the show. For years I was told I *was* the show. For a while I believed, like everyone else, that I had some special talent, because I couldn't see then what I see now: that what I had which was so special was actually what I didn't have – a fuck to give.

I START TO feel tired and hungry and it's only when I'm contemplating going home that I finally summon the courage to speak to Travis. I get a beer from the laundry before I join him at the fire near the back fence. I feel like I'm on stage, holding a prop. I don't want to drink the beer, but I want to look like a regular person who drinks beer.

Sarah is here talking rapid-fire to a girl I don't recognise, both of them sitting opposite to Travis, who isn't joining in their conversation. He is staring into the fire, but his expression is vague. Like he's looking through the flames, focusing on something on the other side. When I first met Travis I noticed he was attractive, but now up close he looks awful. He has the flushed, bloated look of someone who drinks too much. His sandy mullet is limp and oily.

'Is someone sitting here?' I ask.

'Go for it.'

I rest my weight gently on the decrepit wooden folding chair. Travis sips his beer and doesn't talk.

'How are you?' I hardly leave a second of silence before I add, 'You don't have to answer.'

'I'm okay.' He looks at me for a second – maybe checking to see who it was he told to sit – then turns back to the fire. I take a sip of my beer, moving it to my mouth slowly, deliberately, as if a sudden movement might spook him. I take my time to swallow and once I do, I put my hand on my stomach, like I'm expecting it might explode. I don't know what to say to Travis and I feel intensely awkward in our silence, although he seems fine. He doesn't look relaxed, but he seems unaware, vacant.

'He wouldn't want me to be sad,' he says eventually. His gaze has shifted down to his beer.

'If I died I'd want my best friends to be fucking miserable,' Sarah says, before running her tongue over a cigarette paper. I didn't realise she was listening to our conversation, and it seems the girl with her didn't notice either; she looks dejected having suddenly lost Sarah's attention.

Travis laughs at Sarah's remark. A small, sad laugh. He throws a log in the fire and smoke blows in my face. I gag, manage not to vomit.

'I think I should get some fresh air.'

I wait for a few seconds before I stand, thinking Travis might join me, but he doesn't. He doesn't even look at me.

SITTING ON THE kerb between two parked cars, my head hanging low, I try to make out the detail in the bitumen. I can hear the party behind me; I could swear this song was played earlier. Eventually, I hear the ticking of spokes and a light shines from behind.

'Are you okay?' a male voice asks.

'I'm sick.' I keep my head down.

'I can see that.'

'I mean, like, I'm not drunk – I'm actually unwell.'

'Are you okay?' he repeats.

I look up and see the auburn-haired guy from the outhouse. He's standing with his bike, lights and helmet on. Ready to go.

'We've met before,' he says. 'Do you remember?'

I stare at him for a few seconds and then I admire his bike; it's expensive.

BACK AT HOME, in my bed, I can't enjoy our sex. My mind is programmed with a series of alarms ready to interrupt any moment when I start to relax – *I am pregnant, I am pregnant, I read somewhere women's vaginas go purple when they're pregnant.*

Emerging from between my legs, he wipes his mouth, wet with me, on my belly. Kisses my abdomen twice as he makes his way towards my breasts then pulls the lace of my bra down with his forefinger. As he's sucking my left nipple I stare at the brown stains on the ceiling. I think about how much larger than normal my breasts are. I have never had sex with breasts this large. His beard is tickling my waist. He finishes his suckling with an audible, squeaky kiss then looks up at me. 'You're really beautiful.' He is whispering, as though it pains him to say it.

I don't come.

I DON'T TRY to be quiet when I vomit in the morning, hoping it'll disgust him and he'll leave. I want to find him seated on the edge of the bed, lacing up his Vans upon my return. Instead he's on his back, the pillow I was sleeping on now propping him up. The doona sits slack below his belly button. He's reading something on his phone. I don't like seeing a stranger this relaxed in my bed. I stand in the doorway to my room. From here his chest hair is a dark letter T across the top of his pecs and down his centre, with stray hairs scattered around his nipples and belly button. I think about how I'll have to change my sheets later, or at least vacuum away his hairs. He puts his phone down on my bedside table when he notices me watching him.

'You didn't seem that drunk last night.'

'I told you I wasn't drunk.' I stay standing in the doorway. 'I'm sick.'

'I remember.' He smiles.

I think about telling him it's not contagious, but I don't and he doesn't ask.

I don't want to make this guy a coffee. This guy whose name I cannot remember. I remember him telling me his name. I remember him holding his hand out for me to shake before he sat down next to me in the gutter outside the party. I don't remember what we talked about, but I remember him leaning in to kiss me and before he could I interrupted: 'Let's go to my place.'

'I don't have any coffee,' I say. 'Sorry.'

'Don't drink it.' He moves his hands to rest behind his head. He has a tattoo on the inside of his bicep and another under his forearm, thin lines like pencil drawings. His underarm hair is lighter than the hair on his chest and head. 'Coffee's a drug.'

'So's MDMA.' A bag of which is on my bedside table. He didn't offer me any, but pulled it out of his pockets last night with his wallet and keys and the condom.

'That's a good drug.' His eyebrows do a quick up–down.

I leave him in my bed and make myself toast in the kitchen. I take my time eating, breaking it into small pieces. Eventually he appears from my room. Dressed, thank God.

'You really do have a weak stomach.' He's looking at my bite-sized pieces of plain toast.

I don't say anything. He sits across from me and starts eating from my plate. I get the Vegemite and jam from the fridge, then put more bread in the toaster.

'So, what are you up to today?' I stay facing the counter, my back to him.

'This is a nice place.'

I turn around and see he's looking past me, through the kitchen window into the backyard. Like most backyards in Thornbury, ours is concreted, a Hills hoist the focal point. Lining the back fence are pots of herbs, some wilted, some gone to seed – gifts from Annie, who eventually stopped giving us plants and instead started taking them away to repot in her garden.

'It's a bit of a dump, really.' I concentrate on buttering, so I don't have to look at him.

Our house isn't falling apart, but it is cheap. Amid white wrought-iron and Juliet balconies, boxy apartment blocks and weatherboards with psoriasis, our house looks new, but fake. Like a demountable; something that could come flat-packed from Ikea.

'So, I actually have a lot on today,' I say, watching him as he sticks the same knife in both the butter and the jam.

'So do I.' He smiles and stands up. 'Last night was fun.'

I take a bite of toast, fill my mouth with food before I smile back, tight-lipped.

'Good luck with your busy day.' He doesn't try to kiss or hug me and I don't walk him to the front door.

When I hear it shut behind him, I picture him walking up my street alone and suddenly I wonder where his bike is. He rode in the Uber here with me last night. Did he lock it up somewhere at the party before we left? As I slowly make my way through another piece of toast, I try to remember more details from the night, but I can't. It seems that, even without alcohol, house parties are just long blocks of noisy time punctuated by not much. Maybe it's baby-brain, I'm not sure. My only distinct memory is Travis's eyes, glassy and vacant, but in a different way from everyone else's.

When I return to my room, I find a small piece of lined paper on the bedside table. It has the guy's number and his name, *Fergus*, and a small, messy love heart.

I throw it in the bin.

I WAITED TWO WEEKS TO hear from you. We didn't exchange numbers after we slept together, but you could've found me online, as I'd found you. I checked several times a day, hoping to see you there. I remember Sarah saying once when we were younger that the secret to getting over a break-up wasn't to have another relationship, it was just to want another one. As soon as you had feelings for someone, even if it didn't work out, it gave you hope. Possibility is all you need to live day to day. I wasn't going through a break-up when I met you. I'd been single for ages. I wasn't recovering from heartbreak but from boredom. My interest in you was like the striking of a match. It brightened my mind.

I REMEMBER TOSSING up if I should send you a friend request or just a message. I didn't want to do either. What I wanted was for you to contact me. Eventually I landed on the message, but no request.

What are you up to this weekend?

39

I wasn't asking you on a date, but asking you to ask me. You replied quickly.

> Not a lot. You?
> *Not a lot.*

Again, I wondered whether to send you a friend request. I didn't because you hadn't, which I regret now, obviously.

YOUR PROFILE PICTURE is not of you but a beach. It was your profile picture for two years. Then you changed – another photo of a beach, but this one with you in it. Sitting on the sand next to a surfboard, your wetsuit pulled down to your waist, white zinc on your nose, pink skin visible around its outer edges. Drops of water on your shoulders, clear ovals overlapping with your beige freckles. This photo was your profile picture for a year, and then two months before you died you changed it back to the beach. Now I've added Travis and can see all his photos, I have new access to you. I spend whole days in bed, bingeing on it. You and Travis surfed together and went to music festivals. You both had longer hair at uni. Yours was redder then, when you were younger. It faded to blond–pink around twenty-four. You were weedier back then too. Your thighs bulked out over the years, probably from bike riding. There are lots of photos of you with bikes. Splayed on the grass at Edinburgh Gardens, cycles on the ground beside you in a heap. There's a lean girl with dark hair and thick eyebrows, androgynous and attractive. Her name is Virginia and she's at your side in some photos, or the photos are taken by her, of you and Travis. Then she disappears. It

seems you broke up over a year ago. She wrote under your profile
picture after you died:

> Thank you for making me a better person. Thank you for
> teaching me how to make really good passata – I'll think of
> you every time I add sugar and vinegar to my tinned tomatoes.

My favourite photo is of you and Travis. You're seated next to one
another. Drinking coffee, I don't know where, but it's recognisably
Melbourne. You're wearing matching striped t-shirts. Travis's is blue
and yours maroon. You're smiling, your arms folded on the table.
Travis is sipping his coffee, eyeing the camera over his cup. It looks
like such an ordinary and mundane occasion. It's hard to imagine why
someone would've taken a photo, let alone why it's been uploaded.
But you both look so goddamn happy.

I SENT MY first message on a Friday, my second the day after.

> *Want to hang out? Today? Or tomorrow?*

'Hang out' left it open for you to interpret if I wanted sex, or if it
was a date. Three question marks was meant to feign nonchalance,
although looking back on it I now see it would have suggested the
opposite.

You replied that day.

> Hey, sorry. I've now made plans for the rest of the weekend.
> Hope you find something to do! X

I wondered if it was a lie. One that you were forced into after
having said you weren't up to much.

FIVE DAYS LATER you died and I hoped that it hadn't been a lie. It was the last weekend in July, the last weekend of your life, and I like to think you filled it with lots of nice things.

ALL DAY I'M BLOCKING CALLS. Some from Mum, some from Kate. When I don't answer Mum she sends cute photos of baby bucket hats and redundant, albeit cute, baby running shoes. I send her cartoon love hearts in response. Then my phone lights up with her face and I turn it over.

When I told Mum I was pregnant, I didn't say I was having a baby, although of course that's what she thought I was telling her. She was completely silent on the phone, which I hadn't expected, so I went on to clarify. 'I'm not telling you I'm having a baby. I'm telling you I'm trying to decide if I should keep the baby or not.' She wasn't too shocked at first. Not in a bad way, at least. She kept saying, 'Oh my God, I mean gosh. Oh God, I mean gosh.' Even though we were never religious and *oh my God* was something we said a lot, and *gosh* never. I told her the father was in Ireland.

'It's probably a good thing,' I said. 'Co-parenting with someone you hardly know would suck. This is easier in a way.'

I didn't feel too deceitful when I said this because it is true that if Pat were alive, I don't think I'd be having his baby.

'Oh my God, I mean gosh.'

A day later she was stern and rehearsed.

'Think about the hardest thing you've ever had to do.'

I was silent on the line.

'Eva, are you thinking?'

I said yes, but really I was just thinking that the hardest thing I'd ever had to do was probably this.

'Double how hard that thing is. Then think about the most tired you've ever been. Double that. Combine those two feelings and that's one day as a parent.'

'Do you regret it?'

'Of course not.'

It wasn't until I told her I'd quit my job that she went mental. Now she won't stop asking me how I'm going to do this alone. How can I give a baby a future if I don't have one myself?

'I have money.'

'Is it going to last forever?'

'I'll get a job.'

'You had a job!'

And even though I told her the father went overseas, she keeps asking about him.

'Tell me more about this father.'

This father. I'm not sure if she can tell that I'm lying or if, like she says, she just wants me to get child support. Over text she is kind and practical. She was the one who sent *What to Expect When You're Expecting* in the mail. She sends me links to blogs by women who write about being pregnant. I send back lots of cartoon love hearts.

My agent doesn't know I'm pregnant. She emails me audition notices for roles in theatre shows. I ask if she can book me for ads. She calls. I don't answer.

I go on to Kate's website every other day to check if she's taken me down, which she hasn't. My face is still there. My fake face, make-up and lighting filtering my skin, the tight clusters of freckles either side of my nose highlighted. My hair bigger, blacker than in real life. My smile tight, a half-smile. Not because I have bad teeth, but because if I smiled with my teeth my cheeks would puff out, making one of my eyes look smaller than the other. The pointed chin in this photo has already rounded out. All the headshots lined up in a row, like a yearbook for a school only for hot people.

A few weeks ago I asked Kate if I could put her on my résumé as a reference for other non-acting work. She rang me within minutes of my sending the email. I didn't answer and a text came almost immediately after.

> Not sure what I'll say if they ask about your attitude or job commitment.

I replied:

> You could say that I did whatever you told me for six years.

When she rang again I answered and was shocked to realise she was sobbing down the line.

'Why are you leaving me?'

'So many people want to do this,' I countered. 'Hire one of them.'

I made a CV when I first quit but I didn't have anything to put on it other than acting roles and the bartending I did while I was studying. My most recent relevant experience would probably be the play where I had a part as a Domino's employee. I had a lot of lines about margheritas and how they should have anchovies on them. I didn't think it would be difficult to get a job at a cafe or one of the local shops that sells candles and hand cream. I littered the main roads with my CV – High Street, St Georges, the Brunswick East end of Lygon, where all the best restaurants are. I must've dropped into fifty venues when I first found out I was pregnant. I was trying to get in early, before my stomach started looking like a partially inflated ball. So far nobody has phoned me. I wonder how hard these jobs could possibly be, then I wonder if I'm too cocky for thinking this way.

Not having a job is not that different from being a working actor. I'm used to having my days off during seasons, and walking around the house talking to myself is more entertaining than walking around the house trying to remember lines, which is far better than being in rehearsal, where you're repeating the same lines over and over but having someone ask you to do it differently. *Now pretend you're in a hot-air balloon, cut in with observations about the sky.* When I was on show-call I was always working evenings and on weekends so I would go to work just as my friends were heading out. I'd meet them late, after the show. They'd be five drinks deep, Sarah probably eight. I remember the two times I did Shakespeare – *Much Ado*: Beatrice; *The Taming of the Shrew*: Kate – I finished so much later it was harder to catch up. That was when I discovered whisky with beer backs. I used to go to bed drunk and wake up with a hangover. Now I go to bed at the time I used to start drinking and wake up and watch Sarah with a hangover. It doesn't feel very different because I never remembered a lot of what we did when we were out anyway. Physically I don't feel superior to Sarah, as I'm usually vomiting or too tired to move, but it's nice to be freed of the mental anguish. When I used to go out, especially if I was in a bad mood or found myself in a situation where I didn't know a lot of people, I would 'act' the part of myself. Instead of just being, I'd act Eva McMillan. And because I was bored or anxious, I'd drink a lot and wake the next day and go over my words as though they were lines I was studying. Their deeper meaning: I am a dickhead. I don't think Sarah suffers this same level of social anxiety, but looking at her pained shuffling through the house makes me think of my old self. The character of me. And I'm glad that, while I might become lonely, at least I don't have to worry about anything I said to anybody while I was drunk.

While my life feels essentially the same, I know that I am changing. Like my jawline, my abdomen is rounding. Slightly. I think. Mornings, studying myself in the mirror, I don't see it. I slide my hands behind the waistband of my pants and they don't seem tighter from one day to the next. But sometimes, when I'm not expecting it – carrying washing in from the line or on the way to the bathroom – I'll catch sight of myself in a mirror and see that I'm fuller somehow. The mound is there, as small as it is. My nipples are covered in small lumps. They're darker now, too, and look crude on my naked body, like stick-on googly-eyes. It's not so much that I'm different; I'm distorted.

SUDDENLY SELF-CONSCIOUS ABOUT my body – my friends are going to realise I don't have a role as a marathon runner coming up – I stop going out. On Friday night, a week after the party in Coburg, I spend the evening on the couch in front of the TV. When Sarah and Annie try to drag me away, I tell them I need to save money – which I do; I need to save money. I put the news on, trying to be a person who is well informed. I want to be a parent who can answer my child's questions about the world. I watch a story about the drought, how it's definitely caused by climate change. The newsreader announces there will be coverage on the Syrian refugee crisis after the ad break and I change channels. I watch reruns of *Friends*. The friends on

TV talk and laugh – they hate their jobs, but they love each other. Joey and Chandler swap apartments with Monica and Rachel and now they want to swap back. The boys agree only if the girls will kiss. Someone mistakes Chandler for being gay and to him this is embarrassing beyond belief. It's heteronormative and homophobic, but at least climate change doesn't exist yet. Or it's not as bad. Or they just don't mention it. My own friends message me updates about their nights out and when I get a text from Fergus it confuses me. I don't register at first that it's not from Sarah or Annie. I never saved his number and I'm unsure how he got mine.

> Want to get a drink later tonight? F
> *I'm out, sorry.*
> Me too. Want to go home together?
> *Sorry. Can't tonight.*

Between nausea, constipation and lethargy, I may be the least horny I've ever been in my life.

ANNIE COMES OVER early the next morning. She drags Sarah out of bed, her face squashed from sleep. Annie has already played netball this morning so her night must have ended earlier than Sarah's.

'Was the band good?' I ask.

Sarah says they were good, Annie says just okay.

'Was Travis there?'

Sarah answers through a yawn. 'Yeah, he was there.'

'How was he?'

'He was fine,' says Sarah.

'Considering,' adds Annie.

We're always considering now.

Annie announces that we're going swimming.

'You need exercise.'

I'm unsure if her comment is directed at me or Sarah. Possibly both of us. She's bought three new pairs of goggles. She takes them out of their boxes at our kitchen table and gives a pair to Sarah. Sarah puts them on, even though she's refusing to exercise. The goggles cover the purple shadows under her eyes, but I can still see her dry, hungover skin. She sticks her tongue out like a baby gagging, desperate for water.

'It's good for our mental health.' Annie puts on a pair of goggles too. They look like a dentist and a patient, bug-eyed and ready for an extraction, the dentist lying to the patient when she says it won't hurt.

My new, larger breasts spill out of my old bikini top, so we detour via the Northcote Plaza on the way to the pool. I buy a cheap, black sports bra from Kmart and a cup of donuts from the Donut King, which Sarah and I share. Annie doesn't comment on the donuts, but Sarah is defensive anyway. 'It's not like we're exercising to lose weight!'

On our bikes we fly quickly, in single file, down the hill on Arthurton Road.

When I last came to Northcote swimming pool, a few years ago now, I was struck by the diversity. I remember I said, 'You could shoot an ad here.' Young people, old people, people of colour, women in hijabs. Today it's mostly lap swimmers and a couple of mothers with babies, all white. I guess it's the weather; it's not quite hot enough yet to bring out everybody. But, also, Northcote is different now. It's a Melburnian joke that if you drive down High Street from Preston through Thornbury to Northcote you see all the stages of gentrification. Northcote was once like Preston, with lots of international grocers and delis and migrants. Now Northcote is full of cafes owned by people who don't live here and expensive children's clothing stores, and the houses are owned by AFL players. Thornbury sits somewhere between the two. Recently, when Sarah and I noticed a new ice-cream bar in Thornbury, I said to her, 'This place is becoming more like Northcote every week.'

'Northcote?' she said. 'Try Brooklyn.'

I could see what she meant. Thornbury's gentrification seems younger than Northcote's. But maybe that's just another one of the stages.

I HAVEN'T SWUM laps since high school and I get puffed straight away because of the breathing. Running is about controlling breathing. In for three, out for three. Use your feet as a metronome and count evenly. Swimming feels out of control. Every third stroke I turn my head to the side, gasping for air. I try to use the same logic as for running: keep it steady; out for three, in for one. But the one is always desperate. Sometimes I breathe in water and choke and have to stop, standing on the tiles or treading water as I cough. I join the older people in the slow lane and do an easy breaststroke, head above water. I look to the next lane over. Sarah is using a kickboard with Annie yelling from close behind her, 'You can kick harder than that!'

'My bathers are riding up my butt.' Sarah holds her kickboard with one arm, awkwardly jerking her body forward.

Afterwards, we lean back on our elbows on the poolside astroturf. Quiet, except for heavy breathing. I watch the coloured bathing caps in the water making their way up and down the lanes like it's a game of Pac-Man. Sarah and Annie both look alert and slightly mad with white, blotchy skin and red rings around their eyes. I imagine I look the same – my skin is dry and my eyes are itchy. I decide I hate the pool.

'So, how's your mum?' Annie asks me.

'Yeah, she's good.'

'Is she visiting any time soon?'

'Just Christmas.' She comes every second Christmas with her partner, Ken.

'Is she excited?' Annie does this sometimes – instead of just asking, *How did your mum react when you told her you are pregnant*, or, *Have you told her about the father*, she edges towards big conversations, like she's flirting.

I lie on my back and cross my arms over my forehead. I feel the urge to tell Annie everything about my life, but because her mode of enquiring bothers me, I withhold and am vague. I play hard to get, I suppose.

I answer with my eyes closed. 'I'm sure she's worried. Like, I think she'd prefer it if I had a nice boyfriend like James. But at least I'm not married to a fuckwit who's going to repurpose my business without telling me, so you know.' I lower one elbow, making a small window in my arms. Annie and I smile at each other.

Sarah is brushing her hand through the green plastic shag rug beneath us.

'The thing I always think about astroturf,' she says, 'is, like, when do they vacuum it?'

We all laugh.

Years ago, Sarah probably would've responded to my comment, or a similar one from Annie, either sympathetically or awkwardly. Back then, Sarah thought Annie and I talked like this about our families for attention, almost like we were boasting about how dysfunctional they were. Back in the days when I kept my opinions of my dad private, I too thought people did this. If you made some scathing comment about a drama in your life, I reasoned, it meant you wanted everyone else to know about it.

Annie's life changed as we were nearing the end of primary school. One morning, her older brother – her only sibling – didn't wake up. Something was growing in his brain that they hadn't known was there was how it was described to me back then. Years later, I googled aneurysms and I understand about as much now as I did then. At school, Sarah and I were called to the principal's office and handed tissues at the door. I don't remember exactly what he said, only that he ended with: 'I know you girls are her best friends.'

Mum sewed me a new dress for the funeral. I could hear the machine rattling all night. I know now she would've been unable to sleep, worrying about something like this happening to me. I was all she had then. At the funeral, I remember Annie holding her mother's hand as they walked behind the small casket carried by the men. Afterwards, at the wake, Annie showed us her new Game Boy. Then we started year seven and didn't talk about Annie's brother for a long time. It was all a bit much for twelve-year-olds. Annie's parents divorced that summer, but I didn't find out until years later that it was during the intense period after Jonathan's death that her mother's affair was exposed. Her lover showed up at their house one evening, worried because she hadn't heard from her. In the midst of their grief, Annie's mother had to come out to her husband and family. I've never been able to decide if this was a good or a bad thing. If maybe the weight of grief meant a hidden sexuality felt trivial, or if it was horrid heaped on horrid. I guess it was probably the latter, but Annie's mum is still with Janine, so I figure that, despite her grief, she must be happy with how things turned out.

Sarah's parents are happily married, living the boomer dream in a mansion at Noosa Heads. They're always renovating. What Sarah doesn't understand about people in unhappy families, and what it took me a long time to understand, is that you don't make comments about it for anyone else's benefit. It's more about acknowledging your own distance from the pain. It isn't sad – not now. Very rarely in my life have I sat and felt sad about my father. The feeling is done through other actions that you can't recognise as such until much later. Like the time in primary school when I went to a friend's house and, after seeing her parents making toast together, wanted to beat her, so instead I told everyone at school that her house smelled.

Back when Sarah used to party a lot, and therefore cry a lot, I heard friends on the periphery of our lives joke about how she was the one who was fucked up despite being the one who grew up without the fucked-up family. The first time I heard someone say that I realised two things – that Sarah must have told other people about Annie's and my families, and that our other friends don't know us very well, not really.

AT HOME IN the evening, Sarah and Annie try to convince me to go with them to the pub.

'I can't afford it.'

'I'll pay,' says Annie. 'We're just getting dinner.'

They're meeting up with other friends. Friends who will be drinking. Friends who don't know that I'm pregnant.

'I can't express to you how tired this thing is making me.' It's not a lie.

I feel especially nauseous tonight. I blame the exercise. For dinner I boil potatoes and eat them plain, with just a dash of olive oil, a crack of pepper. I don't pretend I'm going to do anything smart this evening. I just put *Friends* on right away. At some point between

Ross dating a student and everyone making jokes about how Monica used to be fat, I get a message from Fergus.

> Tonight?
> *Out again, sorry.*
> So, want to tell me what nights you don't have plans?

I start to reply, *No, I don't.* But as I'm typing out the words I realise he might think I'm being playful. I don't reply until much later in the evening, finishing my message with another 'sorry' before deleting it and hitting send. By this time Monica and Chandler are engaged.

> *Hey, I had fun the other week, but I'm really not in a place to be seeing anybody right now. Maybe I'll see you around.*

I struggle to get to sleep and I wonder if I feel guilty. Eventually I realise it's actually temptation. I know I won't be having sex with anyone once the baby is born, nor when I'm heavily pregnant. Maybe this is my last chance. But despite how sick I feel, what I said is true – I'm really not in a place to be seeing anybody right now.

Fergus doesn't reply.

YOU DIED ON A WEDNESDAY and I found out on the Friday. I came home in the afternoon to find Sarah and Renee on the couch together drinking rosé.

'Isn't it a bit early for that?'

It wasn't early for Sarah to be drinking, but it was early for two people to be drinking together on a weekday.

Sarah stood and went to get a glass for me. 'You know Pat?' she asked.

I was staring at Renee. The whites of her eyes were tinged the colour of her wine. She'd been crying. She had just broken up with Travis, which I'd heard she'd been nonchalant about, so I didn't think it could be that. I was wondering if they were about to tell me Renee was seeing Pat now.

'He died.'

It was Sarah who said it, but I was still staring at Renee.

'What happened?' My brain was limping to catch up. If I'd just been told Renee was seeing Pat, I probably would've asked the exact same thing.

'He took his own life.' Renee looked down at her lap as she said it, as though she was ashamed.

I sat on the couch for hours, staring out the window, watching the world dim and then darken, and listening to them talk. Renee was telling Sarah about Travis. How worried she was for him. I was still stuck on Renee's words: *He took his own life.* If you had taken your own life, it meant that your life was not yours. That your life existed somehow outside of you and you had stolen it. I thought it would make more sense to say you had left your life. Dropped it. Thrown it away. Hanged it. Poisoned it. Shot it. Whatever it was that you did – Sarah did ask, but Renee didn't know. Eventually I circled back to the original idea, though. Maybe that's what depression is. My life might be mine, but a depressed person's life is not theirs. They're already dead and they take their life from the rest of the people living with it.

'What are you thinking about, Eva?' Renee asked.

'The sky looks inky. There are so few stars.'

I felt sick every day for a week. When I found out I was pregnant I wondered if this was when I started to feel it. The book says not, though. Most people can't tell that early. I like to think that maybe I could.

I DIDN'T GO to your funeral. Sarah did. She wasn't going to, as she'd only met you the three times: the same three times I'd met you. Renee was going, as she knew you the best, and she needed to support Travis. But it was awkward, with her having broken up with Travis, so she asked Sarah to go with her in solidarity.

I like funerals. I don't enjoy what they represent – that emptiness of hope. I just enjoy their pageantry. They remind me of amateur theatre, with people who can't act reading scripted clichés aloud. Weddings are the same.

A part of me wanted to go. I thought maybe I could wallow in my grief – or shock, as it really was at that point – in a more active way. I regret now that I didn't. I might have learned something about you. Maybe I'd understand things a little more. But that's also the reason why I didn't go. I wanted to live in my version of how things turned out. The fantasies in which you were alive and we were dating. The truth of the funeral would be too specific. Also, nobody expected me to go. Nobody would've objected to my presence, but I was in such a state that even the effort it would take to wash a black dress was beyond me.

Sarah didn't want to go and was complaining about it.

'At least you'll get the day off work.' I kept making these bizarre statements. I felt like I was floating on my back in water, my ears submerged. I could tell there was noise around me, but it was unin-telligible. All I could hear was my breathing and my heart pumping away; it sounded like it was racing itself. A pregnant woman's heart rate increases by almost half. I didn't know I was pregnant then and all I could think about was your heart lying flaccid and mute. Disgusting without its function. My own body seemed obnoxious. Some part of me must have been functioning in the real world, though, as when I was called upon to speak I did, unsure where the words were coming from since all I'd been thinking about was you.

'I just don't want to have to look at his parents and know that their child chose to do this to them,' Sarah said.

I hadn't been thinking about your parents. But when she mentioned them, I had a strong desire to lie down. Now your parents flit into my mind a lot and when that happens I go to bed, open my laptop and hope the canned laughter jostles them from my mind.

SARAH CAME HOME that night, pissed off and mildly tipsy. She collapsed onto the corner of the couch, almost missing it and landing on the floor. I poured her a Scotch.

'How was it?' I asked her.

'Bloody awful.' She tilted her head back and downed the whisky. 'In the eulogies everyone kept saying how great his life was. But it's, like, clearly not. Clearly his life was unbearable.'

It was strange for Sarah to articulate her complaint in such detail. Usually she'd have stopped at 'bloody awful'.

'How was Travis?'

'Manic.' She held her empty glass out and I refilled it, but with less Scotch this time. 'He was playing music, making jokes. At one point he was talking loudly about the song he was going to write about how much of a fuckwit Pat is for doing this to everyone. A break-up song. I mean, I know the guy's insane, but it was next level. Renee dodged a bullet there.'

I once had a colleague, Nicholas, who was Greek. He played a beefed-up gym junkie in a pilot we shot. The catalyst for the show was the death of a character offscreen. I was that character's sister, Nicholas was the best friend. The pilot began at the funeral. We were young, twenty-three or so. The scene was shot in a church in Melbourne even though if it was picked up, which it wasn't, the show was going to be set in Sydney. There were flowers and extras all wearing black. Older women in hats, which I've never seen at an actual funeral, but often on stage or screen. I didn't have any lines in the scene; the actor who played my father delivered a eulogy. Nicholas and I were seated together in the pew. Between takes, he turned to me and said, 'This is the weirdest funeral I've ever been to.'

At first I froze, thinking I'd forgotten a line, which I never did.

'Do Australians actually do this?' he went on.

'What do you mean?'

I looked around the church. Extras who moments ago had been dabbing at their eyes with hankies were making small talk. I hadn't been to many funerals at the time, but the ones I had been to were similar to this fake one. It was only the hats that didn't ring true.

'In Greece you cry. This hopefulness is weird.'

I didn't think much about it at the time, but I thought about what he'd said as I watched Sarah, limp on the couch, the back of her hand on her forehead like she was feigning having fainted.

I WAS RIDING along the St Georges Road bike path when I started to feel pregnant, although I didn't know then that's what it was. Despite the singular condom, it wasn't my first thought. I demounted and walked my bike, growing heavier and wobblier as I went. At home, I went straight to sleep. My boobs had been hurting, which always happened before my period. Then they kept hurting but the blood didn't come.

The next morning, I was on hands and knees, my neck hooked over the toilet bowl. It was the tail end of winter, so the bathroom tiles were freezing. Between heaves I placed my forehead on the cold floor, which was refreshing despite probably being filthy. I watched the condensation from my slow, shaky breaths appear on the tiles and then evaporate.

It felt like my body was trying to turn itself inside out.

One, two, three days the same.

Since your death I'd felt like a bubble. Wafting along delicately, waiting to be shattered – pop!

I had a pregnancy test in my drawer from a previous scare. They come in packs of two so you can confirm the result. I remember that time being so afraid of falling pregnant that I didn't want to take the second one once the first came up negative. I didn't need a second one this time either; I didn't need convincing.

Pop!

My first thought was to get an abortion. A knee-jerk reaction I'd absorbed when I was young. Young, single girls who get knocked up are nothing. They end up alone, without men or money, and they regret everything. It was the surest sign of failure. I was so used to thinking of conception as something to be avoided at all costs I no longer questioned it. I laughed at the thought of Sarah and me getting abortions together. Girls' day out.

Only an hour after I'd found out I already felt lighter. The sickness had passed for the day and I knew now what that sickness was. I felt present in a way I hadn't since I found out you'd died. The bubble had burst, but what I was facing wasn't endless nothing; it was something. Just like when I met you, a match had been struck.

October

SUDDENLY ONE MORNING I'M NOT sick. Suddenly I'm starving. Money I once spent on alcohol I spend on food. Fruits, especially tart ones, and sour things. Kiwifruit and jars of bright pickled vegetables. Fresh lettuce leaves doused in dressing. I dip carrot sticks in vinegar, not hummus.

I'm unpacking groceries from cotton bags. Sarah is leaning over the kitchen counter, her elbows resting on *What to Expect*, holding it open. She picks at a bunch of grapes, eyes on the book. Her weight is on her left leg, her right leg bent up. She reminds me of a flamingo, all leggy and pale red.

'It says here you should be twenty per cent more hungry now.'

I twist the lid off the vinegar and take a swig before putting it in the pantry. 'I feel fifty, at least.'

'Maybe because you were vomiting for so long. Now you're just enjoying food again.'

'Maybe.'

'It says here you can tell people now, too.' She doesn't look at me as she says this. I know she already knew that. Everyone knows that.

'After today,' I say. 'When we know there's definitely a baby in there.'

'I wonder if you can go skydiving.' She turns the book over, thumbing the pages to the index at the back.

ANNIE ARRIVES AN hour later to take us to my scan. Sarah picks up the conversation in the car as though it was just a moment ago.

'So, you can't go skydiving. Also, what do you mean by definitely knowing there's a baby in there?'

'Lots of people miscarry in the first trimester,' I answer, automatically. 'That's why you don't tell people.'

'Have you looked in the mirror lately? You look like me after I've eaten fructose.'

'I just want to make sure everything is fine before I tell anyone.'

I feel a twinge of annoyance that Sarah doesn't just understand everything I'm feeling. That she accepts I would suffer in silence because of a stupid tradition that made women feel ashamed of their trauma.

I'm meant to have had one scan already. A dating scan to 'confirm the viability of the pregnancy'. Just hearing that phrase made me want to book an abortion. In so many ways this pregnancy is unviable. Anytime Annie or my mum asked about the scan I lied and said I couldn't get in, that I was waiting for a slot to open up. I justified putting it off by telling myself humans had babies forever before they had doctors, and that back then they didn't even have the book. Everyone knows the rules – no darts, no alcohol, no soft cheese. If in doubt: if it's fun you probably can't do it. Some women miss a dating scan because they don't realise they're pregnant. I realised I was, but I didn't realise I was going to go through with it. What

I haven't told Annie or Sarah or Mum is that a part of me has been waiting in case I change my mind. I'd suspected that Annie and my mum might conspire together to convince me not to do this, and if they had I'm not sure what would've happened. A part of me actually wishes they had, because, even if I'd resisted any convincing, I'd be more sure of myself now. Probably. Waiting to see if I change my mind is also the reason I haven't told any other friends. That and the fact I'm terrified of telling them. Not just because some – like Renee and Travis – know I slept with Pat and would guess he's the father, but because I'm scared of their judgement. I don't have a job, but I'm having a baby.

I'm extremely nervous about this appointment.

We stop at a red and Annie slaps down the left indicator. Ticking sounds, like the conversation is being timed. 'How are you feeling?' she asks.

I slump sideways, my ear on the seat's headrest. 'I'm tired.'

'The book says you're meant to have pep in your step now.' Sarah clicks her fingers at me from the back seat, like I'm traffic she's hoping will speed up.

'It's not the same kind of tired,' I say. 'I used to feel sleepy. Now I just feel like I have to sit down all the time.' I close my eyes and let my friends talk about work.

It's Friday and they've both taken the day off for this. Sarah is working from home, officially. She's logged into her emails on her phone. Annie wouldn't be able to half-arse her work like that. She works at a community legal centre and, from what I can gather, deals mostly with domestic violence. This had always been her plan at uni, but I suspected – I suppose shamefully – that like so many people before her, as soon as she got a whiff of what she could earn in the corporate world she might change course.

Annie is the only friend I have whose work is so important. She's also the person who talks the least about it. I don't know if it's good that she doesn't centre herself in her work like some kind of saviour, or if it's depressing she seems so uninterested in her own life. Maybe the work is so depressing she doesn't want to speak about it outside of office hours. Annie knows a lot more about the world than either Sarah or me, but she also seems less perturbed by it. If Sarah and I lament something most people like us would agree is bad, Annie will say something to the contrary. Not necessarily justifying it, but just explaining why it is the way it is.

Sarah started her career doing social media for a local eco-business that made plant-dyed homewares. After exploding their online reach, she was poached by a big ad agency. Sarah seems very good at her job. She'd have to be for her boss to indulge how often she's struck with a last-minute desire to work from home on a Monday.

I listen to my friends talk in foreign acronyms. I feel isolated, as though I'm standing in the wings, observing their real lives from offstage. It's not a nice feeling, but this is how I'd always felt as an actor, so in a way it's comforting. When I wake we're in the sonographer's car park and I realise I was asleep for most of the drive. I rub my eyes, then check my reflection in the rear-view mirror to ensure that I haven't smudged my mascara. I've put make-up on for the first time in weeks to come here. Sarah is doing the same, peering into the rear-view mirror and running her fingers through her fringe.

ALL THE WOMEN here are pregnant. This makes sense, but startles me still. So many big women in one room – beach balls and bowling balls. Some women are huge, not just their bellies, but all of them. Wide-set with flabby arms and fleshy balloon breasts. One woman standing at the receptionist's desk is tiny, her stomach an alien appendage, like a basketball stuffed under a t-shirt. I like the big ladies better, I decide.

'It's like a dog breeder,' says Sarah.

When the doctor was arranging my referral to the hospital where I'll give birth, she started listing the names of midwives there. 'She's a really good midwife, you'll be in good hands with her. She's a *great* midwife.' There are so many women here, I realise now that everyone just has to have someone, good or bad. The doctor also gave me pamphlets and lists. Things I should do and things I can't. I remember her pointing out some of the specific herbal teas; she said they were poisonous to the embryo. I liked that word, embryo. Eventually I will have a baby but then it was an embryo. My affection made me feel maternal. I have a foetus now, grown from the embryo. While we wait, I flick through a booklet of laminated pictures of developing babies. A seahorse becomes a dugong becomes a beetle becomes a doll with terrible posture, shy and embarrassed trying not to take up space. Sarah reads over my shoulder, pointing out parts of the anatomy.

'That's going to be a boy,' she says.

Then I'm on my back, Sarah and Annie behind me. The sonographer's name is Sivan. She squeezes lube over my bare belly and runs the thin plastic wand over me. She turns her monitor to me and quickly – I'm not sure what I was expecting; that it might take a long time to buffer, perhaps – the black-and-grey image of my baby is there. A few seconds after the image, there's sound. The baby's heartbeat is like lying on a towel at the beach, ear to the sand, listening as someone walks past. Intimate, but removed. Loud, but distant. It's fast. I hear Annie sob behind me. She blows her nose.

'Dude, who uses hankies anymore?' says Sarah, then, 'Can you see the nasal bone?'

Sivan nods. 'Yes, that's here,' she says.

Sarah moves in closer to the screen and Sivan points, explaining what we're seeing. She repeats 'normal' and 'healthy' so many times I begin not to believe her.

'You're a bit further along than I'd thought.'

'Look how tiny it is.' I stare intently at the monitor, as though I haven't heard. A pantomime to prove I'm a loving parent, if a disorganised one.

'I'd say you're either fourteen or fifteen weeks.'

'I'm twelve.' I say this confidently, eye contact resumed. I had sex with Pat twelve weeks ago and there was no sex for months before that.

'We start counting from the first day of your last period,' says Sivan, 'because there's no way to know exactly what day the sperm fertilised the egg.'

This makes sense. What doesn't make sense is that this had in some way started fourteen weeks ago, when I'd only met Pat once and we hadn't yet slept together.

Sivan tells me the foetus is the size of an orange. I stare at the image on the screen. It looks smaller than that; a passionfruit, maybe. I'm startled when the ultrasound is over. Just like the abortion, I think. I had a clear idea of what this was going to be, but no idea how long it would take.

Annie and I wait by the entrance while Sarah uses the bathroom. I look around at the women waiting – more beachballs, different ones from before. Mostly accompanied by men, some with other children in tow. They cradle babies with one arm. One lady cleans her toddler, sweeps a wipe all over his face one-handed, pinching it in at the end of his nose and mouth. Women straighten clothes on their kids' wriggling bodies. They wear nice maternity dresses. I'm wearing a t-shirt that says *Show Me Your Riffs*. These ladies have big nappy bags. I'm holding my wallet in my hand.

Sivan enters the waiting room and calls out a name. The woman who stands has no other child with her, but she does have a husband. She looks older than me. I wonder if Sivan will tell her she's doing fine too. I guess she has to. Even if we give birth to kids with heart disease or to future murderers, we'll all be fine because, of course, we all have to be.

AT HOME WE sit in the backyard. I'm in the hammock, Sarah and Annie on chairs with cracking vinyl and rusted legs from years of living outside. Annie has made us all a spritz with orange juice instead of Aperol and mineral water instead of prosecco. Sarah has added a big splash of gin to hers.

'I just wish there was something obvious like my hair changing colour so that everyone would realise I'm pregnant without me having to tell them.' I reach for my glass on the ground beside me, pick out a wedge of orange and stick it between my teeth and my lips, suck it like it's a dummy. I think about how what I said isn't really true. I would've had to hide from Travis if it were true.

Annie stands and starts inspecting our garden, pulling weeds from the cracks in the paving.

'I think you're really robbing yourself of an opportunity here,' Sarah says eventually. 'Seeing people's faces when you tell them.' She jumps up and stands on her chair, lifts her arms high in a V-shape. 'Everyone, I am with child. Also, the father is dead, he topped himself.' She performs an elaborate bow and almost topples off the chair. I wonder if she's already a bit drunk.

'I'm not telling anybody who the father is. I will lie about that.'
I avoid looking directly at either of my friends, but still I can sense
their reactions. Annie looks sad. Sarah is concentrating on her glass,
which she is topping up with more gin.

THE SUN AND the bottle of gin dwindle lower and lower, until eventually it's time to head out. We're going to see Gabriella Cohen play
at the Northcote Social Club. Sarah and Annie bought me a ticket,
a plot to make me go out disguised as a nice gesture. The plan is to
meet our other friends at the pub and have dinner before the gig.
I know the chances of someone asking me why I'm not drinking when
I'm seated at dinner are higher than if I'm standing, watching the
gig. I tell Sarah and Annie I need to have a quick rest first. I almost
have to push Annie out the door to get her to leave without me. I'm
aware my friends are probably complaining about me right now.
I also know they'll be forgiving too. They'll tell themselves they don't
know what it's like to be pregnant, or this tired. I tell myself this too.

I don't really feel like resting, but I have nothing else to do, so
I lie on my bed and think about the friends I'll be seeing. We've
known Renee, Matthew and Ginnie – the Clarke Street house – for
years now, we met all of them at uni. Others, like Travis, are people
who come and go. We'll see them out and drink with them a lot for
a couple of years and then things will shift, move on a little, and
it'll be other people we're drinking with. It was people we knew
through uni, or work, for the first years. Now that we have careers,
as opposed to casual jobs, it's rarer for people to bring colleagues into
the fold and often the new friendships we make, like with Travis, start
from having dated someone. I used to go out a lot and now that I've
retreated I wonder how much I really miss these people. I ask Sarah

about them in the mornings after she's been out. I don't think it's perfunctory; it's not that I don't miss them at all. But when I do, I have years of memories to indulge in. Dancing in the rain, soaked and steaming high at Golden Plains. Driving to Turpins Falls every day during semester break then cramming for exams all together in one lounge room – sharing Modafinil, cigarettes and coffee. Hungover, floating on inflatable boats on the Goulburn River on New Year's Day. A line of six of my friends standing and applauding from the front row of my first opening night. The memories make me feel full and warm. They fill the longing, dull the ache, soothe the soul, any of the clichés. I am lonely, but what I'm longing for isn't friends.

I always thought my adult life would be cleaved like this, with socialising on one side and children on the other. I guess I thought I wouldn't be lonely on this side because I assumed there would be a man with me, which is an odd assumption, given when I grew up it was just me and Mum.

If it wasn't for the promise of seeing Travis, I'm not sure I'd bother going tonight.

I EVENTUALLY MAKE it out of the house, still in plenty of time for the gig. Rather than joining the others at the pub I cycle to the Social Club and go straight to the band room. I stand alone watching the support act – an all-girl rock band, as all support bands seem to have become in the past year. I look around for anybody I know, but the people here are strangers – although, at a glance, they could be my friends: late twenties, same cut of jeans, faded surf tees and shaggy heads.

Eventually my friends arrive. Matthew, Ginnie, Renee holding hands with Sarah. A friend of Renee's whose name I can't remember but who I know I've met before. Travis enters with James and they go straight to the bar. I watch them waiting in line. I don't notice Annie until she's right next to me.

'Feeling better?' she asks.

'Not really.' I smile at her.

Everyone I know greets me excitedly and, seeing their faces for the first time in a while, I remember how much I like these people. The fondness I felt for the memories of them is just a shade of what I feel now. They're all about three pints deep – affectionate and not too interested in actual details about my life, although most of them ask either how or where I've been. Renee keeps her arm around my waist. We stand, interlocked like schoolgirls, facing the stage. The support band – called I Sit Down When I Pee – are playing a track about periods with a simple, repetitive chord progression. The vocals are more like loud talking than singing. Travis is now standing a few feet nearer the front with James. He's drinking a pint, his free hand in his pocket. At one point James makes Travis laugh. He looks significantly more relaxed than when I last saw him at the party in Coburg. At the end of the set he and James turn around and come to stand with Renee and me.

'Do you want a beer?' James asks us.

'I'll come with you.' Renee takes James's forearm. 'Let's go to the front bar, this one is about to be slammed.' She starts to pull him away.

'You guys okay?' James points between me and Travis.

'I'm fine.' Travis tilts the half-full glass in his hand, glances up but then looks back down, avoiding Renee.

'Do you want anything?' James asks me. 'Water?'

I shake my head, then quickly turn to Travis to check he isn't wondering why James would only offer me water. He's not.

The room is filling up as more people arrive for the main act. I watch the crowd for a while. I invent a game to play by myself – if anybody else here was pregnant, who would it be? It's not entertaining, though, as nobody looks like they would be. I turn to Travis. 'How've you been?' I ask. I feel self-conscious about my body. It's like I'm going through puberty again, I'm so aware of the size of my breasts.

'Pretty good.' He takes a sip of his beer. 'The girls said you're not acting anymore?'

'Not really, no.'

'What are you going to do?'

'I'm not sure. Let me know if you hear of any jobs, I guess.'

He nods but doesn't say anything. I think his expression is sympathetic. Maybe it's just vague. I know I'm not going to ask Travis about Pat here, in public, when he seems to be in a good mood. But I'm happy to be talking to him. It feels like progress, whatever that is.

'Have you played here before?' I ask.

'No.'

We lapse into silence and Travis looks around the room. I follow his gaze, wondering if he's looking for someone. I spot Renee and Sarah speaking, their faces only inches apart. When I turn back to Travis he's looking the opposite way.

One of the first things Renee told me about Travis when she started dating him was how excitable he was. 'You know how Sarah never asks what you've been up to, or how you've been, but immediately launches into some anecdote about some person she saw and something that happened? That's him! He loves the most mundane shit.'

When I'd first met him, this impression proved true. Although back then mostly what he was excitable about was Renee. Their relationship only lasted two months. I don't know him well, but what I do know is that he's funny – or used to be, anyway. He likes to muck around, but he's also quick to be earnest. I'm not sure I've ever met anybody else who's so earnest and yet simultaneously hates on so many things. I've heard him wax lyrical about being open-minded and non-judgemental, and then the next moment state that anybody who gets a purebred dog is a moron. His values come from a good place, but I've never heard Travis say anything challenging. His beliefs are the common collective sentiments, regurgitated with no variation, not a lot of depth. Sarah met him before I did and I remember when I asked her what Renee's new boyfriend was like she said, 'He's a bit of an idiot, but he's harmless.'

Gabriella Cohen takes the stage and the crowd applauds. She doesn't say hello, but immediately starts a track.

'Ever seen her play?' I keep my eyes on the stage but turn my head slightly towards Travis.

'A few times,' he says. 'My old housemate used to date her, actually.'

'Oh.' I wonder if he means Pat. I suppose he must prefer to say 'old housemate' rather than 'dead housemate'. I close my eyes and breathe evenly. He's probably had lots of housemates. I open my eyes again and watch Gabriella. I try to picture her with Pat. Her brown hair is wavy and she looks French. From here her skin looks as clean as her headshots. I close my eyes and breathe.

'Are you okay?' Travis asks.

'Yeah.' I open my eyes again. 'I just feel a little sick.'

'Do you need to sit down?' Travis looks around, but there are no chairs.

'No, I'm fine.'

Gabriella finishes a track. 'How's everyone doing?' Her voice is droll, twangy.

Travis hits one hand against his pint glass.

'I've been, um, feeling really sick a lot lately.' I stare ahead at the stage, talking to Travis but looking at Gabriella.

'Oh?' I can't tell if he is confused or uninterested. I pause, waiting for Gabriella to start playing again before I speak. She starts another track, without her guitar this time. She has a tambourine in her hand and dances behind the mic stand.

I close my eyes and count to ten in my head. 'Yeah, I'm pregnant.'

'Oh, wow.' He turns to me. I glance at him side on, then look back to the stage. I breathe quicker for a few seconds and then, purposefully, much slower.

'Congratulations?' His inflection is upwards.

'Thanks.' I do a small nod to myself, as if in agreeance.

I go to place my hand on the orange and then immediately feel like that's over the top and take it away. I keep my gaze fixed on the stage. Travis too seems to be transfixed by Gabriella and yet I can't help but feel watched. My glass is empty, but I tip it all the way up and wait for the final two drops of water to slowly make their way to my mouth. After a couple more tracks, Travis goes to the bathroom. When he returns, he stands on the other side of the room.

AFTER THE GIG the others are heading to Joe's Shoe Store for a knock-off. I decide to go home. Annie insists on joining me for the bike ride and I insist she doesn't. She and James stare at me hesitantly.

'I'm fine,' I tell her, emphatic. I shout goodbye to the rest of our friends, who are already walking south down High Street, and they wave. Travis just holds his hand up like someone stopping traffic. I smile, he doesn't.

I don't know if Travis knows I slept with Pat. I figure it's most likely he does – they were housemates and good friends. What Travis can't know is whether I've slept with anybody else since sleeping with Pat. Or whether I slept with someone the day before I slept with Pat or the day before that. All he can know is that it is possibly Pat's child. But he may not even know that. Maybe Pat never mentioned it.

I coast slowly through Northcote's quiet back streets, and when I arrive home I continue riding a few laps around the block. I love cycling on warm nights. Something about a mild night makes it feel safe to be out late on my own after dark. I let the warm air soak into my skin. I cruise through my neighbourhood and remind myself I'm not trying to fool anybody. I'm just hoping my friends will agree not to know.

At home in bed I write several messages to Travis that I don't send.

EVERYTHING I KNOW ABOUT YOU I can list.

You were twenty-eight – one year older than me.

You were born in Warrnambool. You liked your hometown a lot more than I liked mine.

In primary school you sang Oasis's 'Wonderwall' for show-and-tell and were told that show-and-tell was about *showing* something: you were meant to bring something to class. You never participated again.

You studied environmental science at Melbourne Uni. You met Travis there and he was your best friend. The two of you were living in Fitzroy North when you died.

I'm not sure where you worked and whether it was related to the environment.

The best things I know about you are what cannot be listed. Like that you were attractive in a way that is hard to distil. You were a strawberry blond, freckly boy with crooked front teeth and translucent eyelashes.

I hardly thought anything about you the first time I saw you, but I liked you more each subsequent time.

I HOPE IT'S a boy so he looks exactly like you. I want him to have that sheen of kindness about him.

I DON'T KNOW when your birthday was. I don't know what your parents did or when they moved to Warrnambool. I don't know what they're doing now. I don't know their names. I don't know what music you listened to in the last few years of your life. I don't know where you went to high school. I don't know how you met Travis, who studied creative arts. A few years ago you used to post photos of tables on Facebook Marketplace, you'd built them yourself. Sometimes when I'm scrolling through your old Facebook profile I find things that don't fit with the image I've created of you. You didn't go to a party in your first year of uni dressed as a terrorist – you wouldn't, you wouldn't! I imagine asking you about these things. There is some justification that makes it okay. Or you admit to regretting it. We talk about being young and dumb and exchange our most mortifying memories.

SOMETIMES I THINK about what you must have known about me. You knew what I studied and where. You knew I got a TV role straight out of drama school. You knew I hated acting. You knew where I lived. You knew the sheets on my bed were forest green. You knew most of my friends, but not very well. Did you know that I love ambling through museums alone? And going to the movies on a weekday? Did you know how much I love the people around me, my mother and Sarah and Annie?

It was obvious how much you loved Travis and that made me want to love you.

Sometimes I'm thankful that I don't know some things about you because I think if there is less there then it will be easier to forget. I want to forget you. I want to be old one day, with an adult husband I love in a daggy way, and to not remember you.

THIS IS WHY I hope it's a girl. So there's nobody left who looks like you.

I KNOW YOU have three brothers. I've no idea where they live. I've never been to Warrnambool and I don't foresee ever going.

THERE'S ONLY SO much, and for only so long, that you can control a child's life, and that is a very small amount. Maybe one day our baby will have a friend whose family lives in Warrnambool. There will be some family event and the child is allowed to bring a friend along. Our child goes to this gathering and your parents are there and they will see our child at six or seven or eight years old – the image of you at that age. Their breath will catch in their throats and they will blame the grief.

ANNIE COMES OVER DURING THE week to find me on the couch groaning into a pillow. She asks what's wrong.

'I think I've broken a rib.'

'Maybe your baby kicked you,' she suggests.

'I don't think it does that yet.'

'Your ribcage is growing.' Sarah left the room when I started speaking and now she's back, book in hand. 'It expands to make room for your uterus.'

I keep thinking I'm breaking and then being told it's normal. The other night I spat bright pink toothpaste into the sink – apparently I can expect my gums to bleed.

When Sarah finds the correct page she reads straight from it. 'You can get an exercise ball to stretch or you can go for a walk.'

'I'm too tired to walk.' I shift delicately on the couch.

'Don't worry, Daddy will buy you an exercise ball.' Sarah puts *What to Expect* down and picks up her phone. This is a joke inspired by the book – it opens with a short acknowledgement that not all support people are partners and that not all partners are male, then continues to refer to 'tips for Dads' for the remainder of its pages.

KATE TEXTS TO tell me she has a role in an ad and suggests we meet up in the city to discuss it.

This is unusual. Normally she'd just call with the details of an audition. I ring her, but she doesn't answer. All day I wait for her to ring me back or message, but she doesn't. In the evening I text back to ask where and when we should meet.

The following morning, I lie in bed wondering what to wear. The mound is small enough to cover with a long shirt. It's small enough that an unobservant person wouldn't notice it under tight clothes. Kate will definitely notice: my body was part of her product. Technically it still is. She might just think I've let myself go since I quit acting. This time spent deciding is rendered pointless when I start to get dressed and realise none of my tighter clothes fit me anymore. I can't button up any of my pants. In the end I wear a loose jumpsuit. Such a pregnant thing to wear, I think. Women on TV wear jumpsuits when they're pregnant.

I take the train into town and stare out the window. I'm anxious, but still I manage to enjoy the journey over the Merri. The railway is raised, the carriage gliding through foliage like a giant, slow bird. Below, the creek cuts a thick line, brown and crooked, through the parklands. They could charge tourists to come on this part of my trainline.

Approaching the city, I start to feel anxious. I'm nervous about seeing Kate, of course, but also it strikes me how long it's been since I left Thornbury. I hardly even leave the house anymore. I put a hand to my abdomen, steadying myself.

I'm meeting Kate at a small sandwich shop on Flinders Lane. Walking down Swanston Street from the station I stare at all the people I don't know. It's as though I'd thought that, returning here, I'd recognise everyone, but I don't. Obviously I don't. I pass one small express supermarket after another. A 7-Eleven that I swear I've never seen before. But when I try to think back to what was there I can't remember. McDonald's and supermarkets and 7-Elevens. A four-block radius, copy and pasted over and over until you hit Carlton.

I spot Kate through the window of the cafe. She's on the phone, gazing outside. Her mouth pops open when she spots me. She looks happy and I relax a little. When I approach the table she stands and gives me a kiss on the cheek.

'My most troublesome star.'

Kate does this. Refers to me as *hers*.

When she pulls back from the hug she looks me up and down.

'Are you pregnant?'

I feel the muscles in my face shift, hovering between a smile and gritted teeth. I sit down.

'Is this why you quit?'

'I quit before I found out.'

'I was expecting you'd have a haircut.'

'What?'

'I thought you might cut your hair so then I couldn't use your headshots.'

'I thought telling you I quit would mean you wouldn't use them.'

'What are you going to do for work?'

'Tell me about this ad.'

'There are sets with day care. If you get on a long-running series.'

'I didn't like acting.'

'Nobody *likes* their job, Eva.'

'Don't you?'

'Especially not me.' She looks smug and disapproving.

No pleasantries – we start straight in on my decision to quit acting and we stay there. Kate knows and hates everyone in the industry. Usually when we spoke, she would spend ages bitching to me before we got to the point. The fact that she's not doing this now confirms for me what I already suspected – that she is bitching to everyone else about me. Despite this, she seems genuinely concerned for me and wants to help, but all her help is related to getting me to act again, which, to be fair, is probably the only thing she can do for me.

When the waiter takes our order, I say I'm fine. Kate orders herself a steak sandwich, following up with, 'What do you have that's vegetarian? She'll have that.' As we wait for the sandwiches she looks at me, stern. 'You're as pale as a sheet, Eva. Are you taking care of yourself?'

'I'm trying.'

The sandwich is heavy. Oily bread, falafels the size of golf balls, cheese, garlic sauce, salad. 'I thought agents were meant to force their actors to be skinny.'

'Don't examine it – eat it.'

This is why I'd tried to quit over the phone. When I'm with Kate in person I can't help but obey her.

Over the food we finally talk about the ad. It's for a bank. It's one line. One day's work. It pays well.

'I'm not sure what this is going to mean now.' She points at my stomach as she says *this*. 'I'll have to tell them you're fat. If they're still interested in you, your first audition is on Friday.'

'Thank you.'

'Aren't you going to be embarrassed doing ads?'

'Nobody I know watches free-to-air TV.'

When the bill comes, I slide some money across the table. She pushes it back at me. 'You're still my client.'

Before going home, I detour via Bourke Street Mall and buy myself some new clothes. Plain, sensible work slacks that are appropriate for a bank interview. I'm still in Myer when Kate texts me.

Turns out they love the fat. Goes with the family vibe of the
ad. Emailing through details of audition.

EVERY DAY BETWEEN seeing Kate and the audition, I look at my stomach in the mirror. I stand side on and run a hand over its curve. I don't mind how it looks. A curve, not yet a bump. So far unmarked. I'm still getting used to my new arms, though. And my breasts. Padding, ballooning. Being pregnant is like living in a horror film. First the thing possessing you tries to escape from your mouth. Then it pushes in every direction, expanding you from every angle. Then the finale, all that blood.

I'M SELF-CONSCIOUS AT the audition. Nervous, despite Kate having told them about the pregnancy. Having an agent is sort of like having a parent. They're there to have all the difficult conversations so you don't have to. They also see your life as a little bit theirs. It's definitely under their supervision.

I get a call-back that afternoon and then another the following day. The day after that I get the role – not despite the pregnancy but possibly because of it. We shoot the following week. My role involves staring at my first new home with one arm around my pretend husband and my free hand on my stomach. Our pretend home is as white and well proportioned as my pretend husband. I look to him and ask if he is ready. The same words are spoken by a woman to

her elderly mother as she moves her from her home to a retirement
village. And by a little girl to her friend as they sit on their bikes
at the top of a steep hill. Apparently this bank will help you to be
ready for all these stages of life.

Only an hour into the shoot my arm is tired from rubbing my
belly so much. They ask me if I can rub it higher.

'I don't really have anything higher,' I say. The pregnancy is mostly
in my abdomen right now.

They bulk out my stomach in wardrobe. I rub the pillowy bump
and feel indignant on behalf of my unborn child.

It's one day and well worth the money. A whole four months
added to my timeline or a few big-ticket baby items. I feel like a good
parent, which is a relief, as most of the day I had flashes of Annie,
helping people to navigate the legal system, as I lamely patted my
stomach. Not to mention the guilt of the past few days. I don't know
much about banks, but I know they make their money by investing
in industries that are cutting my child's and possibly my own life
short. I don't know the specifics, because I read the headlines and
don't read the articles. I switch off the radio when the stories are
about burning coal.

At the end of the day my phone screen is stacked with messages.
Annie and my mum are asking how the shoot went and, for the first
time since I brushed him off weeks ago, there is also a message on
my phone from Fergus.

You sure you don't want to hang out sometime?

And a message from Renee.

Congratulations you amazing woman!

Sarah had one too many wines and told everyone a few nights ago.

'Ah, fuck,' she said, walking to my room the next morning as she remembered, one hand to her forehead.

'No,' I said. 'Thank you.'

I get so many messages of congratulations that I wonder why I was so worried about telling people. The thing about babies is that everyone is always positive about them. Even if they're thinking it's an awful idea – because I'm single or because big banks invest money in burning coal, which will make the planet uninhabitable in my child's lifetime – nobody says that. They just say that it's wonderful.

THE DAY AFTER THE SHOOT for the bank ad, I ring Mum. I try to commit to doing this once a week, but I keep putting it off because I don't want to talk about anything difficult. There's a sweet spot I've discovered. If I block a few of her calls she'll be worried enough to be so relieved when she hears from me that she won't ask too many questions. But if I push that line out too far it comes full circle and the only thing she will ask about is the father and how I'm going to eventually work and take care of a child.

I spoke to her only a few days ago, but I know she'll be happy I've done the ad so I call her now, hoping we can focus on that.

'How was work?'

'It was great.' That's an exaggeration.

'Does Kate have any more work for you?'

'I'm not sure. Maybe.' She doesn't.

'You should ask her for more jobs.'

'All right.' I won't.

'Are you okay?'

I'm trying to keep this short and shallow. 'I'm tired.'

'Of course you are. Have you been reading the book I sent you?'

'Yes, thanks so much for that.' I don't know where it is, but I suspect it's in Sarah's room. I change the subject. 'How are *you*, Mum?'

'It's already so warm here, this time of year makes me want to move to where you are.'

She always says this. And any time she visits Melbourne in winter she swears she would never be able to live here.

'I went to the council meeting with Ken the other day. They hardly talked about the issue with the run-off pooling into our yard, but Marg next door said she's getting her stumps checked.'

Mum's partner, Ken, has been having this long-running argument with the local council, which has been recounted to me in detail many times.

Mum started seeing Ken after I moved to Melbourne. The efficiency with which she met him after I left made it seem like she was replacing a housemate. I see him once or twice each year and we're always friendly to one another. I've met his kids. But I feel like I don't really know that much about him. Lately, this issue with the council is mostly what Mum talks about in reference to him. It's tedious, but right now I am thankful for any topic that distracts her from asking about my life.

'So anyway, when are you going to stop being a pain and talk to the father?'

I'm not sure if it was her intention to catch me off guard or if she noticed I wasn't really listening and seized the opportunity to pounce.

'What?'

'I just think it's absurd that you're not asking him for child support.'

I hang up on her.

I'm surprised at how badly my mum is taking this. We've hardly argued or said any terse words to one another since I was a teenager.

But I suppose distance has meant that I haven't had to tell her anything about my life that she would disapprove of in a long time. I've always thought of Mum and me as close – you can't not be when it's just the two of you – but it's only lately that I've realised we were never open about our feelings. We never talk about my father; maybe that's why I thought I could get away without talking about my baby's father. Our version of caring about each other didn't involve a lot of communication. I didn't have a curfew like my friends. I was never banished to my room. Mum and I ate dinner side by side on the couch, watching reality TV. I was filling in for her husband, she was filling in for my sibling. Now it occurs to me that if you have to be a little bit of everything for each other, you're spread too thin to perform any of the roles properly.

She messages me only minutes after I've hung up on her.

You should ask Kate for more work.

This is a thing I always hated about acting. I never felt like an adult. I always felt like I was still at school, with directors and agents standing in for the teachers. I told Kate I quit. I told Mum I quit.

I seethe at both women while I shower. I don't even wash; I just stand under the streaming water, letting it run over my eyes, my hair sticking to my face.

Afterwards, I stare at myself in the bathroom mirror. My hair hangs over my collarbones in lank, black coils. I take a pair of scissors from the bathroom drawer and, without pausing to consider what I'm doing, I cut three inches off each side. I lift a centre section of hair from my back and hold it above my head, scissors at the ready. Then I drop it. Fuck. My darker, larger, nipples stare at me disapprovingly in the mirror, reminding me how I felt yesterday, like a good parent.

Now, if I want to do another ad, I'll need to pay for more headshots. *Fuck.* I blame Mum and then I feel even more pathetic.

I call Sarah. She's going out after work, but I tell her she has to come home first.

'Why?'

'I can't tell you why, but I need help.'

'You're like Britney Spears,' she says when she sees me. She ushers me back into the bathroom. I sit with my head tilted forward looking into my lap, so she can tidy up the back. I don't want to look in the mirror. Not at me, not at her. So I stare at the black curls on the floor, the blood of this crime scene.

I hear Sarah getting ready to leave as I vacuum up my hair. I don't want her to go out, but I can't ask her to stay after disrupting her plans already.

'Bye, Britney,' she calls. 'Don't get up to any more mischief.'

On *Friends*, Rachel gets her dream job and she doesn't have to work as a waitress anymore. On day one of the dream job she has to pour coffee. Monica gets fired and is scared to tell her parents.

Sarah told me to help myself to her leftovers, so I do. After dinner, sleep feels so far away. The minuscule rush of adrenaline from cutting my hair is still pinging around my body. I haven't told Kate yet what I did. Maybe I won't have to. Maybe she won't have work for me anyway.

I feel dumb and reckless. I think of Travis. What would he think of me sabotaging my one way to make money? He doesn't care what I do, I remind myself. Even so, I stew in his imagined disapproval.

Eventually, I send a text. Not to Travis or Kate.

I don't want to hang out, but if you want you can sleep in my bed tonight.

Fergus replies straight away.

I'll come over after work. I finish at 9.

I'm not sure I can stay up that late. I tell myself I can always text to cancel if I get too tired. I go about tidying my room just in case.

I got my first boyfriend in year nine. A surfer, although not a good one, who dumped me after six weeks because I wouldn't sleep with him. I responded to his friends' taunts that I was frigid by sleeping with one of them. That was the first time I slept with a man in an attempt to feel better about myself. My second boyfriend was nice. We dated through years eleven and twelve, right up until the last day of term four, when I told him we should break up because I was moving to Melbourne. I could say it was a mature break-up but I'd be lying. I used the last-day-of-school setting to enact the kind of melodrama I loved. *I have to go. I don't want to wake up one day and realise I never left here. There's nothing here for me.* These are not words I actually said, but I did draw on scenes I'd watched on television when I said, 'I think we should just be friends.' I then continued to sleep with him the entire summer before I moved.

I dated a boy at drama school. We started to argue when I got an agent. We fell apart completely when I landed my first role.

In my mid-twenties I was seeing a married producer. I deflected my guilt by convincing myself it was his, not mine. It was certainly more his, but it was also mine. Eventually I did call it off. I tried to run through the fire as opposed to playing with it. I still got burned. When I told Kate, worried it could affect my career, she said, 'There'd be no girls left on TV if they stopped hiring the ones they slept with.'

On stage I've said, *I love you with so much of my heart that none is left to protest.*

On screen I've said, *I used to think we shouldn't be together because you were my best friend. Now that's why I want to be together.*

In real life I've said, *I'm busy. I'm tired. I just want to be friends.*
Sometimes I've said nothing.

In the past couple of years, I've entered into flings under no
illusion they would be anything but bad – most recently during a
show I was paid well for, with a big-name cast, which was slammed
by the critics for its cultural insensitivity. All the reviews ended by
wondering why my co-star and I would agree to take part in such a
train wreck. You're not meant to read the reviews. Every cast makes
a pact at the beginning of a season not to read the reviews until it's
over. And every cast member in every show reads them. That season
was a long one and we got good houses, in that they were always
full, but bad houses in that the audience were only there to see if
the show really was as terrible as they'd heard. My co-star and I
held hands for our bow, which wasn't scripted. Then I'd bend over
the vanity in my dressing room, him behind me. We'd both avoid
looking in the mirror. Afterwards, he'd leave to shower in his own
dressing room before going home. After only three nights like this,
we stopped speaking to one another off stage.

FERGUS ARRIVES AT nine thirty. His hair is longer than the last time
I saw him and is pulled back into a tiny ponytail, which makes it
look darker red and makes his skin seem paler than I remember.
He's wearing a blue shirt; he doesn't look like he's arrived straight
from work.

'Nice hair.' He leans forward and kisses the side of my mouth.

'I'm eating.'

I turn around and he follows me to the kitchen, where I've been
slowly making my way through the vegetarian pie Sarah left. Rocket,
drenched in vinegar, on the side.

'You eat late.'

'I do.' This is my second serve of dinner.

'Where's your housemate?'

'She went to an exhibition opening.'

'Which one?'

'It's at No Vacancy.'

'Right on.'

He takes a six-pack from his bag and puts it in the fridge. He doesn't ask me if I want a drink, but removes two. He uses a lighter to open the beers, then throws the bottle caps on the table as he joins me.

'That's presumptuous of you.'

'Did I say one was for you?' He tries to be smug, but he still hands me a beer.

I take a large sip and swish it around in my mouth, push it back and forth through the thin gap in my two front teeth. It's an expensive Pale Ale, overly floral.

'So, you don't drink much?'

'I used to.'

I study the beer. A tiny pregnant woman is illustrated on the back of the label with the fine print. A bowling ball, her silhouette a question mark. She's drinking, but from a wineglass. I wonder if Fergus is guessing I'm being evasive because I once had a drinking problem and now don't want to talk about it. I imagine him imagining me drunk, loudly talking over people or vomiting in my own lap.

He talks a lot as I eat my dinner. He's a theatre sound tech and has fitted me for mics before, apparently. He talks about that show. It was years ago, at a smaller theatre. The actors from that show have all gone on to bigger jobs, but not the playwright.

'It's just bullshit she can't get work on the main stage, you know. Just because she's a woman and her characters say "cunt".' He's parroting lines from theatre columnists.

'It's because all her plays are the same. All the characters do is say "cunt".' I don't necessarily agree with this, but it's something I've heard other actors say.

He finishes his beer quickly then goes to the fridge for another.

'So, what's the plan now?' He sits back down with his new beer. I've almost finished my meal and for a moment I think he's talking about the evening, us having sex, before I realise he means my life.

'Find a job.' I stand and take my plate to the sink.

'I have friends who need a director on their show next year. I can put you on to them.'

'I need money,' I call from the kitchen. 'I don't need to like my job.'

'Right on. You're probably too smart to be an actor.'

If he was smarter, he would point out that if all I need is money, I could just be an actor.

I take my shirt off as I walk to my room. I hear him follow behind me. I crawl backwards on my bed, he climbs over. When I take off my bra, he smiles then squeezes my left nipple, tight, between his thumb and forefinger.

'Ouch!'

He laughs, turned on. He pulls my undies off and lowers himself onto his stomach.

'Oh my God, you're so horny.' He stares at me, lightly grazes his finger over the opening. It's the vaginal discharge. I'm lucky if I only have to change my undies once a day now. I worry for a moment that it might make me taste different, before I remember he's only slept with me when I've been pregnant. He lowers his mouth onto me and

I try to relax. It feels good, but I can only relax for a minute at most before remembering the baby, now the size of an avocado. A hiccup of a thought, brief but disrupting. Despite this I come fast and long, which didn't happen the first time I slept with Fergus. After feeling sick for three months, now I'm horny and quickly satisfied.

We do it twice without much of a break between. I fall asleep immediately after the second time. I wake to him kissing my head, telling me he's going to shower. When I wake again, he's sitting up in my bed texting, his hair damp. I get up and go to the bathroom. There's a faint sting at the tail of my stream. I wish for him to be gone so I can sleep alone. I go to the kitchen to get a glass of water and some chocolate. My body is heavy and my mouth feels chalky and tastes stale. I feel like I'm jetlagged. The clock on the oven says it's twelve-thirty in the morning. Sarah's bedroom door is open; she hasn't come home. I return to my room, sit on top of my doona facing Fergus. I unwrap the chocolate, break off a piece and offer it to him.

'No thanks.' He's still reading something on his phone, not looking at me.

'Have some.'

'I'm a vegan.'

'Oh, shit, sorry.' I try to remember if there's a reason I should know this.

'That's okay.' He puts his phone down, shimmies his body until he's lying flat on the bed and rests his arms behind his head on the pillow. 'It was nice of you to offer.'

I don't know if he's suggesting I'm rude. I don't know if I care if he thinks I'm rude.

'Okay, so what's this?' I trace my finger over one of the tattoos on his forearm. It says *Fish & Chips* in a twee typewriter font.

'Stick and poke.'

'Really?' I take his arm and hold it close to my face. The font is far too stylised to have been hand drawn. The letters align perfectly. 'You're lying. You paid for this.'

'It was my first one, actually. I lost a bet on schoolies.'

'So, you weren't a vegan on schoolies?'

'No.' He smiles at me.

'And what happened here?' I lift his arm from the bed and point to another tattoo – *Riley*.

'That's for my friend Riley.'

'Does Riley have a tattoo that says *Fergus*?'

'He does.'

'Too cute.' I drop his forearm. I hear a clattering at the back door and turn my head to listen, expecting to hear Sarah stomp down the hall. It's not her. I picture the door banging in the wind. We're silent. Fergus is looking at me. I turn my attention to a tattoo on his thigh. Larger than the others, but also more obviously hand-done. A wonky love heart with *Baby* and *Angel* inside. An arrow piercing the stencil. I trace my finger along the arrow. He watches me. I don't ask about it and he doesn't say anything. It's so overtly saccharine I figure it must be very real.

'You're really beautiful,' he says.

I feel him looking at me, but I don't meet his eye. I stop tracing the tattoo and take another piece of chocolate. He starts to rub his hand over my thigh; I can't tell if he's being affectionate or is hoping for more sex.

'I'm going to sleep.' I take a sip of water and swill it around in my mouth to remove the chocolate from my teeth.

He sits up and kisses me on the side of the head. 'You go to sleep. I'm going to get that last beer.'

I WAKE TO the sound of the front door slamming. It's morning. For a moment I wonder if Sarah has only just arrived home, then I realise I'm in bed alone.

November

I KEEP SEEING FERGUS. IT'S much the same each time except he doesn't bring beers. The sex is good but our conversations are not. If he says he likes a particular band and I say I don't, he'll say, 'I can see why you wouldn't.' He doesn't elaborate, or if he does it's vague. 'They peaked at their debut.' He tells me I'm smart or perceptive when I say anything, which is ridiculous, as all I ever say is the opposite to what he just said, regardless of whether I agree with it or not. We converse like people who've run into one another and do that awkward little dance of evasion – both move left, both move right. I pull him into me and have sex with him like a person might firmly shift a body aside, to get it out of the way. I'm not sure I've experienced anything like it – sensuous, but devoid of emotion. For me, at least. I wonder if it's the pregnancy. I'm more carnal in so many ways. Feel more in my body at all moments of the day. Once we're finished I slither off. Shiver at the feeling of his slimy, hot meat sliding out of me. He's a sweaty guy. Sweatier than most people I've slept with. In the moment, Fergus's sweat suits our sex – fast and aggressive. Then I come and it's like I regain consciousness and discover I'm dripping and smelly. I shower straight after, then immediately throw the towel I used in the wash. He even sounds like an animal when he comes. A pathetic animal, injured and dying on the side of the road. None of this sounds sexy, but it hardly matters because I come so easily now. He barely needs to touch me. I hope he doesn't take it as a compliment to himself, but it's possible he does think that because I haven't told him otherwise. I've wondered whether or not Fergus has realised I'm pregnant. 'You do have great tits, don't you,' he said the other day, staring at my breasts, which get larger each time he sees me. My avocado is now a mango, so if he hasn't noticed he must be particularly unobservant. I don't waste much time wondering what he knows or suspects, though. Once I've showered, I open my laptop in bed and play episodes of *Friends*. I expect him to say something, to comment on how cheesy or old or outdated it is. He doesn't, so I do. 'You can make fun of me if you want.'

'It's cute.' He watches me watching television. I have my back turned to him and he strokes my arm.

When he leaves, I tell myself I won't contact him again. To his credit he doesn't contact me, but when I do message him, sometimes as soon as the next day, he replies straight away. He invites me over to his place. I ignore the offer and he comes to me.

IT'S LATE ON a Sunday. I'm at my desk, messaging Sarah in the next room. Fergus is in my bed on his phone. I ask Sarah to please do something to make him leave if he isn't gone soon.

> Get him to leave yourself, coward.
> *I'm being as rude as I can. I can hardly say, 'Can you please leave?' Who does that?*

He's been skittish since he came over late this morning, mostly monosyllabic. Occasionally he'd revert to his usual fervent adoration, then it's like he'd catch himself and snap back to silence. Usually he leaves not long after we've had sex, but today, after seeming pissed with me, he's hanging around.

'What are you doing tonight?' He's staring at his phone.

'Um . . .' I finish a message to Sarah but pretend I'm still typing, feigning busyness. 'Well, I'm sending some emails now. Then I'm going to a Red Stitch show.'

'You're seeing Morgan's show?'

'Yeah.'

'No shit. So am I.' He sounds lighter than he has been all day.

I hadn't even considered lying. I hadn't thought I'd need to. And I can't not go. Morgan is an old friend who I haven't seen in ages. The show, which received heaps of funding for development, has been unequivocally hated by critics. Tonight is the final performance. I won't get another chance to see it.

RED STITCH IS a theatre company based in a small red building that looks like a barn on Chapel Street. It's not overly warm when we enter to take our seats, but I know it's going to feel like a furnace soon enough – they're too poorly funded to have good aircon. At least Fergus and I aren't sitting together, since we booked separately. The theatre is about two-thirds full. A couple of people look at me for longer than is comfortable, presumably because they recognise me from other shows. I see a guy I went to drama school with. He hasn't had much success since we graduated and he avoids eye contact. Only seeing one person I know is a relief and I relax for a minute, which feels foreign, and I'm just wondering why I was feeling so anxious when I see Fergus walking towards me with two glasses of wine. He takes a seat next to me.

'Someone might have booked that seat,' I say.

'No, it's okay – look, they're closing the doors.'

He holds a wine out to me but I don't take it.

'Oh, shit, sorry,' he says. 'I totally forgot.'

His eyes dart down towards my lap very quickly and he gives me a small, sly smile before turning his head to the stage. I stare at him as the lights go down. I don't look away until it's completely dark. I contemplate taking the drink in defiance, but know that I will need to pee if I do.

The play is called *Cake*. The opening line – 'I'm going to buy the ingredients today to make a cake' – is followed by a discussion: chocolate, sponges and cheesecakes, flourless or not. It's a perfect opening. Quippy and not thematically loaded, but it gives you an immediate impression of the two characters and sets up a lot of openings for recall later. But I start tapping my foot almost immediately, frustrated by the pace. The actors are lingering on lines, playing hard for laughs. A few times I stop and remind myself I don't need to think like this anymore, imagining myself as one of these people who're imagining themselves as others. Then I remember I can think like this because it's inconsequential and fun to think about now that I'm not acting.

When Fergus finishes his wine, he bends down and takes the second glass, supposedly purchased for me.

'I'm going to leave,' I say to him as soon as the cast finish their bows. 'I don't want to get stuck talking to anyone.'

'Yeah, good call,' he says.

I was hoping that he wouldn't follow me, but he does.

We wait for the train at Windsor station and discuss the show. I thought the script was brilliant. I almost gave it a standing ovation, which I never do. It was so good that, for the most part, I was distracted enough not to focus on how hot it was in there.

'Seriously,' I say, interrupting Fergus's observation about how the play subverted the traditional coming-out narrative, 'if it hadn't been Morgan's play, I would've totally zoned out. It's like a furnace in there. They need aircon. It's absurd.' I wipe my hands under my armpits and then over my shirt.

'I guess you must feel the heat a lot more now, right?' he says as the train pulls in. He quickly glances at my stomach, then steps into the carriage.

I hesitate before following him, tempted to let the train leave without me. It's late, though, and I don't want to wait thirty minutes for the next one.

'Seriously, though' – he opens an abandoned newspaper on the seat across from him – 'I would pay to see Tennessee Williams write a play with iPhones.' He turns pages of the paper, skimming the contents but clearly not reading, like a teenager reads a paper in a play.

'What do you mean I must feel the heat more now?'

It's quiet for a few seconds. He's still staring at the paper but is no longer turning pages. Supposedly reading something now.

'Because you're pregnant.' He's still not looking at me.

'Who told you?'

'Ah, I think it was Jack, who works with Sarah. He might have mentioned it.' He frowns, like he's trying to remember, then returns to the paper. 'An article on the reef dying comes after a royal baby – thank God the newspapers are all going out of business.' He tosses the paper on the seat across from him then finally meets my gaze, not even blinking. 'Also, you're pretty big already.'

'You just said you knew because someone told you.'

'But it didn't surprise me when I found out, you know?'

I feel a tingling of dislike, like static. 'So, I guess now you know why I really can't get involved in anything.'

'Yeah.' He looks at me thoughtfully. 'I mean, you shouldn't need a reason, though, right? No means no, so you shouldn't have to justify rejecting me.'

'I know.' I glance up and down the carriage. The one person without earphones has stopped texting and is now staring out the window. It's dark outside so she's actually staring at her own reflection and I figure she's probably listening.

'Look, I know you don't want a relationship and that's fine. I don't see why you being pregnant means we can't' – he pauses for a moment – 'have fun.' He does a bit of a shrug, a bit of a smile, but not a complete one of either.

'I don't want to do this anymore.' My voice is small and strangled and I hate myself for it.

'Okay. If you don't want to, you don't want to. But honestly, it's fine. I'm not looking for a relationship either.'

When we get to Flinders Street I take the escalator to switch platforms for a train heading north. Fergus is right behind me, following me through the station like we're in a bad movie.

'Don't you have another train to catch?' I ask.

'How are you going to get home?'

'I'll walk from the station.'

'I think it's safer if you don't walk home alone.'

'It's a Sunday.'

'It's dark. I think you should get a tram.'

'Okay, thanks for the advice.' When I turn around, he walks into me. I stand my ground, as does he. We're only inches apart. I hold his gaze for a few seconds. When I turn away, I don't say goodnight, not even goodbye.

I STAND ON the tram for the entire trip home, gripping the ceiling handles hard. A few times I switch ends, marching along the carriage. I have the urge to spit on the ground. I contemplate getting off a few stops early so that I can. I feel my phone vibrate in my pocket. If it's him, I think, I'm going to block his number. It's not. It's a message from a friend I met through Annie, congratulating me, she's just heard. A string of x's at the end of the text. I send back a quick thank you and then I open Fergus's contact. I pause on it for some time before I block it. I place a hand on my abdomen and breathe, in for three, out for three. My breaths grow louder and harsher as my stop never arrives. I'm as relaxed as a woman in a movie breathing her way through labour.

FOUR DAYS LATER I get a message from him on Facebook. He must've realised I blocked his number.

> I'm sorry I acted like a dick. To be honest, I've had a crush on you for ages. Ever since I first saw you act. I was super keen when we hooked up, but could tell you were always holding back a bit. When I found out you were pregnant this made sense and I was upset and pissed off and took that out on you. I was trying to save face and in doing that I ended up being an arsehole. I hope we can be friends, but if you don't want to that's also fair. I really hope it works out for you. You'll be a great mum.

I read it only once then I block him on Facebook.

I TOLD A PSYCHOLOGIST ONCE that I had almost killed myself in the week before our appointment, which was most definitely not true. More truthful would've been to say that it crossed my mind. Suicide crossed my mind, but not the intention to actually do it. It was more that I realised I could do it. I realised I could do it and that moment coincided with a moment of total despair. I was driving home from a work event. One of the parties the theatre companies throw for philanthropists that the actors are forced to attend to suck up to the donors, by allowing the donors to suck up to us. Elitists I didn't know told me stories about actors more famous than me that they'd met at similar events. I shouldn't have been drinking but I was bored out of my mind and trays of champagne kept going by. At the end of the night, as we were leaving, the philanthropists had just sat down for their meal. Their tables were set up on the stage. The person hosting the event began with an anecdote about the stage, how it was the largest in the southern hemisphere. So large you could fit twenty houses on it. Everyone looked around the space. Then the host added, *Obviously not a house that any of us would live in*, and they all laughed. I wasn't plastered, but I was too wobbly to drive.

In the car I was hysterical, crying and gripping the steering wheel. The road ahead blurred. It was late and there were long-haul trucks in lanes either side and for a moment I thought I'd swerved too close to one. The next moment I was thinking that I could swerve into the next lane, give my understudy a chance to shine.

WHEN PATIENTS SAY they are suicidal, psychologists ask them how they would plan to do it. The more thought out the plan, the more serious the case. The psychologist clarified to me that mine had been an opportunistic thought, not a plan.

I knew a girl who was so depressed, so certain she might kill herself, that she took herself to emergency and told them she needed to be admitted. The staff asked her what her plan was, how she was going to do it. When she told them that she hadn't got that far, since she'd decided to admit herself to hospital instead, they sent her home. Not at risk, they said. At home later she swallowed five times the recommended dose of sleeping pills.

I've only known a few other people who did what you did and all of them were adults and I didn't really know any of them, not properly. They were parents of people I knew.

A girl I went to high school with was pulled out of class by the school receptionist. The receptionist did a terrible job of concealing that it was serious. 'Bring your books with you, lovey, you won't be coming back.' The girl did come back the next term, but she was different. There was a sadness oozing out of her. By year ten she was having a lot of sex on the steps behind the science block. That's the only other thing I remember about her. And that she ended up with a top mark at the end of year twelve. I don't know anything about her father except for how he died.

There was the mother of another person from high school, but it happened a few years after we'd left, when the guy was in his twenties. I remember thinking this was less sad. He was an adult. He didn't need a parent as much as a fourteen-year-old did. Then I decided it was far sadder. She was about to retire. Imagine working forever and then nothing.

Another friend's father. Someone I studied acting with. His father had bipolar disorder at a time when mental illness was not considered a real illness. The only treatment for his condition, according to his son, was alcoholism. 'I'm glad it's over,' my friend said. 'He was a vicious man.' This was a far sadder story – both for my friend, who had been put down and threatened for his entire childhood, and for the man himself.

Suicide was said to be common in our parents' generation because people didn't take mental health seriously. Men were meant to be men, which meant not crying, and women were meant to be in the kitchen, but also in the workplace, but being paid less. Depression was not a disease, not a real one.

It's said to be worse in young people now because of the internet. Because of cyberbullying and always comparing our lives with other, better lives on Instagram.

A lot of older men did it after returning from war. Nobody talked about PTSD back then. We say this now as though the fact that we talk about it today stops it from happening, which we know it doesn't.

Apparently people are sadder now than ever before.

A friend of mine once went on a date with a girl who started taking her medication while sitting across from him at a bar. She took so many pills she carried a first-aid kit with her. She unrolled it at the table and told him about her different afflictions, all mental.

He told me this story when I asked him why he wasn't going to see her again. It was evidence she wasn't someone to get involved with.

SOMETIMES I WONDER what would've happened if I had told you any of these things. I'm addicted to the fantasy that if we'd got on to the topic of suicide I could've stopped you. Even though I know that it is just that – a fantasy. Even if I could've stopped you, it's not what happened.

I GET MORE AND MORE tired and eventually I find out I'm low in iron. 'I've been a vegetarian for a decade,' I tell the midwife over the phone.

'Have you been craving meat?'

'No.' It's a lie. I'm craving dim sims. I have no memory of ever having eaten one and yet I imagine exactly what they taste like, salty and fatty. I dream of lashings of soy sauce.

'Often the body will crave what it needs.'

'That's stupid. I can't eat salami. I can't eat any of the good meats, anyway.' I sound like Sarah. I don't even like salami. Or at least I don't remember if I do.

'If you're serious about not eating meat there are other iron-rich foods. You need to eat a lot, though, which shouldn't be hard.' I hear her voice soften a little over the phone. 'And, look, being low in iron isn't that big a risk to the baby – though it can mean the baby is born underweight.'

'So, it'll be easy to push out?' I expect to be scolded for this, but she laughs. There's a sense of camaraderie I've not felt with a health professional before.

'Underweight babies do face certain risks. But, mostly, getting more iron is for your benefit.'

She takes my email and sends me links to websites with information about iron deficiency during pregnancy. I glance at the information – lists of iron-rich foods and risks for underweight babies.

'This is probably why you're exhausted all the time. You have the rest of your life to be a vegetarian. Being pregnant is hard, so go easy on yourself.'

Before we hang up, I ask if I need to come into the hospital again. She answers 'no' with an efficiency that could make me feel relief, that could suggest this really isn't a very big deal, but instead makes me feel like there are far too many babies being born for the hospital to really care for all of us enough.

'There's no major reason for concern. You're fit and healthy.' She finishes the call with, 'You'll be fine.'

I want to say, *But the father killed himself.* But of course I don't.

IN BED AT night I think about dim sims until it becomes too painful. I put *Friends* on, distracting myself until finally I fade off. I wake to pee at 3 a.m. then I can't get back to sleep. I can taste soy sauce in my saliva. I get out of bed and pull on some clothes from the floor. I'm careful not to wake Sarah as I close the front door gently behind me.

It's a warm night; there are insects congregating around a streetlight and the sound of crickets. I start my car and drive – slowly, as though I'm trying not to wake my neighbours – a kilometre down the road to the open-all-hours burger joint on St Georges Road – open since 1945, it proudly proclaims on its signage. I've been here a few times before, always at about this time, but on weekends, when I was drunk. It's less busy now, but I'm surprised to see there are still quite a few people here. Two men, not seated together, both in jeans, only one is eating a burger. Behind the counter it's all men working. I disassociate. Picture myself in this scene like it's CCTV footage. A lone pregnant woman eats a burger at night. The man behind the counter has long black hair and is staring at me.

'What can I get for you?'

'I'm a vegetarian.'

'One veggie burger?'

'No, sorry. I was just talking to myself.'

His face drains of tolerance. The large menu behind him is designed to look like a blackboard, with the menu items listed in cursive font. Dim sims are a dollar each.

'I'll have six dim sims. Steamed.'

'Those are meat.' He doesn't ring up the sale.

'I know.' I feel tears prickling into existence.

He holds my gaze for another few seconds before he starts punching my order into the register.

I take a seat on a bar stool, and a man at the other end of the counter stands and leaves. He tosses a scrunched-up, dirty napkin on the table, takes slow steps out the door. 'Bye,' he calls out to the staff.

'See ya, Bill,' replies the man who served me. He catches me watching and I smile at him, but he turns and goes to the kitchen.

My dim sims arrive in one big bowl. A man in chef's pants delivers them with a squeezy bottle of soy sauce. They taste exactly how I thought they would; they are exactly what I've been craving this entire time. Meat and salt and cabbage and a flavour that is familiar, but I don't know from where or when. I eat one and then another and then another. I feel distinctly replenished, like a character in a computer game whose store of energy has been returned to full. I toy with feeling queasy or uneasy about it, but I don't. I've been a vegetarian for eight years and for six of those I've known that the dairy industry is just as cruel and unsustainable as the meat industry. I've never been a vegan – not because I can't live without cheese, but because I can't stand the thought of having to be strong in the face of flak. People hate vegans.

Q: How do you know someone's not a vegan?

A: They'll make a joke about one.

But, even though I understood the contradiction, I couldn't go so far as to eat meat. I'd be too ashamed to confidently order a steak. Vegetarianism is a safe place where very little attention is drawn to you. Blending into the mass of people who care a little, but not so much they make others feel bad about their choices.

And, anyway, the midwife told me to go easy on myself.

Before leaving I order another three dim sims to take away and at home I sleep soundly, like a log, or a baby.

WHEN PHOEBE IS PREGNANT AND craving steaks, Joey becomes a vegetarian for those months so that no more animals are harmed than would have been otherwise. I imagine this as you and me. I don't know if you were a vegetarian. I think maybe not. I imagine you saying, 'The solution to climate change isn't to stop eating meat.' I picture the photo of you with Travis wearing the t-shirts with matching stripes, and I imagine the baby there, being held up by Travis, its body dangling below its ribcage. That blank, petrified stare that is somehow cute on children. How adorable it is that babies are flummoxed by the world. And you holding a burger, or a steak, so happy our baby is born so you can eat meat again.

MY FANTASIES OF you and me together are perfectly seen, like my real memories of you. They start just after the last time I saw you: the day you left my house and I was giddy with the feeling that everything was about to change. I'd thought I was about to fall in love, with you and with my life. I imagine us going on our first date the following weekend to the cute Italian bar in Thornbury. Or just to the pub in the afternoon for pints, and to the pasta bar on our second date. I imagine our conversations, long ones. I ask you all the things I don't know about you. What is it exactly that you do? Why did you stop making furniture? How did you learn to do that? We laugh over ravioli. I like to imagine that I don't find out I'm pregnant until after our second date, so we get two relaxed dates before we have to get an abortion. I go with Sarah, but you pay. I ask you for half the money, but you transfer me the entire amount. You send me flowers . . . no, you wouldn't actually, but you'd be kind. Then we date. We go on a camping trip. We go to the border of Victoria and South Australia together and drive your parents' Tarago between those big, rocky beaches I've only seen in photographs.

OBVIOUSLY, I CAN'T have this fantasy without feeling sad because you are gone and also because it means, in a way, I am wishing to not be pregnant, which means wishing to not have our child. That's not how I feel, though. I want the baby. It's only in a very convoluted way that I don't. Simply put – I do. And obviously I can't have this fantasy without feeling sad because I'll always remember what actually happened. Not the part where you die, but before that, when you told me you'd made other plans.

I'M LYING ON MY BACK on the couch. My laptop is resting high on my chest – my stomach not flat enough for this anymore – and my neck is at an unnaturally sharp angle. I'm idly flicking through Travis's Facebook account, scrolling down his wall and scanning for anything I might've missed, when a message pops up on my screen from him. He's never messaged me before, nor I him.

Hey, what's your number? I want to ask you something.

I snap the computer shut. He shouldn't be able to know I was looking at his profile, or that I look at it most days. When I open the computer again, cautiously, his message is still there. It could be nothing. But if it was nothing, he would just ask whatever it is he wants to ask in a message. He wouldn't need to call me.

I go to the kitchen, take my time pouring one glass of water and then another. Before I write back, I take some deep breaths. I run my hands over my belly, protective, or maybe just reminding myself it's there. I send only my number, no words. For a long minute afterwards I watch my phone on my coffee table, ominously dormant. Finally, the screen lights up with the call.

'Hello?'

'Hey, it's Travis.'

'How are you?'

I feel the urge to move, so I stand and walk to my room.

'Good. How are you?'

'Yeah, not bad.' I look at myself in the mirror. My skin is smooth and bright. Despite the fact that I'm always sweating lately, I look healthier than I have for a while. Maybe it's the meat eating. My belly is higher up now, pointy. I look pregnant.

'Are you still looking for work?'

'Yeah, why?'

'My parents own a winery in the Yarra Valley. They've got a batch that's been bottled and now it needs to be labelled. It's mundane work but they pay well. I usually take a friend.'

It takes a few seconds for me to figure out why he's telling me this.

'It's not an ongoing gig or anything. I just thought I'd ask you because you'd probably be free and might want the work.'

'Oh.'

'They need it done really soon, though. By next weekend. I'm going to drive up tomorrow. Are you free?'

'Yeah, I'm free.' I can hear the shock in my voice, almost like I'm irritated. It's so unexpected I actually forget for a moment that any money would be helpful.

'It's two days work. Or you could just do one day if you'd prefer.'

'I'll do two.'

'Great. I'm going to stay at my parents' place, so you'd need to drive yourself there and back. It's less than an hour away.'

'That'll be fine.'

He gives me the address then rings off.

THERE ARE TWO very similar photos of Pat and Travis together. The photos were both posted in November but several years apart. They're sitting at the same wooden bench in each picture, surrounded by wine bottles. It's hard to see the detail of the room they're in as the lighting is dim. In one, they are both looking at the camera. In the other, Pat is looking at Travis and Travis is looking at a wine bottle in his hands. Pat is smiling, maybe laughing. That's what I've always focused on: the way he is looking at Travis. Now, looking at the photo again, I can see other details. That Travis is running a hand over the surface of the wine bottle. That there's a reel of shiny white sticker paper on the bench beside them, almost neon in the darkly lit room. Wine bottles stacked in crates in the background.

I usually take a friend, he said. I return to Travis's profile and scroll through his photos, searching for the barn, the dim lighting, the wine. The only two images like this are with Pat. Did he always take Pat?

Travis said he thought to call me because it was late notice. He assumed I'd be free, which is true, I have nothing else to do. I'm suddenly overwhelmed with appreciation for the gesture and the fact that my life is so empty right now and I start to cry, hard. No warm up, my face is wet in an instant. I rub my bump and try to feel happy for my baby. This might be the closest we get to being with its father.

Eventually I wipe my face and pick up where I was before Travis called. Scrolling, searching, scrolling.

I'VE NEVER HEARD of Kangaroo Ground, but it's on the way to Healesville, which I have heard of, although I've never been there. The route is confusing and I have to keep checking the map on my phone at traffic lights. I'm anxious about being late. Not because this is like a real job, but because I don't want to look unappreciative. This offer must mean Travis likes me, I realise. Or he doesn't dislike me, at least, if he's willing to spend two days with me. The idea of spending more than five minutes alone with Travis makes me nervous. I've made a list of questions I want to ask and I rehearse saying them in ways that might sound off the cuff and also in ways that mean he doesn't have to answer, not if he doesn't want to.

I know I didn't know him as well as you did, but I really liked him when I met him.

I was surprised how sad it made me, given I didn't know him that well.

I can't imagine how hard it must be for you.

It's okay to not be okay.

KANGAROO GROUND IS stunningly green with long, winding roads through rolling hills. I stop at a small store, which looks like a cottage, with a red corrugated-iron roof. I buy a salad and cheese roll, suffocated in cling wrap, a thick layer of margarine visible.

'You just passing through?' The woman behind the counter is middle-aged and blonde.

'I'm here to see a friend.'

'They local?'

'Yes. His name is Travis.'

'Oh, the Millers. Have you been there before?'

'No. I have directions, though.'

'Their street is the second right once you dip down the hill. Number nine – you can't miss it. Big blue house, beautiful.'

The directions come in handy, as the reception drops out just past the store. The woman was right: the house is beautiful. Big but not pretentious, weatherboards and tall rectangular windows. I'm about to phone Travis when I see the front door open; he jogs across the lawn. He looks different – dressed in cargo shorts and Blundstones, unfashionable sunglasses. It suits him, I think, the country. I wind down my window and he bends to speak to me, one hand on the roof and one on my door.

'Come up the driveway,' he says. 'There's space for you to park along the side of the house.'

I drive slowly behind him as he walks up the drive and points towards a carport. There are two other cars here already – an old Landcruiser and an expensive-looking sedan. I'm glad to be parking behind these two cars. I'd be scared of pulling in next to one and scratching it.

Travis doesn't hug me when I get out of the car.

'Come this way.' He opens a gate at the back of the carport. I follow him into his parents' backyard. 'How was the drive?'

'It was fine. I've never been out this way before.'

'I love it here.'

The property is huge. There's a steep slope at the back of the house that leads down to a small dam and a paddock. The grass is a bright, pale green. Travis leads me towards a large shed next to the dam.

'They don't grow the grapes here,' he explains. 'They have a vineyard over in the valley. They bottle it there too. We're just labelling. It's a small batch.'

He turns and smiles at me. For a second, I think I've never seen Travis like this, happy and excitable. Then I remember he was always like this when I first met him.

He unlatches a tall door to the shed and holds it open for me. One side of the space is filled with pallets of wine, stacked high, each stack taller than me. It looks like a big 'small batch' to me. There's a large workbench with some bottles already lined up and rolls of labels sitting ready.

'Don't worry. We don't have to finish all of them.' Travis is looking at me looking at the pallets.

'How will we get them all down?'

'We have a pallet jack,' he says. 'We just can't use it drunk.' He throws me a quick smile. 'So, anyway, I've already unstacked the first few pallets over that way. The stickers are all here on this table. I've done the first few bottles so you can see.'

The sticker has a minimal design. A cream label with an illustration of a grapevine. Basic font, italics.

'What wines are these?' I ask.

'These ones are pinot noirs. Those over there are chardonnays, we'll do those tomorrow. They won an award for that wine recently. Take some bottles at the end of the day. Save it for next year, maybe.'

'I'm sure Sarah will drink it before next year.'

I concentrate on Travis's laugh, try to discern if it's impatient or affectionate. It's hard to tell.

He carries a tall stool over to the workbench. 'I got you this,' he says. 'So you don't have to stand all day.'

It looks like it might be hard for me to balance on, but I don't mention this. I'm touched he's so eager to help me.

I get started labelling while he sets up a speaker and puts on some music.

'Feel free to DJ,' he tells me.

He removes a few more pallets of wine from their stack and eventually sits down and joins me labelling. 'Don't worry if you fuck any up, by the way. That can just be a bottle for you to take home.'

'What if I fuck up all of them?'

'Then we'll soak them in warm water and rub the label off. And then you'll be fired.'

'So, do you do this every year?' One of my rehearsed questions. It almost feels nostalgic, like I'm remembering lines.

'Yeah, since I was sixteen.'

'You never wanted to make wine?'

'My brother does that. I wouldn't mind holding off on joining the family business.'

'Classic youngest child.'

This was a comment Renee made about Travis after she broke up with him, when he was incredulous, trying to convince her she was wrong. I'm worried Travis might ask how I know he is the youngest, but he doesn't.

'Do you have siblings?' he asks.

'No, I'm an only child.'

'Classic actor.'

We both smile.

Travis is being chatty and friendly, but I realise quickly he's not relaxed. He labels some bottles, then stands and goes back to the pallets for more, even though we still have plenty ready to label. He doesn't just leave an album to play, but changes tracks individually. He narrates what he likes about each song, emphasising off-beat notes, subtle background percussion and good lyrics. Some I recognise – Sampa the Great and Nick Cave – but others I haven't heard before, long-winded instrumentals. Unlike the last few times I've seen him, he doesn't leave silences in our conversation. After two or three seconds he'll circle back to what we were saying before. He's manic, in a friendly way.

'How's your band going?' I ask.

'I still love it. But also I don't. We don't make any money. We tour but we have to stay in hostels, get flights at six in the morning. It makes it really hard to hold down an unskilled job when you have to take weekends off all the time.'

I don't feel sorry for him now, having seen his house, but I resist the urge to point this out. 'At least people go to your gigs,' I say. 'In indie theatre you have to do all the work to get a show on, then you have to perform it to an audience of two people.'

'Didn't you get a TV slot straight out of uni?'

I watch Travis delicately lining up a sticker on a wine bottle, placing the corners in exactly the right place, then smoothing his hands over the label. I don't know what to say. I'm stunned, having been presented with this mundane fact about my life from a person I thought didn't know me that well. I wonder if his concentration on the bottle in front of him is feigned, if he's avoiding looking at me, but realise I haven't watched him label any others so I can't be sure. I realise now that it's possible Travis has invited me here for the same reason I agreed to come: he suspects Pat might be the father of my child and he wants to get information about me, about my baby. I stand from my stool and steady myself at the workbench.

'Are you okay?' he asks.

'I think I need a break.'

'We can stop for lunch now if you want.'

'It's pretty early.'

He smiles. 'First lunch.'

I follow him to the house. We go up the stairs to a large, square verandah and through glass sliding doors into the kitchen, which is simultaneously modern and not. A large island bench with a stainless-steel counter that matches the splashbacks, and wooden cupboard doors with chipped white paint.

Travis opens a fridge and takes out a bottle of cold water, pours me a glass. 'Is there anything you can't eat?'

'Like, everything. But don't stress – it's okay if I eat things occasionally. Also, I bought lunch at the general store.' I take the salad roll from my bag.

'Oh, their rolls are the best.'

'Sorry – I should've bought you one.'

'Tomorrow.' He keeps smiling at me after he says things, pointedly, like a parent trying to keep a child happy.

I take a sip of water. He takes a bag of bread rolls from the cupboard and starts unloading ingredients. Salad, different kinds of cheese, avocado and spreads – Vegemite, jam, peanut butter. He also takes out crackers and a few tubs of dip. He makes himself one sandwich and then another. When I finish my roll from the store I eat some biscuits. He asks me about being pregnant and I'm wary at first, but he doesn't talk about the father, or even about my not having a job. He wants details of weird physical sensations. Can I feel the baby in there? What body parts does it have already? Can I feel where those are? I keep my answers short, but I make sure to smile and meet his eyes.

After lunch we get back to work. We turn the music up and I choose a few of the tracks – Cash Savage and Sharon Van Etten. We're much quieter than we were this morning and I'm pleased that he feels comfortable in our silence. Occasionally I take breaks, stretching my arms and standing from the stool. At four Travis calls it a day. We're nowhere near halfway through the labelling.

'We still have a lot to go.'

'It doesn't matter if we don't finish it,' he says. 'My parents will do some themselves. Are you right to get home?'

'Yeah.'

He leads me to the carport and waves me off from the gate. As I back out of the drive and am trundling slowly down the street, I wonder what he'd have done if I said I wasn't right to get home. Would he have driven me himself? Or invited me to stay? As I drive, I dissect everything he said over the day, wondering at any deeper meaning.

It's peak hour and even though I'm travelling against most of the traffic, it's still excruciating. I take my phone at red lights and search for Travis's band. They're called Working From Home. Travis does vocals and guitar. It's a lot dreamier than I'd expected – slow rhythms with a lot of synth and keyboard. In most tracks I can't actually hear any guitar, but usually Travis is singing. Most of the lyrics are vague and open-ended. Things like: *'I get lost with space.'* The band released an EP last year that had six tracks much like that. There's a new single, released more recently, that sounds different. Bare, plonky keyboard notes playing a simplistic melody. I almost go to double-check it is still Travis's band, then I hear the vocals.

'I hate you.'

I almost laugh when I hear his voice, breathy and overly earnest.

'I used to love you, but I fucking hate you. I wake up and I think of you. I go to bed and I think about how much I fucking hate you.'

I look at the date of the release – a little more than a month ago. The song must be about Renee. I wonder if she knows about it. It's one of the worst things I've ever heard and I play it twice.

THE NEXT DAY I arrive and let myself into the backyard. I have salad rolls from the store for each of us. When I enter the shed I see Travis has already started, a large dent made in the wine bottles from yesterday.

'I couldn't sleep last night, so I just kept labelling.'

I'm not sure what to say so I just smile.

'Don't worry, we'll still pay you the same amount.'

Still not sure, still smiling.

I get to work labelling and let the silence stretch for a bit. He has the radio on today. A meteorologist is explaining that the temperatures recorded this month are hotter than previous years. He makes predictions for the approaching bushfire season. Talks about incineration as an inevitability. I really want to change the station and can't believe Travis doesn't. Here where his parents live is so green. In summer it must be so dry. My skin feels hot and uncomfortable, like clothing that doesn't fit.

Eventually, when there's a break in the broadcast, I ask if I can put music on.

'Oh, sure.' He sounds dazed, as though he wasn't even listening. Or maybe he's dazed because he was. I try to find something light and happy on my phone, which takes a while.

I ask Travis his plans for the rest of the week, then the weekend.

'I'm not sure.' He's fixated on a label and for a moment I think he is going to stop there, but eventually he continues. 'I might stay here. Have a weekend in the country.'

'That'll be nice.'

'My parents will be here.' I'm not sure if he's saying that makes it more or less nice. 'What about you?'

There's a sadness when he asks this, an inhalation of breath that I'd been expecting. I'm acting so much like Annie right now I almost laugh, a private joke with myself. 'I'll go to Renee's birthday party. At the Clarke Street house.'

My logic is that if I can get him to talk about Renee, we'll be in a sad vein that will make it easy to transition to Pat. I reason that he'll find it hard to talk about Renee without mentioning Pat. His death, at least. She broke up with him less than two weeks before his friend died. Whenever I saw Travis and Renee together Pat was there too.

What happens next is what I intended, but not what I expected. Travis is pouring his heart out, talking about Renee. How much he loved her, how he had a sense – he didn't know why – that this might be it. He told his mum he was going to marry her. He didn't sleep for three days after they broke up.

I feel sorry for him but also think he's being absurd, talking like what happened to him was a great injustice. He says he hopes every day that he will run into her – on his way to work, maybe, or just shopping for groceries – but he can't face the party. The idea makes him want to vomit. He's so dramatic it's almost comical, but Renee said he was like this: excitable.

I hardly have to say anything to keep the conversation going. I sit, labelling, letting his feelings gush everywhere. After he has gone over their break-up in detail he says, 'And then . . .' He doesn't continue. I want him to keep going, to talk about what happened after, but he falls silent.

'It must've been horrible.' I concentrate very hard on my bottle. I count to five in my head, telling myself that at five I will mention it. I will finish the sentence: *And then Pat died so soon after that.* One, two, three –

'Let's talk about something less depressing,' he says. 'Do you like The Peep Tempel?'

'Sure.' I don't know who they are.

The second half of the day we spend almost in silence. We listen to two Peep Tempel albums and then switch back to the radio. We learn about how families can navigate their child's internet use, interspersed with tips on how to make their gardens and kitchens nicer.

At the end of the day Travis thanks me, walks a box of wine to my car.

'Thanks so much, Travis. I really needed this work.'

'I really needed the company.' He sounds flat, unenthused. I don't know if he's still thinking about Renee or if he's sad to see me go.

'You should come on the weekend,' I say.

'Maybe.' He taps the roof of the car twice as I'm backing out of the drive then steps back and holds his arm up in a salute.

Driving off, I watch him in the rear-view mirror as he walks back inside the house.

I GO TO Renee's birthday on the weekend hoping to see Travis, but he doesn't turn up. At first my friends comment on how big I'm getting. Later in the evening they comment on how quiet I am.

'I'm tired.' I stay for just over an hour. At home I can't sleep.

I IMAGINE TELLING YOU I don't like Travis's band. I wouldn't go as far as to laugh at them – he's your best friend, after all – but we would see them together and you would know they're not that good. You would nod your head, smiling with your eyes closed, a little exasperated but very affectionate.

I REMEMBER THE night at The Tote, Travis saying that anybody who didn't like The Drones just didn't like music and how you reasoned with him, reminded him of a band he didn't like who most people did. You reminded me of Annie, although less resigned. You said everything as though it was hopeful.

Travis needs you, I think. Someone to temper his hyper-enthusiasm. I try to imagine how the two of you might have met. If you had a class together or if you met through someone else one of you had a class with. I can't really picture it – how someone as extroverted as Travis and someone as composed as you started talking. I imagine you meeting more and more times, speaking more each time you met. When did you fall in love? I want to ask you these things, not Travis. The way he spoke about Renee, his feelings rolling and rolling, all messy like waves, was absurd. How much he had to say about a two-month relationship with someone who, by the sounds of it, wasn't even that kind to him. What would he do if I mentioned you? I think he'd probably say nothing.

December

DAYS SLIP AWAY AT THE speed of hours. Each morning when I wake, it's with ennui – here's another eternity to fill with nothing. And yet it's December, soon I'll be in my third trimester, and it feels as though that has happened far too fast. My stomach is firm, not fatty. It's rounded and harder to push on. My baby is lengthening, thinning out. Now it is a papaya and next it will be a grapefruit.

Sarah has me doing pelvic floor exercises, so that I don't wet myself. We sit side by side on the edge of the couch. Leaning forward, like we're anticipating something.

'Like you're trying not to wee,' she tells me.

I contract what I've always thought was my bladder. It feels awkward and wrong. I've no idea if I'm doing it properly, but the ritual feels responsible so I go along with it.

'One, two, three . . .' Sarah counts us to eight. We do it again and again. Every day when she gets home from work.

As well as the pelvic floor exercises, Sarah sings to me. The book says it's a way for the father to connect to the baby, to make the baby feel an attachment to his voice. Each night she sings a different song, but mostly she only knows the first verse and chorus of anything, so once she's made it to the end of the first chorus she circles back and starts again.

Suddenly I'm struck with the idea that being this obviously pregnant will help me get a job. Isn't that who you want handing you a loaf of sourdough? A smiley pregnant woman in a linen apron?

I PUT ON a nice floral wraparound dress – one that used to actually wrap around me but that I now wear with shorts and a top underneath – and take the last of the stack of résumés I printed off months ago. I take the tram north on High Street to Preston, which is not a strip of shops I threw myself at last time. The owner of a cafe congratulates me when I walk through the door. I haven't yet got used to strangers acknowledging my pregnancy and I'm confused, wondering if she's referring to the résumés that I'm clutching to my stomach. She tells me to take a seat. I order a cup of tea and place my résumé face down on the table, suddenly embarrassed. An unemployed parent. Instantly I realise the fact I'm this pregnant will mean I definitely won't get a job. Nobody would hire someone they know is going to leave soon. As quickly as I was convinced this was a good idea, I now realise it's stupid.

I sip the tea and scroll on my phone. I got a message from Travis yesterday. He sent through four hundred dollars for the labelling. I feel like the amount is absurd, but having seen his family home I don't feel guilty. I spent a lot of time wondering what I should write back to him, before finally writing a simple *Thanks*. I want to write something more now.

Keep me in mind for more work.

I had fun, thanks for thinking of me.

Thanks for the cash, but honestly I just wanted you to tell me if you know why your friend died.

The walk home is difficult. The days have already pushed past thirty degrees and my hands are swollen and tender. My feet too – bloated and red like a baby's. At home I wet a tea towel and drape it over my body. I collapse onto the couch and turn a fan towards myself. I know I should regret not applying for the job in the bakery, but I'm so used to the torpor now I'm not even sure if I'd be able to work again.

'I'm going to ask Mum for Dad's money,' I say aloud to no one.

After he died my father left a smallish lump of cash that was meant for me. I told Mum I didn't want it. 'You have it. You put up with him longer than I did.' She's mentioned it a couple of times over the years. When I first moved to Melbourne. When I was nearing the end of drama school. Any time I went a few months without a job. I always told her I didn't want it. Eventually she stopped mentioning it. We haven't talked about it for a few years now. I know that on some level I must have accepted months ago that I was going to fall back on that money now.

Mum and Ken are coming to Melbourne a few days before Christmas and we'll have Christmas lunch together before heading to the coast for a holiday. While I'm dreading giving Mum so much opportunity to question my choices, at least I'll have an escape valve: James's parents live in the town where we'll be staying, so he and Annie will also be there. I decide that before I ask Mum for money – for *my* money, I remind myself – I'll go shopping and use the money from the ad shoot to buy things I need: sensible, mothering things, like a crib and a pram, so that when I'm asking for *my* money she will see how responsible I am being.

SARAH AND ANNIE come with me to Northland. We used to spend weekends at the Sunshine Plaza when we were teens. We bought cheap make-up with our pocket money. Walked through every level of the complex, even the ones with shops we didn't need to visit. Sauntering and sipping thickshakes from Wendy's. Cold in the aircon with our short shorts and thongs. Stopping to chat to people we saw at school every day. Wasting time because we were teenagers and we had so much of it.

Annie is cynical, Sarah is hungover and I am content in their company. An expensive swimwear store advertises that if you don't buy food you can afford their bathers and look good in them too. Annie is quizzing Sarah on legislation, asking about guidelines in advertising material.

'Stop walking so fast,' says Sarah.

Both of them cheer up when we enter the baby store.

Sarah holds up a pair of tiny Converse high tops. 'You have to buy these!' She uses the small shoes like finger puppets, tap dancing them on my shoulder.

'I'm having a baby not a toddler.'

Little jumpsuits increasing in length inch by inch are lined up in rows – tiniest to still tiny. So many phases to pass through so fast. Just like pregnancy, where every two weeks is a new fruit. It strikes me now how often I'm going to have to do this. How quickly a baby grows and how many new clothes I'll have to buy. Maybe that's why there are so many women pushing prams around the shopping centre.

My friends coo, holding out t-shirts the size of hankies. Sarah comes at me with a pink jumpsuit, lays it over my belly. 'Does it fit?' Annie takes a photo of us, both turned to the camera, both laughing. Sarah's index finger pointed at my round belly.

We race prams up the aisles. Taking the corners fast, telling ourselves we're testing the steering. They're all so large, the tyres thick like mountain bikes'. I say they remind me of SUVs and jokes about soccer practice are made. I want something small and easy to use. I use the word 'zippy' to the sales attendant. We take up much of her time and eventually leave without buying a pram. We do buy a crib, though. Pale slats of wood. A sweet jail for the white stuffed rabbits in the store, their blue and pink bows their prison uniforms.

It's a long time since I've done this: browsed shops, happily spending money. We stop at the food court before we leave and share a large serve of fries. Annie rips open the paper bag and we pick at the fries like birds. I look at the teenagers seated around tables together, not eating. Looking at their phones and sharing so much. 'Have you seen?' they say, passing the screens to their friends. 'Yeah, I've seen it. Did you see Jake's comment?' My friends are looking at their phones too. But we're silent, private in our scrolling. I know they're most likely just reading emails, nothing I'd be interested in, but suddenly I'm wondering if maybe they have their own secrets. I try to imagine what kinds of things they might hide from me, but I can't. I never told Sarah or Annie about labelling the wine with Travis. I'm afraid they might judge me for spending time with him, given I haven't told him about Pat. But this isn't a secret. Just something I'm not mentioning. If either of them heard about it and asked me, I wouldn't lie. Secrets are more protected, covered in untruths.

'Have you felt the baby kicking yet?' Sarah asks.

I realise my hand is resting on my bump, absent-mindedly.

'No, not yet.'

'That's completely fine,' she says. 'All the books say not to worry. It might not happen for a while.'

I DO THE rest of my shopping online. I feel calmer this way. I don't have to move, don't have to remember my pin number, and everything looks nicer onscreen, photographed with studio lighting.

I spend long mornings in bed, thinking about Travis and how we will not be friends much longer. He's not going to visit me and my crying newborn. We're hardly friends now. I think about messaging him every day. I type out texts that become so long they're more like letters. I spend time editing them and then I delete them. There's no chance of me getting drunk and deciding to send them. No chance of Travis finding my phone and reading them. But still I delete them. And still I write them. It must be cathartic, because I keep doing it.

ONE DAY IN THE MIDDLE of the month there is a knock on my door and it's Mum, two weeks earlier than expected. I'm wearing a dressing gown with tea spilled on the lapel and here's Mum on my doorstep looking tired but happy in a maroon dress that's wrinkled – not because she doesn't iron, but because when travelling she wears clothes that are deliberately wrinkled so that it doesn't matter if they get creased in her bag. She's not wearing make-up and her hair is a sleek grey bob. She must have stopped dying it. Maybe she's trying to look more like a grandma.

'Surprise!' She hugs me. Mum is not one for surprises and she only hugs on occasions that really call for it, which I suppose this is.

'I was just about to get changed.' Already, I am lying.

I'm conscious of her alone in the house while I shower. Conscious of the dark layer of dust on the windowsills and skirting boards.

I retrieve the one nice dress I can still fit into from the bottom of my washing basket. It feels moist and grubby. I flap it like a sheet a few times, loosening the dust, hoping to de-wrinkle and air it out.

'I can't believe you bought a crib!' Mum says when I walk out to the lounge.

'I'm getting ready.'

'Look at you.' She hugs me again. There's something affected about her manner. When someone who doesn't usually hug hugs you twice in a short period of time you should feel nervous.

'I thought you weren't arriving till the twenty-third?' I say.

She breaks away from the hug, but keeps her hands on my shoulders.

'I thought I'd surprise you.'

SHE'S STAYING IN the St Georges Motor Inn at the end of my street. It's a brown-brick building with a tall wall surrounding it and would be attractive enough if it weren't for the huge yellow-and-black signage that's always flashing *Vacancies*.

'Why are you staying here?' I ask.

'It's cheap and it's close to you.'

'You could've stayed with me.' I would've dusted the skirting boards.

'I don't want to be a bother.'

'It wouldn't be a bother if you'd told me.'

Mum's luggage is open on her bed and she starts to hang her clothes.

'These dresses are so great for travelling.' She runs a hand swiftly down each one, inspecting it before placing it in the cupboard.

We catch the tram to Fitzroy North and get morning tea at the bakery on Scotchmer Street.

'This is quirky.' Mum pulls her chair in close to our table, making room for customers passing behind her.

'You know that book I bought you last Christmas? The author's husband designed this store.'

'Oh, okay.' She looks up and around the bakery, from the ceiling to the counter. 'That's random.'

When our drinks and pastries arrive, she sits up a little straighter. 'Now . . .' She pours me a glass of sparkling water. 'You are eating meat, aren't you? You have to eat meat.'

'I'm eating meat.'

'Good. And what vitamins are you taking?'

I repeat what I've already told her over the phone. I'm eating the right foods, drinking lots of water, taking the prenatal vitamins. She lists. I list.

Thankfully she doesn't ask about Pat. Not yet.

Afterwards, we go across the street to the IGA. I follow my mother through the aisles, bored and impatient. She compares prices before putting anything in her trolley.

'This supermarket is expensive,' she says as she fondles mangoes. 'No wonder your generation is broke.'

'I don't usually shop here.'

'Good,' she says. 'Now, what have you been craving?'

'You don't need to buy me food, Mum.'

'No, but I'd like to.'

'Dim sims.'

'You like those, do you?'

She reads the ingredients on each of the packets of dim sims in the frozen food section. 'Are you sure you want these?' she asks before she puts the packet in the trolley.

I try to help her with the bags on the tram, but she insists on carrying them herself.

'I'm pregnant,' I tell her. 'I'm not dying.'

'I'm old, but I'm not dying either.'

Back at my house she unpacks the groceries, telling me to relax and rest. When I've visited Mum on the Sunshine Coast as an adult, I've marvelled at my ability to revert to being a child in her presence.

Waking in the morning and parking myself on her couch, switching on the TV and flicking channels until I find something merely watchable. Asking her what's for lunch rather than looking myself. Or if I did look, I'd stand with the fridge door open, staring, asking her what was for lunch. This transition into the old version of ourselves is harder here. As she unpacks the shopping, Mum opens almost every cupboard trying to work out where things go. I'm conscious of my pantry's lack of order. The pantry moths' glossy webs in the muesli and flour. She refuses my offer to help and I don't insist. I'm tired. I fall asleep to the sound of her chopping vegetables.

When I wake, she's placed two steamed dim sims in a bowl on the coffee table, a salad on the side. She sits on the couch opposite with her own salad. I feel heavy and ugly, my eyelids the weight of concrete. I can't be bothered speaking, especially not about anything serious, not even about anything bland. It strikes me now that with Mum here weeks before we planned, I'm going to need to host her. Without a job, I have no reason to leave her for long periods of time.

'When is Ken arriving?'

'The twenty-third.' Mum is looking around my lounge.

'Why are you here so early?'

'I wanted to see you.' She's looking at a particular print on our wall – a photo of a monstera plant, far healthier than any of the actual plants we have in the house.

'What do you want for dinner tonight?' I ask her.

'I'll be out tonight so you don't need to worry about me.' She pokes a fork around her bowl, spearing individual chickpeas and pieces of cucumber. I wait for her to elaborate on her plans for the evening, but she doesn't.

'Where are you going?'

'I've got plans.' She opens her mouth wide, shovels in the big forkful and returns my stare. 'Do you think mothers don't have lives?' She smiles knowingly. Clearly, she's hiding something.

WHAT HAPPENED WITH my father was theft, in the literal and the metaphorical sense. Mum worked in retail in her twenties and climbed her way up to floor manager at the first Myer in Brisbane. I don't know how she met my father. I assume I asked when I was very young; it seems such an obvious thing to wonder. By the time I thought to ask again we hadn't mentioned him in years so I refrained. What I do know has been pieced together from years of off-hand comments and a couple of conversations I wasn't meant to overhear. He came from a reasonably well-off family; my mother did not. He worked at a bank. What he did there I don't know, I just remember the rectangular name badge. After they were married my father helped Mum open her own store near where we lived in a suburb an hour or so out of Brisbane. It was a homewares shop that also sold jewellery and accessories. Aprons, tea towels, decorated crockery, gift cards. I remember teddy bears with silky fur and sitting on the counter, being smiled at by the customers. Mum had the store for eight years and business was good for most of that time.

Although the business was in Mum's name, like many women of her generation she was raised to allow her husband to handle the money. She handled the customers; he handled the numbers. And besides, he had come up with the cash needed to open the shop in the first place. Dad paid Mum a standard wage and himself a modest wage. The store did a steady trade. Customers loved Mum and she loved them. The house they lived in was being paid off and I was born.

Along with claiming a raft of tax benefits available to small business owners, it turned out my father was also contributing to his super far more generously than the amount that was being paid into Mum's. Eventually – I'm not sure exactly when because Mum isn't sure exactly when – he started investing the profit from the business in shares. He made some money and then he lost some money and then he lost a lot. He continued to invest poorly and lost more. His debt was growing and growing. Mum had no idea it existed until the day he told her they'd have to liquidate to pay it off. The debt belonged to the business. Mum's career and her income were both gone, along with her connection to her community, the source of so many friendships for years. She wasn't in trouble with the law, the investments hadn't been illegal, they were just stupid. That's what a lawyer told her. The house had to be sold as well as the business. When they divorced they were both left with what they had when they entered the marriage. Mum, nothing. ('Not nothing,' she would correct me. 'I have you.') Dad, some family money.

One of Mum's regular customers had a holiday house that she offered us rent-free for four months. That's when we moved to the Sunshine Coast, just the two of us. I have a few memories of that house. It was old – the couple were intending to either renovate or bulldoze and build something knew – with different wallpaper in every room and thick floral carpet that was always dusty no matter how often you vacuumed. It smelled like mould and the ocean – degradation and freedom.

The photo of me on my first day of school was taken out the front of that house, soon after we moved. I'm holding a blue backpack with both hands. Smiling widely in a baggy checked school dress reaching halfway down my shins, and a red jumper. Pigtails tied with one red bow, one blue. The fact that Mum had the energy to arrange coordinated hair ribbons at this time now baffles me and breaks my heart.

Mum got a job in a store much like the one she had owned. She never liked the Sunny Coast, I always knew this. But I'd been made to move once. She didn't want to uproot me and make me go to a new school. Once she'd saved some money we moved from the decrepit holiday house to a modest rental where we stayed for good.

Between then and my father's death nine years later I saw him rarely and Mum and I talked about him even less. I'd meet him in the school holidays. Mum would drop me off at a shopping centre between Brisbane and the Sunshine Coast. She would sit with me in the food court until she saw him approaching from a few hundred metres away, then she would stand and walk away. He would escort me around the shops and buy me clothes and takeaway McDonald's. He'd ask me how school was. I'd answer in monosyllables.

He died of a heart attack when I was fifteen. On the day of his funeral I'd assumed Mum was just dropping me at the funeral home, but when we arrived she turned the car off, then sighed heavily before getting out. I was thankful she did. I'd been nervous of what people would think of me if I didn't cry, but Mum didn't cry either, so I felt an iota of ease. People kept offering her their condolences and she just smiled in a strained and sad way. I remember feeling baffled by how gracious she was to all the people who'd loved him. When they said, 'Sorry for your loss,' I wondered which loss they were referring to. We never spoke of him at home. If he had to be mentioned she referred to him as '*your* father' – he was mine, not hers. His funeral was the first time I realised that maybe she didn't hate him; maybe she loved him. I sat through the service and heard people I didn't know talk about a man I didn't know and I tried to recall my early memories of him. The time before the betrayal. Could

I recall a trip to the beach or him making me dinner, driving me to birthday parties, the kinds of banal acts of love that I remember my mother doing a thousand times? I couldn't. To this day he is a vague figure who lurks in the corner of my memories, his face obscured.

Years later, when I was in drama school and had to use grief as a memory to motivate emotion, I considered whether I regretted a lost opportunity for a relationship with him. Did I carry guilt?

Yes.

Could I use this feeling to inform my work on stage? This curdled feeling – the sadness and anger that sloshed around in me like oil and water – could it be distilled into a facial expression, a posture?

No.

This was possibly when I started to question the technicalities of acting. Was it really possible to replicate an actual life? It always felt like we were acting just one thing, when in reality we were feeling everything all at once.

I'VE HEARD PEOPLE SAY THAT becoming a mother changes your relationship with your own mother, instantly and forever. People also say that women become mothers when they find out they're pregnant, while men only become fathers when their babies are born. I've decided at least one or both of these generalisations is bullshit, as my relationship with my mother is unchanged. Over a week and a half we cycle through the same conversations, never coming to any different conclusions. She insists that I adhere to rules about pregnancy that existed when she was pregnant with me. If someone is smoking in a public space she takes me by the shoulders and pulls me away. She encourages me to walk every day. We amble very slowly along the creek all the way to Coburg Lake. She brings bottles of water with her everywhere we go.

She starts early on the subject of the father.

'I'm not allowed to become stressed at the moment, Mum.'

'You're about to learn a new meaning of the word stress. And you're going to keep learning that for the next eighteen years.' She narrows her eyes at me. 'Make that thirty.'

She moves on ever so slightly by asking if I'm trying to meet someone new.

'I'm trying to save money.'

'If you don't go out you won't ever meet anybody.'

'I could go on a dating app.'

She scrunches her face at this. Not complete disgust, but distrust. The face she'd make if her meal is a bit too salty. On this topic I realise I haven't thought about Fergus in some time. I have the thought, then drop it easily.

Mum wants me to act again and doesn't believe the pregnancy should hold me back. 'There are so many ads for prenatal vitamins. I see them every day.'

'Pregnant people in ads aren't actually pregnant; I've been pregnant on television before, remember. Anyway, I want to find something else.'

'Get a job in casting.'

This isn't the worst idea and I make a mental note of it without telling her.

'I just want to find something I can do that I don't hate and that I can fit around . . .' I stumble on the word *family*; it seems to refer to something much larger than my own circumstances. 'Something that I can fit around a baby,' I finish.

We always disagree at the same points then leave it there. Watch the ducks on Coburg Lake and eat the sandwiches she's made.

Almost every afternoon she leaves me alone, tells me I need sleep. If I insist I don't need sleep she says that *she* needs sleep. One afternoon I leave her at the motor inn, then, instead of walking home, I cross the road to the KFC and sit in the window. Only ten minutes later I see her standing on the opposite corner. A car arrives and she gets in.

My first thought is that she's having an affair, but I don't believe it for a second. It's a cliché, that's the only reason I thought of it. Apart from not thinking she would leave Ken, the only way she could meet someone living in Melbourne would be online and I can't see her doing that. I try to consider any possibility, no matter how far-fetched, but there are only two I can imagine. Either she is organising some kind of surprise for the baby – buying a car seat or a pram – or she's sick and going to see a specialist. Given the frequency of her heading out alone and her lack of flexibility and the lies, the latter seems most likely, but it's too awful to imagine so I try to put it from my mind and hope to God she's having an affair.

I don't ask her outright where she's going, but the next time she suggests we part for the afternoon, I whine and tell her I don't want to.

'Why are you being so needy at the moment?'

I poke her on the shoulder. 'Beep!' I use a high-pitched voice. 'Beep! Beep!'

It's a game we played when I was little. When I misbehaved she'd say, 'Don't push my buttons, Eva!' and I'd run at her, my little index fingers high in the air: 'Beep-beep! Beep!'

'Just you wait,' she says to me when I do it now. She smiles at me with so much love.

THE HARDEST PART OF TELLING Mum about you isn't even that you're dead. Because that, at least, is concrete. If I told her about you, surely she would ask me what you did, and the truth is I don't actually know what you were doing when you died. I know what you used to do and what you'd been studying. You talked about your degree and your old furniture making. You didn't talk about what you'd been doing day to day in those three weeks I knew you. Maybe it was nothing; maybe you were that depressed.

It's embarrassing to admit that I don't know what you did, but also that was the great thing about you. Spending time with you wasn't an exchange of tired niceties. It was an exchange of odd facts and laughter. Conversations just pinged between us. We didn't need to reach out for the easiest topics.

Telling her about you would be like trying to describe a dream. Something I enjoyed so much that if I tried to put it into words, sentences, paragraphs, the holes in the timeline, the gaps in the logic, would become chasms. They'd spread so far apart, the threads of the narrative I have would disperse. I'd be on the precipice of a vast gorge.

Right now, I feel as though I'm on a narrow hiking trail. Annie and Sarah are with me, one walking ahead and the other behind. I'm surrounded by bush. Isolated, but safe. I can't see that far ahead, but I can see where I need to step next.

WHEN I DO END UP asking for the money I'm defensive and irritated.

We're in Sivan's clinic waiting for her to arrive. I'm on the examin-ation table, ready for the ultrasound. I'm relieved that Sivan is doing this second scan, as every time I visit or speak on the phone to the hospital, I'm with a different midwife. I'm grateful for this shred of consistency. Mum's in a chair, looking at her phone. She's wondering about the weather for tomorrow. There's a storm coming and she doesn't know if we'll be able to walk in the morning.

'It says the cool change will come through at three o'clock, but it's going to be nice early. I'm buying an apartment.' Her eyes are still on her screen. Her two statements roll together seamlessly with no pause, like she's trying to force some obvious metaphor about a storm.

'Are you selling your house?' I ask.

'That's Ken's house – it's his to sell. I'm using the money your father left and buying a small place in Coburg. I'm going to move to Melbourne.'

'That's my money!' I don't raise my voice, but I turn my head sharply to look at her. We are exchanging affronted stares when Sivan enters and asks how we are.

'We're fine!' says Mum, overly cheerful.

'Have you felt the baby kick yet?' Sivan asks me.

I shake my head. I'm utterly shell-shocked and I think Sivan mistakes this for fear.

'Don't worry, it's different for everyone,' she says. 'Some people don't feel it until much, *much* later than this.'

I haven't been worried about the kicking, but everyone keeps asking me about it so I wonder if I'm meant to be. I find Sivan's insistence off-putting. Not as though she's saying, 'Everyone else is normal,' but like she's saying, 'Some people are even more abnormal than you.' She asks Mum if she is excited.

'Yes, oh yes, I can't wait,' she says, before going on to mention how her generation never got all these scans like we do today.

When the baby appears on the screen I start to cry. Sivan smiles, misinterpreting my tears. I envy my child, curled up on its own away from everyone. Mum leans in close to the ultrasound and grabs my hand. The baby's heartbeat is amplified. The sound of a water bottle shaking, again, again, again.

'Gosh, that's fast, isn't it?' Mum says.

My own heartbeat feels faster.

Sivan points out the curve of the baby's spine, the heart, the arms and legs, a hand. She measures the body parts. She lists all the organs. Everything is correct, everything is as it should be. The baby is an ear of corn.

'You're doing great,' she says to me with a big smile.

BACK AT THE motel our conversation goes in circles, like most conversations we've had since Mum arrived, but louder. She's using my money to put a deposit on an apartment, she will move here, Ken will visit every month or two. Mum will work part time and help me raise the baby. She should be able to handle the small mortgage, but Ken will step in if she needs help. She reminds me I said I didn't want the money. I remind her I wasn't pregnant when I said that.

'You said you had enough money,' she tells me.

'Because I thought I could have *this* money.'

'I don't think you realise how hard raising a child alone will be, Eva. Do you know why I didn't drink for ten years of your life?'

'Because you were taking care of an infant?'

'No, because I thought if I got drunk enough I'd probably kill myself. I was barely holding on. I never liked it on the Sunshine Coast, you know that.'

This is true but also thrown out as a reminder of my debt to her, everything she gave up for me.

'What about Ken?'

'Eva, I'm not sure why you're saying I should do what makes my partner happy.'

'I'm saying you should do what makes *you* happy, not what you think is best for me.'

'Well, you're not really telling me that, because you're saying I can't have the money.' She signals the end of the argument with a key change. Tone and volume both lowered – 'I'm doing this' – pace decelerating – 'for you.'

It ends in tears – mine. I sit on her motel bed sobbing loudly. She pats me on the back but doesn't hug me. More like the mother she used to be. Kind but practical. Less indulgent.

Given only days ago I was worried my mother might have a potentially terminal illness, I should feel relieved and grateful she's not dying. I realise that is what I should be feeling.

I've been self-righteous in our argument. Going back on my word. Blaming her for a decision I made without thinking through the consequences. 'It's my money,' I kept saying, emphasis on a different word each time until eventually it was every word. '*It's. My. Money.*'

Eventually I leave. I don't look at her on my way out and I feel awful for it.

'Sarah!' I scream when I get home. I go to her room, but she's not here. I ring her, sitting on her bed. I've hardly spent any time with her since Mum arrived. I get her voicemail but I've no idea what to say so I just groan then hang up.

She rings back a few seconds later.

'Where are you?' I ask.

'I'm at my work Christmas party. Where are you?'

'I'm coming.'

'Okay, but wear something hot.'

I open Sarah's closet and find a fitted black dress stretchy enough to expand over my abdomen and thickening arms. It's not weather appropriate, though; the sleeves are long. It will be hot in the wrong sense of the word. I order an Uber then realise I need to save money and cancel it; the cancellation costs me ten dollars. I walk to the tram stop instead. I glare at the motor inn through the window of the tram as I pass by.

'YOU'RE WEARING MY dress!' Sarah is exuberant, not pissed off, obviously drunk. The party is in a sparsely furnished warehouse. There are thin fluoro tubes tracing the perimeter of the ceiling but they don't appear to be emitting actual light as it's almost too dark to see in here. Angular people saunter through the space drinking posh beers. Introductions are made via references to other people. 'You know Eva McMillan. She knows . . .' People nod in recognition. They look at my belly, but don't congratulate me. Sarah's dress is creeping up the backs of my legs and I've never been more self-conscious about being pregnant. I end up in conversation with a handsome man I've met once before. His name is Max and I don't remember much about him, but I dimly recall having formed a bad impression of him. He asks me what I've been working on lately, what I've been in.

'I'm taking a break,' I say, then add awkwardly, 'For a bit.'

'You were in that series set in New Zealand, weren't you? You must know Gary Andrews.'

'Maybe.'

I don't know Gary Andrews, but Max continues to tell me about him. I nod, not listening. Sarah has left me for the other side of the room and I can hear her voice reverberating around the warehouse. 'Oh, shut UP!' She punches some man in the arm with her free hand, her other hand clasping a girl's. I take my phone from my pocket. 'I'm listening,' I tell Max, before I put my head down and ignore him. I text Annie asking her to come here. I return my gaze to Max, but repeatedly check my phone as I wait for her to reply.

'Anyway, do you think you'll act again?' he asks me.

'Oh, maybe. Hey, when did your company change their logo design?' I ask, pointing to the logo projected on the wall.

'Oh, that was me!' He starts to tell me in detail about the work that went into it.

I don't think anybody here would judge me, or even notice, if I drank a beer, but I resist the urge. If I'm going to drink, I at least want to be standing near someone who will protest so I can look them in the eye while I do it anyway. The canapés are lavish and nobody but me is eating. I do laps of the space, having seconds. Each time I pass Sarah she gives me a squeeze and a smile. Eventually, I pass her and she doesn't react. Her eyes are glassy and wine is splashed on her top in two places. People are talking around her but I can tell she's not hearing them.

'Let's go home,' I say. I don't want Sarah to make problems for herself at work.

'Do you want a bump of coke?' She grabs my arm, her eyes open wide with possibility.

A few of her colleagues do a double take, then laugh. I see in their looks the familiarity of their amusement – they've seen Sarah like this before.

Sarah talks at them, loudly. 'Eva is usually really good. She's not eating eggs or ham.' She hiccups.

'Let's go home,' I repeat.

'I'm going to take Charlie home. She's so cute!'

'She left,' I lie. It might be true, though, as I can't see the girl she was flirting with earlier.

I drag her out. She doesn't protest, but she also doesn't move her legs. I keep having to push her slightly. She trips for a few steps and then is still again.

When we get to Brunswick Street, I steer her towards the tram stop.

'Are we going to Annie's house?' she asks.

'Actually, yes,' I say. 'That is where we're going.'

Annie hasn't texted me back, which is unlike her. (Though before I stopped drinking she used to not reply if it seemed like Sarah and I were getting loose together). Out the front of her house I call her and she answers. I drive the three of us back to Thornbury in Annie's car. We stop once on the way for Sarah to vomit, which she is at least able to warn us about. We spend the night on the floor of the bathroom. I tell Annie about the money and about Mum.

'How did she get the money?' Annie asks me.

'She's had it since he died.'

'So, it wasn't like in a trust that only you can access?'

Realising I don't know the answer to this makes me see how oblivious I am to money. Just like Mum was.

Annie and I exchange sad smiles across the bathroom floor. I rub my abdomen and shuffle my butt bones that are growing more and more tender on the hard tiles. Occasionally Sarah chimes in, her voice echoing around the toilet bowl.

'Fuck your mum, it's your money.'

It stinks in here.

Annie sleeps in my bed and in the morning we drive Sarah to the airport. She's flying to the Sunny Coast for Christmas. Large black sunglasses cover half her face, but you can still see her scowl. She lies on the back seat with an icepack on her head, too nauseous to sit up straight. When we get to the airport, she doesn't even thank us for the lift.

'Look at these people,' she says. 'Going to the Gold Coast for Christmas holidays. What fuckwits.'

'Bye,' we call as she plods into the terminal.

She flaps her hand out behind her dismissively, like she's shooing away a fly, some annoyance. I notice she's wearing my t-shirt.

ANNIE AND I pick up James and the three of us go to the pool. They do laps. I loll on the side, rest my head on my arms, listening to the water filtering around below me. It reminds me of the baby's heartbeat. A few times I think it might have kicked, but I'm not sure if I'm just feeling the water moving around my stomach. I breathe and try to stay calm. I can feel the anger at Mum seething through my body alongside my heartburn. I envisage her living here and realise how convenient it will be to have her nearby to babysit. Not just convenient: necessary. I don't have a job. Even if I had one, I'd have to pay for child care. I need her to do this and she is doing it. I just wish she was doing it without my money.

After our swim, Annie and James seem reluctant to drop me home. They offer to cook me dinner later.

'I'm fine.'

Mum has also offered to make dinner. She rang, then, when I didn't answer, texted me.

> I'm sorry you're upset. Let me cook you dinner. We'll figure
> something out, it will be ok.
> *It's ok. I just want to go to sleep.*

I go to bed with a bowl of muesli and a banana. I open my computer and search for meditation guides, ones that promise to bring on sleep, to help you drift away quietly. They sound like they're meant to help you die. I listen to the recordings all the way through. Soft voices slowly list body parts – like there's a full stop after every word – and ask me to focus on them. My toes are swollen, my back hurts, my lungs are crushed and my legs feel thick and heavy.

After two failed attempts at meditation, I take my phone, unblock Fergus's number and text him.

> *Hey.*
> *How are you?*

I lie on my back, my eyes closed. Already, I feel calmer. Like maybe now I could meditate and it might work. It's less than a minute before I get a reply.

> *Is this real?*

Hi again.
Hi. How are you?
I can't sleep.
Maybe because it's six o'clock.
I can usually sleep at any time.
Nowadays.
But not today.
Is something wrong?

Probably that I'm doing this.

I'm not sure if anything is wrong.
Sorry. I know that makes no sense.

The screen shows me he is writing a response. A long response, it seems, as I wait but nothing comes through.

Also

I butt in before he can send his long text.

I'm really horny and all alone.

The screen goes blank. He's no longer writing whatever it was.

Really?
Really. Really. Horny.
That's so hot.
For you maybe. I'm all alone.
Want me to come over?
No. Just tell me what you would you do if you could be here
with me.

My phone lights up with a call. Fergus's name on the screen. I answer the call, but I don't say anything. I just hold the phone to my ear and breathe.

'Take off all your clothes.'

'I'm already naked.'

'I'd spread your legs wide apart and shove my face in your pussy. Lap you up.'

'I'm very wet, there's a lot to lap up.'

'Good. I'd tickle your clit with my tongue until you come.'

'That doesn't make me come, you should know that. Don't you know that?'

'I'd lick you until you were wetter, wetter, wetter, then I'd slide my fingers in you and make them wet with you.'

'Yes.'

'Then I'd place them on your clit and rub you until you come.'

'Keep fingering me while you do that.'

'And I'd feel you coming on my hand.'

I rub furiously on myself and when I come I moan excessively loudly. I can hear him on the other end of the phone: rhythmic breathing, gathering in speed.

'What are you thinking about?' I ask.

'You.' His response is breathy. Like someone talking while running. 'I'm thinking about coming on your pregnant belly.'

My eyes widen and I stare at the ceiling, expressing shock to myself. I'm holding my phone with two hands, listening closely to silence.

'Are you there?' he asks eventually.

'Do you want to come on my pregnant belly?'

Almost the second I ask, I hear his whimper. It's long and it's loud, but it still sounds pathetic. After, there's the sound of both of us breathing, heavy and slow. Breathing until eventually we're in time with each other. I fall asleep immediately after I hang up. I sleep for half of the next day.

ANNIE ENDS UP STAYING IN Melbourne for Christmas instead of flying to Queensland or going with James to his parents' house. When I ask why, she's rabbity and vague. I don't push her as I guess she's staying for me, not wanting to leave me knocking around the house on my own, knowing how tense things are between me and Mum. I forgive Mum quickly, though, in the way you do forgive your parents. I'll be annoyed at her forever, while also recognising how much I owe her. Also, the fact remains: I need her. For a few days I try shifting the anger from her to my father. In a roundabout way I can always make anything his fault. But it's a sad and pointless anger towards the dead. It's directionless and only ends up making me furious at no one, or at myself.

Mum and I go out for croissants and tea to clear the air before Ken arrives.

'The thing is, Eva, what do you think is going to happen when I die?'

'Don't talk about dying.' I've actually been thinking about this a lot lately, even before I was suspicious she was sneaking off for doctor's appointments. Having a baby pushes both me and Mum into older roles: we're not just child and parent now; we're parent and grandparent. Her inevitable demise seems much more real than it did before I was pregnant.

'That's what being a parent is, Eva. Your life does not end with you anymore. It continues on after and you have to think about that.'

What she's saying is that the money is still mine, technically. It will be mine after it is hers. She's right and I feel guilty, but also indignant.

Everything feels normal enough. We laugh about something a politician said on the news. She shows me a video of a comedian doing a parody. She also shows me photos of the apartment she's thinking of getting. I think I feel happy, until I hug her goodbye at the motor inn and walk home. In bed I roll over, unable to get to sleep. She could've asked me first, I think.

ON CHRISTMAS DAY, Annie and I cook lunch together at my place. We roast a chicken, dowsed in butter and rested atop half a loaf of bread. We play Christmas albums and wear old t-shirts that end up splattered with fatty oils. When it's almost time for Mum and Ken to arrive we change into dresses. Annie bought mine for me for Christmas – a proper maternity dress, with a mound sewn into the bodice – along with a book of essays by women writing about pregnancy and child rearing. We wear jewellery and put on make-up even though we're not leaving the house. I feel like we're little girls playing dress-ups and performing a pantomime for our parents.

Mum and I have always celebrated Christmas, but it never felt authentic. I know this is partly because my reference points growing up were American – festive knitted sweaters; snow; food and drink that sounded exotic but wasn't, like eggnog. But even locally, our celebrations felt like a charade. Mum never pretended my gifts were coming from Santa. She says she did when I was a baby, but stopped when I was around five. I've no memory of this, so as far as I'm concerned she never did it. Mum said later it was after Dad left that she stopped. It was no longer some fun game she and my dad were playing, it was just a lie. I think also it was because we were poor back then. 'The kids who get the most presents,' she would say, 'are most likely the meanest ones.' And even before I became vegetarian it seemed pointless to cook a roast for two people.

Annie and I spread a red bedsheet over the dining table and put Christmas crackers beside each plate. Everyone has two glasses, one for water and one for wine, though I have sparkling apple juice instead of wine.

The lunch is easy, low-key. We talk about Mum's move. Ken says he is able to work remotely, meaning he can visit for weeks at a time. Mum is looking for a part-time job. They will both ease into retirement. I ask Ken about his children. I've met them before but struggle to remember what they do. It turns out there's a tennis coach and a real estate agent, there's a grandchild. Mum and Ken ask Annie about her career. Her boss has just told her that she's pregnant and will go on maternity leave in the middle of next year. Annie may be asked to step into the role. It will be a big step up, and a pay increase. She'll ask for flexible hours, though. There are nods at the table as we agree that work–life balance is important. We discuss names for the baby. After about thirty seconds any seriousness is gone and we're being deliberately terrible, competing for the worst name.

'Gretchen.'

'Roger.'

'Karen.'

Once the chicken is finished, Ken and I pick at the sourdough mattress on the bottom of the roasting dish, soggy with butter and chicken drippings.

'This is delicious,' Ken says.

'This is the best Christmas dinner we've had in a long time.' My mother pats her partner on the back and smiles at me. Her happiness infuriates me, which makes me feel like an arsehole.

'Don't get used to it,' I say.

'I guess you won't have time to whip up something so decadent next year,' Ken says.

I try to envisage next Christmas. Usually, it would be my turn to travel north for the holidays, but Mum will be living here. I can't imagine Ken wanting to miss a second Christmas with his family. But also, my baby will still be so small. I probably won't want to travel with Mum if she goes. I guess I'll be a vegetarian again? I try to imagine any Christmas, two, three or five years from now. I can't possibly know when, if ever, it'll be worthwhile to make so much food again.

I THINK ABOUT YOUR FAMILY. This would've been their first Christmas since you died. I wonder how they commemorated you. A place set for you at the table. A gift with your name on it under the tree. Maybe none of that. Possibly someone cooked, then all the food went cold. Everyone pushing pork around their plates in silence. No New Year's resolutions.

Everything is a countdown for me now, as people like to remind me. Fifteen weeks to go. Last Christmas without a baby. Last summer. Last days I can wake and think of myself first. Better get sleep while I can.

Your family's grief moves in the other direction. First Christmas alone, first New Year. Whenever your birthday is, that will be a first too. I've been waiting for this. Checking on your Facebook page and Travis's. I figure there will extra posts when that happens. Each time I check and it's not your birthday, I feel a little relieved, but also worried. What if I never find out? Then I feel relieved again – maybe I don't ever want to know.

All the rest of your family's birthdays – your parents and your brothers – those will be firsts too. A sad collection of events will pile up, like the years, crash mats erected around a memory; it will hurt less each time they think of it.

GOOD RIDDANCE TO a shit year. I figure we'd all agree with that.

ON NEW YEAR'S EVE ANNIE is adamant that either she spends the night in with me or I come out with her and James. They've been invited to dinner at the home of one of James's colleagues. She reassures me it'll be a quiet night, only a dozen or so people.

'Another of his colleagues, Simon, is cute,' she adds. 'And single.'

'If he's interested in dating a pregnant woman, I'm not interested in him.'

She nods, a grim smile. I insist she goes without me.

'Okay, fine. But let me make sure you have a nice night alone, anyway.'

I swallow my irritation at her suggestion my life is not nice.

We spend the afternoon together making raspberry jelly. We blend frozen raspberries with sugar and soak gelatine sheets ready to set it in the fridge. A pregnant woman's cocktail.

I feel a flickering behind the wall of my abdomen, one I've felt a few times now, and my hand goes to my stomach.

'Is the baby kicking?' Annie asks.

'I don't think so.' I do think so. It's nothing like I thought it would be, but it must be that because what else could it be? I don't know how to explain this, so I just say no.

When Annie leaves late in the afternoon, I pick up the book she gave me for Christmas. I read one essay and start the second then put it down. Sore tits, pummelled bladders. A mention of a vaginal canal being cut and all I can think of is Mum at her sewing table, nipping just the edge of a sheet of fabric and then tearing swiftly and the entire thing coming apart.

I fall asleep to Monica and Rachel arguing as Rachel moves out. They scream everything they dislike about one another. And then they hug and cry about how much they love one another.

Suddenly Annie is shaking my shoulders gently.

'Eva,' she whispers. 'Happy New Year.'

I grow more disorientated as I wake and realise it's dark outside. I fell asleep on the couch with the lights on.

'What are you doing here?'

'I wanted to see in the new year with you.'

It's twelve twenty. Annie is carrying a string bag. Peeking out the top I can see two candles, several long sticks of rosemary, a big handful of eucalyptus leaves.

'Do you have a lighter?'

She tiptoes to my kitchen, with exaggerated quietness, and starts opening drawers. Her movements are slightly saggy; she's drunk. She finds the long stove lighter then pushes the drawer shut. The cutlery crashes around.

'Sorry,' she whispers.

I shake my head and smile. 'Nobody's home.'

She opens the drawer again and bangs it shut loudly, and laughs.

With the string bag over her shoulder and the lighter in one hand, Annie opens the back door. I get up from the couch and follow her. She drags a metal drum from the back of the yard – the drum we use for fires in winter. She asks if I have any paper. I go inside and see the book she gave me for Christmas face down on the coffee table. I want to burn its inconvenient truths, but of course I can't do that with Annie here, so I find some old scripts. She starts a fire in the drum then breaks the rosemary into pieces and throws them in. Leans in to smell the smoke, like she's cooking. I've no idea if this theatricality is irony or drunkenness.

She gives me two sheets of paper and a pen, and tells me to write my wishes on one sheet and my fears on the other. We're going to burn them both.

'Isn't that symbolism a bit off?' I ask. 'Throwing both your fears and your wishes on the same fire?'

'They are equal parts of your life, Eva.'

The plan is that we will watch the fire smoulder down and then Annie will create a garden bed and scatter the ashes in it. Our fears and our wishes will help grow the vegetables and fruits we'll eat in the new year. It seems overly sentimental, not the kind of thing that Sarah would tolerate, which makes me wonder if Annie is actually being very genuine.

'So, we eat our fears in our vegetables?' I ask her.

'We are our fears.' She's overly intense for a moment, then she laughs. Relieved, so do I.

I stare at my pieces of paper. The first thing I think of is the vaginal canal, the image of it being torn. Then I think about money. Possibly having to pretend to be other people again. I think about Pat. Is my biggest fear the possibility that he never liked me at all? It doesn't really work as a fear, given that even if it's true it's something that has already happened.

Under fears I write: *My baby.*

Under wishes I write: *My baby.*

I hesitate before throwing the lists in the fire, despite how stupid this is; it feels a little aggressive to incinerate something representing my child.

Annie has already done hers. She's staring into the flames. So animated a moment ago, now she looks vacant, her expression hanging off her face.

'What did you write?' I ask her.

She shakes her head, pulling herself back to me, then smiles. 'I wished that your baby is as great as you are.'

'What about your job?'

'My job is fine. I don't need to wish about that.'

She picks up some sticks that are gathered at her feet and starts dropping them into the flames one by one. She doesn't ask me what I wrote.

I get the jelly from the fridge and divide it into two bowls. Annie finds half a bottle of wine at the back of a cupboard. One of the bottles I labelled with Travis, which it seems Sarah has opened at some point. I wonder what he is up to tonight. I envisage him high, still harping on about Renee.

I ask Annie about the dinner and she says it was fine.

'One of the couples announced they're pregnant.' She doesn't say this as though it's exciting or not exciting. She doesn't elaborate.

'Poor woman,' I say.

I tear off one of the old script sheets and throw it in the flames.

MY BIGGEST FEAR IS BECOMING your parents. I see a child running across a street as a car rounds a corner. All the swimming lessons and everything they learned from prep to year two is obliterated. All that work leading to nothing. The vessel for all that love, shattered. Love left flooding everywhere, dampening everything. Is this why I don't tell Travis about the baby? Because I don't want to meet your family? I don't want to look into their eyes and think, this is what I'm gambling. I could end up like them.

SHOULD IT BE my biggest fear that our natural resources are being exploited by a government I didn't elect? A future where the planet has warmed, the crops have died, and there is only genetically modified food to eat. Maybe our child will be able to google something just by closing its eyes. One day corporations will be more powerful than governments. Arguably, they already are.

I WISH FOR simple moments. Holding each other, skin on skin. Pushing a pram along the path that Mum and I walked, all the way to Coburg Lake. Making homemade playdough. Constructing things out of Lego. Having nice colleagues. Making small talk with other parents at a school gate in the afternoon. Sharing the banalities of our days over our walk home, itself a banality.

I WISH FOR you to be alive, but I know I can't have that. So instead I wish for the feeling I had just after I met you. Something to anticipate. Having somewhere to be tomorrow or, better yet, someone to be there for. I wish for someone to love and to love me back.

January

WHILE WE'RE AT THE COAST, the other end of the state is being incinerated. The front pages of the papers show acres of scorched earth; a koala drinking from a water bottle; a smiling fireman, now deceased, holding his young child. News reports attempt to quantify the destruction – hectares burned; animals killed; homes destroyed; lives lost.

Starting the morning with such blunt horror then going about a seaside holiday feels absurd. And yet, here we are. It's not like going home to Thornbury will change anything, I tell myself, which doesn't make me feel any better about anything.

The house we're renting in Mount Martha is large, bare and smells woody, like sawdust. For a few days this confuses me. The pale floorboards in the kitchen are actually laminex. I put my nose close to the tortured wood coffee table, but it smells fruity, industrial. On the fourth day, I go to charge my phone in the lounge and I notice the small canister filled with liquid plugged into the wall. I look closely and see it's labelled 'Rustic Barn Scent'. The town is full of these contrived details. Cafes serve salads in jars and sandwiches on wooden paddles.

Still, it's nice here. It's green and smells like gum leaves and the ocean. You can hear kookaburras in the morning and see rosellas in the trees. I watch Mum and Ken together. Her hand is always on his back, their banter is easy. He measures half a shot of Scotch into her Diet Coke every afternoon and phones restaurants before we go out to check that they can make dishes for her without the garlic and onions. They play chess, jibing one another while always laughing. One morning Ken can't find his swimmers for the beach. He left them on the line last night and now they're gone. He suggests the rosellas took them.

'Well, I guess we're going to Sunnyside now, hey, Debbie.' Ken winks at Mum.

She rolls her eyes. 'They'll be in the car.'

'What's Sunnyside?' I ask.

'It's a nude beach down the road in Mount Eliza.' Mum's voice is impatient, but not without affection.

The dumb joke irritates me. As does their perpetual fussing over the most minute details of their days – which beach, which cafe, what time of day. I realise my annoyance is partly driven by jealousy. I'm dreaming of being fifty, with my own grown daughter or son and a man I love easily. I'm impatient for it. I'm not content in this place of flux; I'm ready for what's next.

My growing unease with my life is paralleled by my discomfort in my body. The mound has become a mountain and I constantly need to pee. I pee before we leave the house and as soon as we arrive anywhere. We only visit the cafes that have toilets and I know which ones those are. Being on the beach helps. It's sweltering and I can loll in the shallows, not having to make a bathroom trip every eight minutes. Relief for my hands and feet that balloon after seconds in the heat. In the water I am lighter, I'm not coated in sweat. I've had to buy bigger swimmers: a small tent that covers my breasts, which are large and streaked purple. My body is marked like a map – cracked earth and waterways. My stomach is always itchy and I remind myself of a man with his hand on his crotch. I waited for the baby to kick for so long and now I'm wishing it would stop. I have an appointment over the phone with a midwife from the hospital. She tells me to count the kicks. Ten in two hours is good. I don't count. There's easily more than that.

We see Annie and James every day and a few times we all have dinner together. James and his father go out diving for mussels one day and we eat them cooked with garlic and chopped tomatoes and heaped on top of crusty homemade bread. James's family's backyard is large, green and bursting with vegetables. The salad is always from the garden – rocket, tomatoes, zucchinis, eggplants. A grapevine grows over the verandah and bunches of fruit dangle from above like decorations. They must love Annie, I think, and it's obvious they do. James's mother calls her Ann, which none of us do. 'No, Ann doesn't like beetroot,' she tells Ken when he's assembling burgers for dinner.

Annie is different around them. She's always reticent, even with Sarah and me, but when she does speak it's clear she has been listening intently, thinking through what to say next. She's more agreeable here, less technical. Watching her I realise how I could be a blemish on her perfection, the single, knocked-up friend. She never treats me like this. Instead I'm doted on.

James's parents are friendly, intelligent and retired. They both cook and will tell you about the recipe they used, taking the cookbook off the shelf. The same with their summer reads, which are stacked beside their wicker chairs in the sunroom at the back of the house. They start talking about a book and at some point they'll go retrieve it; they like props, it seems. James's mother offers me more water.

Asks if I need to lie down. She likes to talk about pregnancy, shooting smug glances at the men. I'm acquiescent, placing my hand on my belly and acting the part of a happy pregnant lady. I appreciate her attentiveness and feel guilty that it only makes me feel more lonely. A single person with a big belly. Not laughing any louder as the night goes on, my water not making me drunk. As much as I am lonely, though, at least I don't have to ignore questions about getting married or engaged, which Annie and James do every day.

This would be a lovely backyard for a wedding – if you'd like a small event, that is. Better watch her, James. I smile at Annie as she smiles into her drink. James doesn't respond to the teasing but doesn't seem bothered by it either. He put a deposit on an apartment recently. He and Mum talk about stamp duty and I don't listen. Jokes about baby brain are made.

Afterwards, we stroll back along the beach to our rented house. Mum and Ken hold hands, Ken carrying their sandals in his free hand.

'James is so lovely,' says Mum. Every night she says it.

MUM PUTS FACE washers in the freezer for me in the mornings and at night I take them to bed. Lay one over my forehead, let the cloth soften and feel the water melt over my face.

I message Fergus from bed, send photos of my naked torso in dim lighting, legs spread. Me on my side, my large breasts melting over my bed. Sometimes I will send a photo followed by nothing.

Too tired to chat tonight. Sorry.

He pleads.

You can't do this to me.

182

He never sends me photos of himself, which I'm thankful for. Sometimes I'm asleep even before I read his replies. Never for long, though. My legs cramp. My pelvis hurts. So I message him again. Any time before 2 am he will reply straight away.

Other nights we have phone sex, sometimes for hours. Me under the sheets to muffle my voice so Mum and Ken don't hear. Occasionally I'll text him in the morning to say I woke up horny. He responds right away and I don't. I wait until I have a moment at the beach, write that I'm about to go swimming, describe how my breasts are spilling out of my top, and then I put my phone in my bag on the sand and walk to the water, where I loll with Annie for hours, leaving him waiting.

This summer is scorching and the beach is heaving. Brightly coloured beach boxes line the shore as far as I can see and remind me of being little, when I would line up my Polly Pockets, a colourful housing estate on the floor of my bedroom. This beach is full of families. Teenagers, whose Wild Turkey cans we find in the mornings, swim further south where they try to impress each other by flinging themselves from the rockface into the water. The few people our age are just north of here, on a secluded rocky beach, which, because of the steep incline you have to walk to access it, is free of screeching children. I wouldn't be able to waddle my way down that hill, which is why we are here and, despite the lack of quiet, I am calmest at the beach, when it's just the two of us.

'Look, that will be you next year.' Annie is pointing to a woman standing knee deep in the water wearing a long white linen shirt, her black one-piece visible beneath it, and a big straw hat. When her hands are free she rests them on her hips, but mostly her hands aren't free. She grabs at two toddlers in the shallows. Pulls them apart when they're wrestling. 'Don't lick your sister!' I hear her say.

'That's not me. *That's* me.' I point to a young girl in a floral bikini, dipping a fat baby's toes into the water as it chuckles pleasantly.

'She's the babysitter.'

'Don't just say that because she's young.'

'I'm not just saying that. I know she is. That baby's family is renting one of Ian and Maureen's properties.'

'Which one of their properties?'

We smile to one another. I relish this time with Annie, recapping moments from dinner the night before, joking about making a lasso for her to capture James with. We talk about names for the baby, seriously this time.

'Have you heard from Sissa yet?' Annie asks.

'No. Have you?'

'No. But, you know, I'm not pregnant. It would be nice of her to check in.'

Whatever we say about Sarah, the last comment is always the same, always from Annie. 'She was so smashed that night.' Her gaze is far off across the sand, unfocused, as though she's thinking some deep and profound observation.

I don't indulge her wanting to complain about Sarah, because I don't want to spoil this time. A weight is lifted – literally, as the water holds me up, also because I'm away from Mum and the stress of thinking about money or what I'm going to do for work. I feel free and relaxed, like my baby, comforted as I'm submerged.

I want to see you

Fergus sends me this message almost every day. I respond by reminding him that I'm in Mount Martha, as if this is an explanation, as if when I'm home I'll see him again, though I'm not sure if that's true. Occasionally I remember the last time I saw him, when he gave me permission to dump him, which puts me off. But more than that, it's my body. Inflated and stretched. The pale pink marks on my belly growing darker. A red line splits me down the middle. It's smeared and fuzzy, like a scar. I look like I've been cleaved in two and poorly sewed back together.

Texting Fergus is like porn, an imaginary place where even I feel desirable.

THE MINISERIES I FILMED IN New Zealand is being replayed on free-to-air. Mum and Ken watch it late in the afternoon, even though they've seen it before. I'm so skinny. It's all I can think and I don't blame Ken for saying it in exactly those words. In the first episode I'm being held captive by a threatening man. I'm in a dank room in a filthy grey dress. Squatting on my haunches, dirty legs. My arms are sticks. My cheekbones ridgelines down my face. My make-up streaked brown to look like dirt. It's such a popular genre, this – young girls being held captive.

'Can we watch something else?' I ask.

'I can't remember what happens,' Mum says. I wonder if she's thinking this will entice me to act again.

One day I'm in the ad break as well. Standing with my hand on my fake belly, which is about the size of my belly as it is now, although I look very different, my arse and jawline fuller . *'Are you ready?'* the TV me asks – a version of me who thought she *was* ready, that this ad was somehow adequate preparation.

After the ad break I'm out of the dank room. Dressed in blue skinny jeans and a pale pink blouse that is bunched at the shoulders, not the kind of thing I'd ever wear in real life.

'You people are all the same,' the television me tells a television police officer. 'You just wear different clothes.' I remember the line well. It was one of the sound grabs for the trailer. I'd hated it. Too overdone. Hitting the viewers on the head with a hammer.

'WE SAW YOU on the TV!' James's father is wearing a brown apron. He puts his knife down to kiss me on the cheek then raises his glass of chardonnay.

'I was really skinny, wasn't I?'

Annie laughs from the couch where she is reclining, also drinking white wine.

'Maureen and I watched it when it first aired. I thought I recognised you from somewhere. And then Ann told us you were in *Much Ado About Nothing* last year.'

'Mmm.'

'Who was the other woman in that, Maureen? She was in that new police drama.'

I stop talking and let Mum fill in the gaps. She tells Ian what awards I was nominated for, which is a much longer list than the ones I won. They talk about the other actor, the one who was in the police drama. It was a depressing show about a woman struggling to cope with her child's death, like all mothers in stories. They're either beaten by their husbands or have lost their children to war or disease. No happy mothers exist in fiction.

'So, do you have anything lined up?' Ian asks me.

I look to Mum, wondering if she's going to keep talking for me, but she doesn't.

'No,' I say. 'Nothing lined up.'

Steak and potatoes, followed by fruit from the garden, sliced and placed atop ice cubes. At the end of the night, as we're saying goodbye, James's dad says, 'Could be a little star you're cooking up in there!'

I smile, thank him for the dinner. Annie is in the kitchen washing up. I can't see her face, but I can feel her smiling too.

IN BED I message Fergus.

   Ok.

I'VE NEVER BEEN TO A nude beach. I realise when I arrive that the picture I've had in my head is a teenage boy's wet dream from some American movie, I don't remember which one. I'd imagined blonde bombshells, but the first people I see are a cheery, camp couple who smile at me as they walk along the shore.

'Nice day for it,' one of them says, striding ahead.

I'm dawdling deliberately – others might think I'm only here to enjoy the view, like I've accidentally stumbled across the beach. I was hesitant to come, but it was the only place I could think of where I could be sure I wouldn't run into anyone I know. I imagine bumping into James's parents and have a small laugh to myself.

It's not a long walk from the main beach and, while it is pretty – a small pocket of sand backed by shrubs, a sprawl of shiny black rocks becoming mossier as they meet the water, gentle waves slopping happily in the inlet – it strikes me as not very private. I know from my Google search that the northern section of the beach is exclusively for gay men. Looking northward, I can't see anyone's penis, but I can see well enough to tell they're naked. The shoreline continues in both directions to other, regular beaches, where I envisage people looking over to us here, judgemental or perving. I'm not sure what I was expecting, but I feel exposed.

I spread my towel on the sand behind a beach hut and park myself on it, protected from one side. I don't get undressed right away, but survey the other beachgoers. There's one couple sitting side by side on towels and reading. The man is wearing a cowboy hat. Beyond them is another woman on her own, clothed.

It's much quieter than the main beach.

I slip off my sandals and my beach dress but leave my bathers on for the time being. I feel the sun hot on my skin. It's probably doing me damage, but I let it for now. I keep looking around at the other people, but nobody seems to notice me, or care. As I settle in, I realise I feel relaxed in a way I haven't in weeks. I'm mildly nervous about seeing Fergus, who didn't hesitate before agreeing to meet me here despite it being more than an hour's drive from the city. But also I'm calm, alone for the first time in a while. Eventually, I slip my bathers off. I take a few deep breaths, like I would if I was running, in and out, even. I'm thankful now to have already applied sunscreen, realising how uncomfortably sexual it would be for Fergus to rub lotion on my body here, even with bathers on. I lie down on my back, raise my arms up and over my head and stretch my legs. I spread them just a little. I urge a breeze to come so that I can feel it in my pubes. I close my eyes. I won't be able to stay like this for long, the baby's weight will squash my lungs, but for a few moments at least I relax into it.

'You look nice.'

I open my eyes and see him standing over me. He's had a haircut. A clean symmetrical bowl cut, which is fashionable but not summery.

'I like your hair.'

'I had it done over a month ago.'

I stare at him, trying to decide if he's making a point of how long it's been since I've seen him. He stares back, then, after few seconds, he smiles. He drops his towel and lowers gently onto the sand. He surveys everyone here, like I did when I arrived. One of the older men has been for a swim and is now drip-drying. Fergus and I sit together quietly. I exhale loudly, act exaggeratedly relaxed.

'How did you know about this place?' he asks eventually.

'My mum's partner made a joke about it.'

He turns to me and feigns a sleazy look. We fall back into silence and I watch him watching me, his eyes running over my body.

'I'm huge now.'

'It suits you.'

'I've got cellulite.' I raise my legs and show him the underside of my thighs, deliberately coquettish.

He laughs, asks me how my holiday has been. I summarise what I've been doing the past two weeks between sexting him.

'Are you going to join me?' I ask.

He drops back onto his elbows, but still doesn't undress. 'I don't know,' he says.

'What do you mean you don't know?'

'Well' – he turns onto his stomach, moves his face in close to mine to talk – 'I don't think we can get naked together. Like, be a naked couple here. Wouldn't it be odd?'

'That couple over there is naked.' I point to the man in the cowboy hat reading next to his partner.

Fergus looks over to them and then back to me. 'Aren't they strange, though?' he whispers.

We both laugh.

We laugh all afternoon. Fergus is working on a summer musical and he recounts the horridly sexist storyline. He asks me about Mum and Ken and I tell him about my family, even my dad. I ask about his Christmas and learn about his family. He has two younger sisters, which I find hard to picture. He talks about them affectionately and I realise I can hardly imagine him being anything other than desperate to please, the way he is with me.

When we move from the sand to the water he finally gets nude. I can't help but stare at his penis, which, unlike when I've seen it before, is small and dangly. I feel embarrassed, as though I'm witnessing something too intimate. The tide is low and we have to wade out, out, out until we're covered. Once the water is deep enough we swim circles around one another.

Fergus is more relaxed than I've ever seen him. He doesn't agree with everything I say or try to match his opinions to mine. If there are silences, he lets them be.

I've swum out deeper here than I've been used to in Mount Martha. Treading water is harder work with my big body. Occasionally I need to rest, wrapping my legs around his torso and letting him take my weight. My protruding belly touches his flat one. He puts his arms around me loosely. Calm, not fervent. It's the most enjoyable time I've ever spent with him. Possibly the only enjoyable time.

Walking from the water back to the sand I feel self-conscious, expecting the other people here to stare, but nobody does. Resting again on my towel I survey the dots of water on my body, glistening in the sun, soon to be absorbed or evaporated.

'I think I love the nude beach,' I say to Fergus as I envisage a future as a single, hippy mother, whose child doesn't want to know she goes nude swimming.

He doesn't comment.

After three hours that pass easily, we walk back to the car park together. He carries my bag, I have the towels.

'So, when are you back in Melbourne?' he asks.

'We leave in three days.' I'm walking behind him and he doesn't add anything else. Doesn't ask if we're going to see each other. 'It's weird,' I go on. 'The next time I see my mum I'm going to have a baby.'

'That is weird.' He turns his head back to look at me, but he doesn't stop, he keeps walking.

When we reach the car park he hands me my bag and I hand him his towel and we hug goodbye and then we kiss, soft and closed-mouthed. Not long, but with a gentle affection.

'Get home safe,' he says.

'YOU SEEM VERY relaxed,' Mum says to me that evening. She and Ken are watching the finale of the miniseries. On television I'm rigid, sullen in a witness box. In real life I am lying on a couch opposite Mum and Ken. I pretend to be asleep and don't answer.

THE NEXT MORNING over breakfast I write a message to Travis. I try to write it quickly. Try not to overthink my words. A combination of the same sorts of sentiments I've been drafting for months. I'm not telling him anything he doesn't know, just reminding him that I'm here. I send it without even rereading it.

Afterwards, I sip my tea and look across the back garden that is bright with morning sun. I listen to birds screeching and wonder if I'm anxious for a reply. I guess that I will be eventually, but right now I feel calm.

FOR OUR LAST night in Mount Martha we have booked dinner at a restaurant on the Esplanade. We order seafood platters for the table. Crunchy tempura crab and flaky white fish. Everyone but me knocks back oysters, ordering a dozen more and then a dozen more. After dinner we go to a wine bar. It's upstairs and has a balcony that overlooks the street. It's expensive, but acting bohemian. We sit on cushions on the floor and drink from large, stemless wineglasses. I drink fancy lemonade with homemade ginger syrup and rosemary. Our parents comment on how nice the bar is. Annie, James and I spy on the people on the street below. Annie and James are on their third wine and getting silly.

I manage not to think of Travis for the whole evening. I forget about the message I sent him until I get home and am idly scrolling on my phone before bed. I reread what I wrote:

> I know we're not very good friends, but I am here for you if you would like company or to talk and you think it might help. I am also very sad. I know I wasn't as close to him as you were, nowhere near, but I thought he was a really nice guy. These things affect everyone. Feel free to ignore. I hope you're ok.

Maybe I should've added a 'Happy New Year' or 'Belated Merry Christmas'. Although, on reflection, it's probably better I didn't. He probably hasn't been feeling that festive.

THE RENTAL NEEDS TO BE cleaned before we leave. I waddle around with the broom, struggling to sweep, and Mum tells me to sit. I lie on the couch while she and Ken work around me, and feel more like a child than ever. Afterwards they drop me at James's parents' place. Annie and James are driving me home while Mum and Ken are headed straight to the airport. Mum hugs Annie goodbye and they're giggly.

'Next time we see each other there'll be a little baby!'

'I know!'

On the drive home we ring Sarah. She got back from the Sunshine Coast a week ago, which was the first time I heard from her since we dropped her at the airport. She sent me a text:

> I read about a CEO whose baby didn't like breastfeeding, or
> bottle feeding, so she jellied her breast milk.

No hello. No context. I replied:

> That's gross.
> I think it's beautiful.
> So do I.

After that, she messaged every day. Bored, impatient for us to return. We invited her to come to Mount Martha, but she refused the offer and continued to tell us how bored she was each day.

Now her voice complains through the car's speakers. We listen to her talk about Queensland. I realise that when Mum moves, I'll have no reason to go back there. I feel little sadness about this and it makes me feel old.

Sarah tells us about going out to a club on the Gold Coast. Partying with schoolies kids and sleeping with one of them. He called her vagina her 'minge'. We haven't laughed this hard in weeks. I'm worried for my delicate bladder. And yet, like boiling water taken off heat, something inside me settles.

I USED TO GRAZE TRAVIS'S socials looking for you, but lately I've been expanding. Yesterday I spent an hour looking through an album of a holiday he went on without you, a road trip through Victoria and New South Wales. He slept in a swag that he strapped to the roof of his car between destinations. Another boy and two girls were on the trip. They had a cast-iron jaffle maker that one person is holding in the fire in almost every shot. There's a particular photo of Travis I keep returning to. He's sitting on a log beside the camp fire. One of the girls on the trip is seated next to him and it looks like they're talking. Her expression is serious, staring at the ground. Maybe she was just studying a bug there or she was telling him she hates her job, she doesn't know what she wants to do with the rest of her life. Travis is bent forward, elbows on his knees. His face is turned towards her, trying to look into her eyes that are fixed on the ground. I think at first that maybe she's upset and he is trying to cheer her up. I laugh to myself when I imagine being isolated in the bush with Travis. Maybe she is tired of him and he is bustling for her attention.

In the next shot only their heads are visible above a body of water that is bursting with reflected sun. You can't see much detail, everything is over-exposed, but you can tell they're both laughing.

TRAVIS SHARES PETITIONS to stop Adani. He shares articles about how all cops are bastards. He asks people to come to his gigs using memes: men playing saxophones in cafes, a slug holding a flute. He shares the video of the koala drinking from the water bottle. There are photos of him with friends standing on rocks with views behind them, beers in hand.

I look up his parents' winery and browse photos on the website. Expansive shots of the orderly grid of a vineyard, close-up shots of the tightly coiled tendrils of a grapevine. There are photos of Travis's father and his brothers making wine and then there's a photo of you. I hadn't been looking for it and it knocks me from within. It's possible to be winded by grief, I've learned. You're with Travis, walking between barrels in a large dark warehouse, both wearing aprons and tall, sturdy work boots. I'm not sure if you'd worked there or the photo was taken to make it look like you had.

I save the photo and shut my laptop. The purpose of looking at this stuff is to learn more about you and yet each time I do I feel indignant, hurt by even the tiniest facet of your life that surprises me.

February

IT'S ANNIE WHO TELLS SARAH I'm going to move. It just makes sense; we can't live together with a baby. She tells her when I'm not there and then later the three of us have dinner – mussels in a tomato sauce, James's dad's recipe. We drag our kitchen chairs close together, crowding around one corner of the dining table. The laptop is open and together we read ads on rental websites, people looking for rooms. Sarah won't live with anybody who likes sport or describes themselves as active. Also, she won't let anyone who has a cat or a dog move in.

'I can't trust someone if they have a pet, but not a home.'

We look at places for me. Annie says I need a new bathroom and a small courtyard. 'If you don't have a backyard you'll get postnatal depression.'

It feels like online shopping for a new life. I picture myself in these flats, a version of me who has a job and dusted windowsills. And a baby.

OUR FRIEND GINNIE moves out of the Clarke Street house and Sarah takes her room. I find a small one-bedroom. Mum has to apply to go on the lease herself, because I don't have a job. There's a moment where we wonder if she will be accepted. She's at an age when most people retire. Annie says if Mum is rejected she will apply for me, and I feel at once like the luckiest and the most pathetic person in the world.

Sarah and I start bumping out our home. As she's moving to a house already set up, she lets me keep the furniture.

'Also, you need it,' she says. I suspect Annie has told her to let me have it. To show I'm grateful I do as much of the packing as I can. I'm slow, but at least with no job I have entire days to fill boxes, which is about how long it takes.

My back hurts, my heart burns and my feet keep swelling. I have terrible acid reflux. This is because my muscles are relaxing, I'm told. It's the reason why my back hurts and my posture is out of whack. I picture the muscles around my stomach, oesophagus and pelvis drooping over my skeleton like pancakes, the image so divorced from how I feel – trapped in pudgy armour. I'm sweating all the time. At night I wake up drenched.

SARAH AND I do laps of the empty house before we leave. We pat the walls and vanities the way people tap a newly purchased TV set or the boot of a car before it drives off. I feel like I'm walking around a bare stage, the set either yet to be built or just stripped down.

I hire a van, not a removalist, and Annie and James help me move. They arrive early in the morning and the first thing Annie does, without even saying hello, is tell me to get changed.

'It's going to be hot today. Don't you think you should have short sleeves on?'

She's like this for the rest of the day. I go to lift something and she'll stop me. 'I'll get that.'

I can't even make a cup of tea without her telling me to do it her way. It's excruciating, but I can't tell her to fuck off because I need the help.

Since I can't lift things into the truck, I insist on driving. I'm only moving around the corner. About four streets north, the other side of St Georges Road. A small block of five flats. I'm worried about moving to an apartment with a crying baby. 'What if my neighbours hate me?' I say to Annie.

'What are they going to do? Call the cops?'

This is a rather Sissa thing to say, I point out. Annie looks at me, shocked, but then she smiles. We both do.

Sarah and I never knew our old neighbours. When we first moved in, we were still young enough to stay up all night drinking, even on weeknights. 'It'll be easier if they hate us,' she'd said. 'We won't have to try to please them.'

I think now how I will make an effort to knock on my neighbours' doors and introduce myself. This feels like a very adult thing to do, until I admit to Annie and James I'm embarrassed about being pregnant and alone.

'They'll wonder where my partner is.'

'Maybe you can go with her, James.'

We all laugh.

The new apartment fills fast with the old furniture. The ceiling is lower than in the old house and the fridge looks huge. The couch takes up one whole wall. The second couch closes off the space and we decide I don't need it. Trying to fit my old things into a smaller space feels too significant; too obviously a metaphor for life shrinking, closing in around me.

Annie says I'll need a new coffee table. Not right away, but the glass-topped one I own won't be safe once the baby is toddling around. I need to get the heater tested for carbon monoxide and also I need a barrier to stop the baby from reaching it. She walks around the house kicking sharp corners of the skirting boards. 'I wonder if we can baby-proof that.'

Baby-proofing, I joke, sounds like you're trying to protect the house from babies getting in.

Annie fills the house with indoor plants. She read an article about air pollution and how bad it is for everyone and, of course, if it's bad for everyone then it's worse for pregnant women. Apparently six houseplants will cleanse my air. Then she sees the walls have been freshly painted and decides to buy another three.

Annie makes me feel small, bossing me around like she has to do everything for me. I wish that she could resign herself to these little things, like the way she is when we talk about the world's bigger problems.

AT THE END of the day we order takeaway Indian. I tear the side off an empty cardboard box and place it on the kitchen counter, so the curries don't stain the white benchtop. They look like open tins of paint lined up in a row, dark green, dark orange, brown. Annie and James drink a beer each. We're exhausted, so nobody talks much and the silence screams of Sarah.

It's not like I'll never see her. It's not like I ever thought we'd live together forever. She was a shit housemate anyway . . . A conversation with myself in my head.

Sometimes I'm happier without James and Annie around and it makes me feel awful to admit it because they do so much for me.

I'm not allowed to be irritated with a friend who will offer to go on a lease for me, but I am. Sometimes my envy of Annie scares me. I get jealous of Sarah too, but also not, like when she sinks four champagnes at a wedding ceremony and then vomits in a vase on the table at the reception. It's easy to see the ways in which I don't want to be Sarah, whereas Annie is objectively perfect: job; boyfriend with a job; never gets too drunk. But there's something about her acquiescence that I pity. Has she never felt the desire to veer from what is generally considered acceptable? I'm not sure what's sadder – if she's wanted to, but restrained herself; if she has never wanted to; or me, thinking that quitting my job equates to some kind of emotional enlightenment. I feel superior and then like an arsehole. I resent her any time I feel judged for doing what I'm doing and I feel superior to her any time I feel smug for doing what I'm doing. Sometimes I wonder if I'm wildly depressed and actually have been for a long time and sometimes I wonder if I understand more about myself than most people do. I often wondered this when I was an actor. Do actors have more insight into the human condition because they spend so much time analysing people's motivations? Or are they completely misguided and actually understand nothing?

THE FIRST NIGHT in my new home I'm awake until late, getting used to the sounds of the building. It's a quieter street than the old one, which means less background noise for the creaking walls to compete with. I hear my neighbours next door when they flush the toilet. This I don't mind, signs of life. Someone nearby to hear me scream. It's the sounds in the walls that disconcert me. Like my body, shifting and moving within yet outside my control.

I MESSAGE SARAH in the morning.

> *Miss you.*

I send a photo of myself seated alone at our old breakfast table. *What to Expect* is here. I offered it to Sarah, but she'd already finished it, which I know I won't. I stopped caring what was going to happen two-thirds in. I've succumbed to this state. My body is not mine but belongs to my child. Like being an actor, I am a vessel for someone else's idea.

My phone chimes with Sarah's reply.

> Omg I missed you so much I couldn't sleep last night.

For the next few days I document my life in five-to-ten second videos that I send to her. It starts with sharing our meals: we phone each other to have company while we're eating. Which leads to my sharing photos of the books I'm reading. She sends a photo of her drinks. Which leads to us texting when we're going to bed – a photo of me blowing a kiss. One day Sarah messages me:

> Ok, I'm going to the toilet now.

The whole thing descends into us recording our own farts and messaging those to each other. It's delightfully disgusting and helps me to miss her less.

When I'm not messaging Sarah, I spend my time shopping for healthy food. I no longer want to eat dim sims; the thought of them actually makes me sick. I cook myself nice meals that I eat in small doses. With the move done now, I notice the absence of Mum and take comfort in the fact that I miss her. With everyone back at work, the sudden lack of company is depressing, but also hopeful. Family gives you an automatic comfort, a rhythm to your life.

I manage to fill the days by making schedules out of nothing. I schedule Education Time in which I try to learn things about the world so I can be an informed parent. I listen to the news until the point it depresses me and then I read. I work my way through the Zadie Smith novels I've owned since uni. Inevitably I fall asleep while reading; this is Relaxation Time. I walk laps around my neighbourhood – Active Time. Mum and Ken bought me a pram for Christmas. It sits by the door of my flat, perpetually ready to leave. I practise pushing it back and forth on the spot, but it doesn't move comfortably on the carpet. My bike, too, is rested against the wall in my courtyard, collecting cobwebs. I long for the weightlessness of riding along flat roads and spend the afternoon looking up baby bike seats online. I buy more jumpsuits, watch my bank balance deplete and spend afternoons folding the baby's small clothes into drawers.

None of it is particularly exciting, but I find comfort in my routine and I feel more relaxed than I did last year.

I'M SURPRISED TO realise how put out I am that Fergus hasn't contacted me since I returned from the coast. We haven't spoken since the day at Sunnyside. I think a lot about whether I want to see him. I did enjoy his company on the beach. Having sex would be nice. But then I hold my hands on my stomach and remind myself I shouldn't.

When I ring him, it's deliberately impulsive, I dial before I can stop myself. He sounds happy to hear from me, but neither of us mentions how long it has been since we last spoke.

'I've been thinking about you,' he says.

I don't respond, unsure if this is teetering into phone sex or love or breaking this off – whatever this is.

'I'm on production week for a musical,' he says. 'Been doing fourteen-hour days back to back, but we open Thursday. Do you want to come to opening night? I can get two free tickets to the show and the after party.'

I don't really want to go. I've never liked musical theatre. But the party means free food, free booze for my plus-one and also something to do. An excuse to make my friends spend time with me.

'Can you swing three tickets?'

'I'll see what I can do.'

TWO NIGHTS LATER we're going – Annie, Sarah and me. I haven't been to an opening night in a long time and the buzz in the foyer intoxicates me a little. The three of us have a daggy portrait taken in front of the media wall. There are small bowler hats on sticks, matching the costumes from the show. Sarah places one on my large belly.

The musical is about a young, tap-dancing girl who moves to the big city to become a star. I never had to act this archetype, thankfully. I've pretended to be a nurse, a teacher, a housewife and a writer, but I think this role would be beyond me – trying to understand why anybody would want this life. Especially *this* life. Musical theatre is even more gruelling than talking theatre, with six-month seasons.

The show is sexist and culturally insensitive, but the tap dancing is good. It's pure escapism that requires me to abandon every critical faculty. I don't like this kind of show, but I do admire its lack of pretension. Actors I worked with – those who worked in 'serious theatre' – and writers I met love to call themselves artists. They talk about creating empathy and telling the stories of our time in order to understand it. They say, 'We tell ourselves stories in order to live,' as though what we do is a great triumph of catharsis for the human race. Actually, we tell ourselves stories in order to live with ourselves. If you are an artist, you are actively participating in the distraction of thousands of rich people who should be very worried. Does Greta Thunberg go to the theatre? I doubt it. I'm not saying this is necessarily a bad thing. Writing and acting might even be noble pursuits, distracting a doomed race. What I don't like is pretending that what we're doing has any grand meaning. Musical theatre, at least, knows that it's a glittery, smiley distraction.

Annie, unsurprisingly, has trouble succumbing to the escapism. 'What does Fergus actually do?' she asks me at interval.

'Fits the cast for mics.' He definitely described his work in more detail when we were at the beach, but I've forgotten the specifics of it. I feel Annie watching me, waiting for me to go on.

After the show we attend the party in the theatre's large function room. Sarah and Annie take glasses of wine from a tray passing by. I shuffle us around the room, chasing the canapés. I run into someone I knew from drama school. I can't remember his name, but I remember his face, and Sarah and Annie are talking to one another, saving me from having to admit that I can't introduce him.

'I heard you quit the biz.' He gestures to my belly when he says it.

'What have you been up to?' I ask.

'I'm on *Harry Potter*; my swing is filling in for me tonight so that I could come and see Lola perform.'

I don't know who Lola is. 'How is *Harry Potter*?'

'It's a long season. But, you know, what's the alternative? Auditioning for three years and not getting any work?'

'Right,' I say. 'So at what point will you realise you have the worst job in the world?'

He laughs, claps me on the shoulder and says he has to go talk to Lola. I feel bad after he leaves. I'm almost tempted to chase after him, to tell him that, actually, I admire the work he's doing. But there's probably no way I can articulate my thoughts on non-art theatre without offending him more. Social anxiety firmly settled now, I want to leave. We haven't seen Fergus yet and Annie thinks we should wait. Sarah turns away to chase one last free drink. While she's gone, Fergus finds me and Annie. He kisses me on the cheek, introduces himself to Annie and asks if we liked the show. Annie tells him she thought it was culturally insensitive. He agrees with her and they talk about representation in musical theatre, whether it is better to abandon shows altogether or attempt to modernise them. I only half listen; I'm scanning the room for the guy I went to drama school with, trying to remember his name. Eventually Sarah returns with two wines. She drinks most of one in one long gulp, then pours the remainder of it into the other glass – two glasses of wine looks like one quite quickly. I laugh; luckily for Sarah, Annie is engaged enough in her conversation with Fergus that she doesn't notice.

'I think I'm going to head off,' I say, interrupting them. 'I'm tired.'

Annie nods. 'I'll come with.'

'Thanks for coming.' Fergus hugs each of us. 'I'll speak to you soon,' he says quietly into my ear.

Sarah tips her head back and downs her big glass of wine.

The three of us are quiet on the tram back north. I'm observing the drunk people here. Their bodies are flung around like rag dolls whenever the tram stops. 'I'm a Capricorn,' one drunk says to another. 'I say what I want.'

'Fergus is nice,' Annie says. I turn and see she's watching me watching other people.

'Yeah, he's nice.'

I'm aware of Annie studying my reaction. I keep looking down the tram, even once the drunks pile off together. Annie and Sarah both get off in Collingwood. Annie is going home and Sarah is meeting other people out. I continue on to Thornbury alone. I take my phone out to message Fergus and thank him for the tickets, and see he's already sent me a message.

> What are you doing?
> *On the tram home.*
> Can I come over?

I'm too tired to even entertain the thought, although I do entertain it a little.

> *Not tonight.*

MY RELATIONSHIP WITH FERGUS BEGINS to resemble what it was at the old house. I don't love the sex, but I don't hate it, and I'm bored so I keep inviting him over, almost every day.

It's harder to get into a rhythm now. Hard to find a position that I'm comfortable in two days in a row. We try with me on top, my heavy belly resting on his lean one, but my leg starts to cramp.

'Lie on your back,' he suggests.

'I can't breathe if I do that.'

I lie on my side and he awkwardly manoeuvres himself between my legs. It works for about twenty seconds and then it doesn't.

'Can you use your mouth?'

I can't. I just can't get myself there, my belly presses hard into the bed. He wants to go down on me but I'm too self-conscious. I soak through three pairs of underwear a day lately. In the end I'm on my hands and knees, Fergus behind me. Unsexy, but convenient. When the baby kicks I can't help but take it as a request for us to stop. I don't come easily like I did in the second trimester. Actually, I hardly come at all.

Fergus keeps turning up. He lists new positions we can try as he's unlacing his shoes.

'How do you find this stuff?' I ask one day when we're eating lunch afterwards.

'Do you realise how many women write about it online?'

This is how it's different from before: we spend time together, and it's this part I enjoy, eating noodles on my couch. We start watching a television series together. Not *Friends* – something with fifty-minute episodes. I usually fall asleep and when I wake, he's headed off for his evening shift.

One day I even go to his house. When I visit anyone's house for the first time, I picture myself living there and then judge the person according to how much I enjoy the imagined life. He lives in a semi-detached brick place on one of Carlton's long, straight streets. It's filled with nice furniture, which, unlike mine, is nicer the closer you look. I inspect the wood of a tall record shelf and he tells me his friend made it from rescued Tasmanian oak. A dark leather couch is shiny and unscratched. On the wall there's a large framed print of a dense forest. It matches his houseplants, which are bursting out of clean pots. The house is perfectly arranged and clearly expensive, and I feel attracted to him in a way I never have been before, picturing my life like I did when I was younger – cool, and casually rich. My materialism bemuses me. I'm probably not as perturbed by it as I should be.

I wonder if his housemates know about me and, if they do, what they know. I picture Fergus laughing over wine in this kitchen as he tells them what it's like to have sex with a pregnant woman. I feel a twinge of annoyance. Then I realise that if one of them were to walk through the door and have no idea who the pregnant woman sitting in their house was I would be hurt.

We don't talk about what it is we're doing and I don't think much about it. Most of the uneasiness I feel is not about our feelings but about the sex. How each time we do it now, it ends up with him masturbating, his gaze fixed on my stomach. His face goes dark red before he comes and he looks too intent, unhealthily serious.

I bring this up at dinner one evening when Sarah and Annie are eating at my place.

'That's so normal,' Sarah says. 'Remember Ryan? He had a fetish for sleeping with pregnant women – *specifically* women pregnant with someone else's baby.'

There's silence except for the sound of snow peas crunching; we're eating stir-fry. If my friends and I are going to talk about this – my sleeping with a man who's not the father of my child – we should do it now. It's unlike my friends – or anyone, I assume – to never ask what is going on with someone I've been seeing for this long. But I've never been pregnant before. I search their faces for judgement. Sarah looks expectant, clearly hoping I'll elaborate, Annie is very interested in her bowl. The conversation moves on to Sarah's new housemates at Clarke Street.

'They're all always working,' she says. 'When they're not working, they go for runs. Renee is joining a junior board for an arts festival.' She shudders exaggeratedly and repeats, '*Junior board.*'

'Why do you care?' asks Annie.

'Corporate art wank pains me.'

Sarah leaves after dinner and Annie stays to do the dishes. 'I spoke to Renee,' she starts. I think she's going to say something about Travis so I stop wiping the bench and turn to her. 'They invite Sarah out with them, but she never goes. She'll only go out with her work friends because they're the ones with good coke. She crashes into the house wasted at five in the morning, then is a bitch to them on Sundays when they won't spend time with her.'

I'm not really sure what Annie is telling me. I don't know if she's venting or we're teetering into a bigger, more serious conversation. 'Why do they care?' I ask.

'You heard her tonight.' She turns to face me now, her hands still in the sink. 'She's bagging them out because they're not getting hammered with her. Like it's an affront to her if someone wants to go for a run in the morning.'

'They knew what Sarah was like when they said she could live with them.'

Annie doesn't say anything. There's just the sound of cutlery sliding around the bottom of the sink. Annie's frustration with Sarah is similar to Sarah's frustration with her housemates. Annie takes it as an affront that her friend isn't living her life the way she is. She drains the sink and takes a dish towel to start drying.

'Leave those,' I say.

'It's okay.'

'Dishes dry themselves; tea towels were invented to sell linen.'

Annie folds the towel and hangs it on my oven door. 'Do you have any tea?' she asks.

'Sorry, I should've offered.' I start making a pot.

She's no longer complaining about Sarah, but she doesn't seem to have anything else to talk about. She drinks her tea slowly as if she's putting off going home.

'How's work?' We hardly talked about Annie over dinner. This happens sometimes. She won't talk about herself, so she gets left out of the ring-around.

'Okay,' she says. She's blank for a second then not. Her expression changes, as though she's just shaken herself awake. 'Good, actually,' she adds. 'I'm being awarded this thirty-under-thirty thing – for significant achievement under the age of thirty.'

'That's amazing.'

She shrugs. 'I think a lot of people get them.'

'What do you get?'

'Résumé wank.'

I suspect there is actually more to it than that.

'That's amazing, mate. Honestly, we should celebrate.'

She smiles, drains her tea and leaves.

IN BED AT night I think about when Mum was here. How obvious it was that she was keeping something from me. I get a similar sense from Annie now, though she's subdued about it, as if her secret is not something exciting. I also think about Sarah and I wonder if Annie was trying to tell me to pull her into line, as though Sarah is my responsibility.

I find Annie's irritation more irritating than Sarah's behaviour, yet on the weekend I decide that instead of staying in reading I'll go to Clarke Street to check on her. We have brunch on her back deck then spend the afternoon at All Nations Park looking at other people's dogs. Renee comes with us and I realise how much I have let other friends drift from my life since I've been pregnant. Renee started a new job months back without my realising. Matthew is on a work trip to London. Renee asks me about pregnancy and about the baby, but I don't say much, letting Sarah answer for me. I want her to ask me about something else but realise I have nothing else to talk about. I have no job or job prospects, and my romantic life is limited to a guy I don't think I'm interested in. All I have to share

are my small joys – a pleasing turn of phrase in a book I'm reading, the eggplant my neighbour plucked from his veggie patch and left on my doorstep, the feeling of my baby kicking in a moment I was feeling lonely. For some reason, we never talk about these things.

Just before the sun sets, we walk back to their house, stopping in at a bottle-o on the way so the girls can buy a slab.

'I bet you can't wait until the baby's born and you can drink again,' Renee says.

'I guess. But it's not like I can have a few wines after dinner when I have a baby sleeping at home.'

'Yes you can,' says Sarah. 'I'll come over and take care of it.'

This is hardly reassuring, but I don't comment. We sit on their back deck and watch the sun go down over the city. From their back porch you can see a flat sprawl of houses and greenery leading all the way up to the storybook cluster of skyrises in the distance. Watching Sarah and Renee, I don't sense any of the tension that Annie hinted at. Sarah is looking at her phone, objectifying boys on a dating app. She matches with someone on there, shows us, and Renee says she went on a date with him recently.

'He was fine,' Renee says. 'Nothing wrong with him.'

Sarah peers at his photo. 'Did he go down on you?' she asks.

Renee nods.

Listening to Renee talking about men she's dating, I'm reminded of Travis and I realise that, amid moving, I haven't thought of him nearly as much lately. He never replied to the message I sent him in Mount Martha, which probably should be driving me crazy. I feel guilty suddenly, which is stupid given my obsessing over him wasn't helping anyone at all.

'Have you spoken to Travis recently?' I ask.

If Renee is surprised by my question she doesn't show it. 'No, not for ages.'

'That's always sad. When you lose touch with an ex.' This isn't true, but I've said it. As always when it comes to Travis, I'm not even sure what I'm fishing for.

'We weren't together that long,' she says. 'I mean, I'd hardly call it a relationship.'

Although I thought Travis was overdoing his pain, I feel a little hurt on his behalf by Renee's nonchalance.

'He was so obsessed with you, though.'

'He's obsessed with everything he does.' Renee shrugs and looks out to the city behind her.

Sarah stands. 'I'm getting another beer.' She goes back inside.

'I haven't seen him in ages.' I know this information is uninteresting; my ability to loiter around this topic is about to run out.

'He has a gig next week.'

'Really?'

'I think it's next week.' Renee takes her phone from her pocket to check. 'Oh, shit – it's tomorrow.'

'I've never seen his band.'

'They're okay.' She puts her phone back in her pocket. 'A little over the top.'

'Kind of like him?' I ask.

She laughs.

Sarah returns with beers for her and Renee.

'Do you want something?' Renee asks me. 'We have ginger beer, or juice.'

'I'm fine.'

I spend another hour on the balcony with them. I connect my phone to a speaker and select tracks for us to listen to. I play some of Travis's music, but Renee doesn't comment so neither do I. We don't actually talk a lot and it's relaxing. By the time I leave they're four beers deep and on to their fifth. Renee gives me a big hug at the door, holding on tight. 'Stop being a stranger.'

I don't say I will, but I squeeze her back.

AFTER FORGETTING THE MESSAGE I sent Travis from Mount Martha, I stay up for hours thinking only of it.

Maybe he saw it while he was busy and then forgot.

He must get lots of these kinds of messages, surely.

Maybe he wants nothing to do with me.

But then why would he have invited me to label the wines.

Maybe he's found something out since then.

I message Renee the next day.

> *I'm thinking I'll go to the gig today. Want to come?*
> *What gig?*
> *Travis's.*

I toy with feeling guilty for using her to get close to Travis. But it's not only that – I enjoyed her company yesterday and she told me not to be a stranger.

I get the tram down High Street late in the afternoon and meet her in the front bar of the Northcote Social Club. I haven't been here since we came to see Gabriella Cohen months back. My stomach is so much larger now and I feel out of place. I want to feel righteous, as though it's absurd that pregnant women shouldn't go to gigs or even pubs, but I've stopped doing any of these things of my own accord, so I guess on some level I believe it. Renee is here on her own, which pleases me. I didn't message anybody else, but I figured she might invite her housemates.

'What's Sarah up to?' I ask as I sit across from her.

'Nursing a sore head.' Apparently they'd stayed on the deck until midnight the night before, at which point Renee went to bed and Sarah went out. Renee tells me about a woodwork course she's doing on Sunday mornings and shows me photos of a table she's building. When it's time for the show we walk into the band room. She's barely drunk any of her pint. 'I just want something to hold while we're in there,' she says.

'So, are they good live?' I ask.

'When I first saw them I thought so,' she says. 'But that was when I first saw Travis and I just wanted to fuck him.' She smiles.

The crowd is not as large as when we came here to see Gabriella Cohen, but it's decent. A few people wave at Renee, but we don't speak to anybody else. The band walk on stage wearing matching outfits: pairs of dark green workmen's overalls. The two other band members – a male drummer and a girl who plays the synthesiser and keyboard – stand quietly as Travis picks up his guitar. Without speaking or looking at the audience, he starts to play. Not chords, but a melody. The lighting is dim and there's a faint haze of smoke over the stage.

I haven't seen Travis since we bottled wine together and he doesn't look well. I'm not sure if it's the lighting on stage, but his skin is dull and he has dark bags under his eyes. His expression is serious and moody, which I guess is part of the act, but I don't think it suits him like the farm did.

The gig is slow, flat and pretty boring. A few people standing near the stage are interested, eager, but other people are shifting from foot to foot, talking. Some people leave.

'This is really different from the stuff I listened to,' I tell Renee.

'Yeah, this is their new EP,' she says. She doesn't seem either bored or interested; she remains relaxed and fairly calm. It's obvious how someone could be enamoured of Renee: she's so unfazed, so cool. It's no wonder she and Travis didn't work together. I was nervous to come here today, wondering if he would be unhappy to see me, but I'm beginning to feel less anxious. With Renee around, nothing could be awkward. I get a water from the bar and when I return the band is playing a song I recognise. It's the one I heard in the car; the one I thought was about Renee.

'I know this song,' I say.

'This is about Pat,' she says.

I put my hands straight on my stomach when she says it. Everything goes fuzzy for a moment. Fuzzy, but amplified, as though I'm underwater.

'Are you okay?' Renee touches my arm.

My hands are still on my stomach. 'Yeah, I'm fine. I just . . .' *I just can't move. I just can't think of a lie.*

'Do you need me to get you something? A water?'

'I'm going to go home.'

Renee is looking at me, concerned. 'Eva, are you okay?' she repeats.

I nod. Try to shake whatever expression I have off my face. 'It's nothing, really. I just get tired really quickly now.'

I lean in and kiss Renee on the cheek, press myself against her and give her half a hug.

'I'll walk you home,' she offers.

'I'm fine, really.'

She doesn't follow me, but Travis's words do. They taunt me from the stage as I leave the band room. '*I used to love you, but I fucking hate you. I wake up and I think of you. I go to bed and I think about how much I fucking hate you.*'

AT HOME I listen to the song again. The lyrics are full of anger, but the melody and tempo are melancholic. I know sleep will be impossible tonight, so I put the song on repeat and flick through all the photos of Travis and Pat again. I wonder at myself the way I used to wonder at the people I was pretending to be. Renee knew that song was about Pat. Maybe she knows more than that. I'm like a schoolgirl. Desperate to be near Travis, but useless in his presence, mute and intimidated.

I used to love you, but I fucking hate you.

The only person I can imagine being angry at for their suicide would be Sarah, because I'd assume it was because she was reckless. The more I think about it, though, I realise I would be angry at Annie too – angry that she didn't ask for help. Initially this has the feeling of a breakthrough, like I am closer to understanding something. Soon, though, I just feel more confused.

As I lie here, heartburn starts to radiate through my body. I go to the bathroom and find that I've run out of antacids; I'd meant to pick some up when I was out earlier. I grab a pillow from the bed, clutch it to my body, bury my face in it and scream. I scream loud and long, stifling the sound with the pillow, like I'm both the attacker and the victim.

A REVIEW DESCRIBES WORKING FROM Home's new EP as a complicated mix of upbeat tracks with serious vocals. Another review describes it as teenage angst music. I read an interview with Travis.

'I wrote the EP as a response to a friend passing away. I'd never really experienced grief before then and it was not like I'd expected it.'

I think about his words for days. Not what he had expected. I try to imagine my life without Annie or Sarah, but I can't. Beyond being angry at them for their suicides, or in shock at whatever else might have happened, I can't envisage what possibly goes next. I've known them so long. It's like trying to imagine having amnesia. What is there to expect?

OVER THE NEXT few days I read and reread the interview with Travis.

'Not everyone is going to like the album but that's because it's meant to be messy. It's not meant to make sense. Given the mass commodification of popular music, some people might consider it more like performance art.'

I feel like this is a cop-out. An excuse for why his music isn't pleasing to listen to. It's how I always felt with experimental scripts – art given as the reason why a playwright was unable to wrangle his ideas into something coherent.

The interviewer asks Travis what is coming up next for him and he says he's going to hit the road. Not on tour, but alone. He's going to throw his swag in the back of his car and travel around Australia.

I feel weirdly dejected on reading that he's leaving. Abandoned. Offended he hasn't told me his plans. I'm aware how unreasonable I'm being. Not letting anyone in, then blaming everyone for how lonely it is out here on my own. Awareness isn't making me act any differently, though.

I play the song a lot. It's not a nice song, but it is about you. I play it and rub my belly. Something of you for our baby to enjoy, now, when it can't understand what the song is actually about.

I'M NOT AROUSED AS I wait for Fergus to arrive at my house one afternoon, only lonely, so when he does arrive, I suggest we don't do it.

'Is everything okay?'

I'm surprised by how surprised he looks. Startled, like he's afraid of what I might say.

'I have my period.'

At least he laughs with me.

We go to the Thornbury Picture House. It's relatively new and I've never been. An old Australian film is showing, something Fergus loves and I haven't seen. Before the film we eat panini at the Italian place a few doors down and he tells me a lot about the director, the shooting, how significant it was in the eighties to have an Australian film not set on a beach. I'm sitting across from the old Fergus, the one who irritated me when I first met him. I wonder why it is that this annoys me: something as innocuous as liking a movie. I suspect his enthusiasm is put on. Or maybe it's that his enthusiasm feels like a rebuke: like he thinks I'm not capable of feeling that passionately about something. I think about what I would say if I was going to do this, talk at someone about something I've enjoyed – like the book I've been reading, *Swing Time*. Quotes I underlined: 'I experience myself as a kind of shadow of a person.' How I thought the celebrity from Bendigo wasn't very well drawn. All the parts of motherhood, the war between mother and child. But I can't be bothered articulating these thoughts. Maybe I don't want people to think I'm feigning substance, which I so often thought Fergus was doing when I first met him. More than that, though, I think a part of me wants to keep my love for that book, the joy I had reading it, to myself. My epiphanies are secrets for me alone.

After the film, we walk back to my apartment. I feel like the story happened in front of me and I was hardly aware. I have nothing to say, but this doesn't matter as Fergus is talking and gesticulating, moving his hands ahead of his body in circles, like he's showing wheels moving. I've found myself wondering lately whether I could be with Fergus. On paper, he would be a good partner. He has a job and he isn't racist or homophobic. But there's something in the way that he is aware of his privilege, how he mentions it and acknowledges it, that doesn't seem genuine. Like he knows it's something he's supposed to say, not something he believes. Like his obsequiousness, it seems mannered, learned to please. The real problem, though, is I just don't like him that way. I don't mind him. I even look forward to seeing him sometimes. Occasionally I read something and make a note to tell him about it later. But I always tire of his company eventually. I don't know why, but I can't help feeling a little sorry for him.

He walks me all the way to my door.

'Do you want to come in?'

'I guess I should go to work.'

'Okay.'

We smile at one another. Usually we kiss goodbye, but this time we hesitate and it doesn't happen.

'Is everything all right?' he asks.

'Yes. I mean, I don't know. I just don't really know what we're doing.'

I'm uncomfortable having this conversation outside. I don't want my neighbours to hear. I feel horrible looking Fergus in the eye, but when I look down I see my bump and I don't want to look at the baby either.

'I don't know either.' Fergus is looking at me.

We stand awkwardly at my door. We hug. Fergus gives me a small, sad smile and leaves.

Later, before I go to bed, I write Fergus a message.

> *I'm sorry things got awkward today. I should've thought more before you came over what I was going to do/say. Now I have had some time to think about it: I said to you a long time ago, before you asked me out the first time, that I'm not in a position to see anybody and this is more true now than ever. We were going to have to stop this some time, and now seems as good a time as any. I'm sorry if I led you on or anything. I didn't intend to. Having said that, I'm not really sure what I was intending. I guess I wasn't thinking.*

I add, *I hope we can be friends* at the end then take it off. Add it on and take it off for about twenty minutes. Eventually I send it without.

I tell myself that if Fergus hasn't responded in two weeks, I'll message him again. I manage two days.

> *Reply. Please.*

He answers immediately.

> *I don't have anything to say, but if you want we can be friends. I'm not mad at you.*

I'd been so anxious to hear from him it felt like I had morning sickness again. I exhale reading his reply, but, like running cold water over a burn, the relief doesn't last. I wish I'd waited the two weeks. It was an easier awful feeling, worrying about Fergus. Now I'm back to feeling shaky and unhinged, thinking about Travis. Wanting him to contact me. Wondering if I should message him. Wanting to know that he registers my existence.

THE BABY KICKS me throughout the day, harder now. It used to be a fluttering, like swimming legs. Now it's like someone pushing me in the back, but coming from within. I joke with the girls that my baby is angry with me already.

'That's a good sign!' says Sarah.

I'm breathless. One of the midwives told me to go for short walks every day. I'm light-headed before I even reach the end of the street, so I walk around the apartment. I constantly knock into things. The bench. The doorframe. I open a drawer and it hits my belly. Sleep doesn't happen in large blocks anymore. I wake every hour, needing to shift position, unable to breathe or with my legs cramping. I wish I had a job, so I had something to distract me from my physical pain, but also thank God I don't have a job. I catch hours of sleep at any moment I can. This is what I imagined labour would be like. Walking in small circles, intermittent sleep and moments of relief. It's close enough now that it's harder for me to avoid thinking about giving birth. I sit on the floor of my room with no pants on, spread my legs in front of the mirror and watch my vagina contract as I push. Sometimes after I do this I feel buoyed, ready to punch labour in the face. Other times I collapse on my bedroom floor, breathless and bereft. There's an episode of *Friends* where Rachel, Monica and

Chandler watch a birthing video. Rachel can't look; she's too scared. I'm scared of the aftermath, the permanent damage to my body described in the book of essays Annie gave me. My body is like an elastic band. The pregnancy is stretching it out, out, out. After the birth it snaps back in but slackened, beaten. Never back to what it was. I'm afraid of that, but in a sickening way I'm looking forward to the main event. I've attached a symbolism to my being ripped open. I see it as something that will change me irrevocably, marking the fact that this part of my life is over.

Annie and Sarah come with me to a birthing class at the Abbotsford Convent. It's run by a woman who looks to be in her early forties. I figure this is deliberate: they need someone who's given birth more than once, but not someone who did it too long ago. Other women here are with their male partners, except for one lesbian couple. They smile warmly at Sarah and Annie and me and it feels like we've been accepted by the coolest girls in the room. We learn about labour, the signs you're going into it, false labour, how to tell the difference. Sarah takes notes. We're handed plastic models of cervixes and pamphlets on breathing techniques. We're encouraged to make a birth plan and given a long list of things to consider – drugs, positions, comfort items. We're told to make sure our support person is familiar with the plan as when we're in labour we won't remember our own names, let alone a plan.

'Just as there's no right or wrong way to give birth,' the facilitator says to the class, 'there's no wrong way to provide support. Just do your best and listen.'

Sarah rolls her sleeves up when the pamphlets come our way.

At the end of the course I feel bored and frustrated, like I might as well have attended a workshop on what careers our children should pursue after school. Like acting, there are different methods of giving birth: Lamaze, Bradley, Alexander, Lecoq, Meisner. I've decided I'll approach labour like I approach acting – don't think too much, just do it.

We eat delicious pasta at the convent for dinner. Sardines and currants with soft, chewy house-made fettuccine. The girls share a bottle of red and for the first time in a while I crave alcohol. I allow myself one glass. I smile smugly at the waiter who pours it and will someone from the birthing class to walk by and see me drinking. I barely touch it, though. Just two sips make me feel blurry and I feel guilty.

After dinner Sarah gets a digestif and then a Scotch. I order dessert. I get up to pee at one point, leaving my friends at the table. I stay on the toilet for a while after I'm finished. I take my phone out, always on private call mode now, and phone Travis. Hearing his voice on the other end of the line brings me a strange comfort. I've taken to calling him in the early hours of the morning. When he answers, it's always the same. He says hello, and when I don't say anything back he says it again. I stay on the line, silent, with the overwhelming feeling that we're both thinking about Pat and also that I'm possibly losing my mind.

'Hello?' he says now. There's silence and I will him to say it again.

Then I hear the bathroom door open and I quickly hang up. I usually let him hang up.

A second later I hear Sarah's voice, loud and echoing against the tiles. 'Eva?'

'Coming.'

'Do you need help getting up?'

Since finding out that Travis's song is about Pat, I've been feeling the same as I did when I first found out he died. One step removed from everything, hardly aware what I'm doing from moment to moment. But, still, I find myself splitting the bill with my friends, driving them both home, asking what they have on tomorrow and saying goodnight. I think I'm acting fine, although I don't feel fine at all and I wonder if my friends can tell that something has changed. If they can, I reason, they probably assume it's the pregnancy.

THERE'S SOMETHING I HAVEN'T ADMITTED to you yet. It's about Virginia, the one with the striking face and thick eyebrows, who you taught to make passata. After I saw her comment on your Facebook page I clicked on to her account and trawled through her photos – looking for you, obviously. But there was nothing I hadn't already found on Travis's page. There's a photo of the three of you sitting on bikes in front of a suspension bridge over the Merri. You look sweaty and lively. Her smile is wide, her face alight with laughter.

Underneath, you had written:

Fitzroy North Riders.

Virginia had added:

Watch out.

After your death Travis had gone back and added:

Riders for life.

Virginia echoed:

For life.

I googled her and found she teaches yoga at a studio in Brunswick. I searched the studio's website and found photos of her looking sweaty but content, with lean, sinewy arms. Missives of health and wellness under the photos. The reason I'm mentioning all this is that very early on – you were dead, I knew I was pregnant, but I hadn't told anyone – I went to one of her classes. It sounds insane, but it wasn't really. It was just a yoga class. I scanned the studio's timetable, found out which classes she taught, then booked myself in for her next session, which was at three o'clock that day. I arrived at the studio and told the woman at reception that I was there to do Virginia's class. She told me Virginia was not in that day and that she would be taking the class instead. 'I'm pregnant,' I told her. She was one of the first people I told. She reassured me she would let me know if any positions weren't safe.

I wasn't sure what I was trying to achieve by stalking Virginia, but I guessed that the reason she wasn't at work was because she was too upset. Can't teach a yoga class crying.

I did the class. I held my body in ways it didn't want to go until my muscles wobbled, all the while trying to breathe on command, and I decided then that you had left her. You broke her heart once, now twice. I wondered if maybe your relationship didn't work out because you were too sad.

I never went back to the yoga studio. I didn't try to find her again – although occasionally I look at her online.

AFTER THE BIRTHING class I had a dream about being in labour. Virginia was there, coaching me through the contractions. She held my hand and told me to feel my body and be in touch with it. She exhaled with me, loud and breathy. She told me if one position was uncomfortable, I was welcome to change. I woke suddenly from that dream, gasping. It was morning. For a while I lay in bed and imagined you being my support person. I tried to envisage you rubbing my back and counting through contractions. The image was absurd. We were never at that stage of comfort with each other. I wouldn't be having the baby if you were here. We wouldn't have been doing this together.

Just for a moment, I felt relieved that you're dead.

FOR THE REST of the day I looked at photos of you, my old favourites. Comforted that they still made me sad.

March

I'M IDLY LOOKING ONLINE FOR baby clothes when my phone rings. I almost answer without looking at the caller ID, expecting it to be Mum, as she usually phones me in the afternoon. Luckily, I see the name shining across the screen before I do – it's Kate. I drop the phone like it's something hot. Stare at it vibrating on my floor. I never actually had to tell her about cutting my hair, as I was growing so much bigger she wasn't able to book me for more work anyway. No more banks wanted young, smiley mummies. I've only heard from her once since the ad aired. A blunt, smug text saying she can't believe I'd give up real work to do that. I don't intentionally let the phone ring out but am paused in shock so long that it does. A moment later I get a voicemail alert.

Her voice is irritatingly comforting, like hearing a familiar pop song I once hated.

'Eva McMillan, you need to call me back.'

The wave of affection I feel for her surprises me. This was the same message she always left, no matter what the reason for her call.

239

I ring her back right away. I know if I think about it too much I'll get nervous, psych myself out of speaking to her. And, anyway, I'm bored.

'Eva McMillan.' I hear an intake of breath; she's smoking.

'Kate Gascoyne.'

'How's life on the other side?'

Other side of acting or other side of womanhood? I'm not sure which she means. 'It's okay.'

'For a brilliant actor, you're a shit liar, you know.'

'To what do I owe this pleasure, Kate?' She doesn't like to get to the point.

'You've been nominated for a Logie for best supporting actress. For your work on the miniseries.'

'*Supporting* actress?'

'I know, right? It's, like, just because you don't have balls you're a support – and you'll never guess who's nominated for best male talent.' And on she goes. It's hard to get her to stop talking. Before she can finish a thought, she starts another, so when she finishes her second point she then has to circle back to the original subject. I go to the spare room and refold the baby clothes in the drawers – not because I need to, but because it's something to occupy my hands.

'So, why the fuck did I call you? That's right, the nomination. You have to accept it.'

'Do I get any money if I win?'

'No, just honour.'

'Oh, well no, then. I won't accept.'

There's silence on the line, but for breathing. She's exasperated or smoking, probably both.

'It just seems pointless. I'm not acting anymore.'

'You know the production company will be able to get more money if they have more nominations.'

'Even nominations for a supporting role?'

'Don't take it too personally.' Her tone softens.

There must be a reason why Kate is keen for me to accept the nomination. It reflects well on her too, I suppose.

'How are you, anyway? Are you eating?'

'I'm eating a lot,' I say.

'How are you paying for it?'

I surprise myself with how candid I am now. I admit that I think I couldn't get a job because I'm recognisable.

'They probably thought you were only wanting something between gigs.'

'If only everyone knew how shit being an actor really is.'

'So, does this mean that once you've popped that pound of meat out you're going to want some work from me?'

'No,' I say. 'Or maybe yes.'

'No or maybe yes.' She laughs, then coughs, gravelly, down the phone.

'I want to work in casting.' If it weren't for this fact, I doubt I would've answered Kate's call. I've been trying to gear myself up to ask her about it for weeks.

I hear her sucking on the end of her cigarette. She's quiet for so long it reminds me of my calls to Travis, listening to him breathing down the line.

'So,' she says eventually. 'Little Miss Rock-the-Boat comes sniffing around for a job.'

I want to remind her that she called me, but I resist. It's the best approach to take with Kate: blunt and ruthless.

'I can't get you a job in casting,' she says.

'Can you get me anything?'

'How fast can you lose your baby belly?'

'I don't want to act. I would be good at casting, though. I know a shit actor when I see one – I've worked with enough of them.'

'You have to hate actors to work in casting.'

'I do! I do!'

'You hate yourself. It's different.'

When I'd first told her I was quitting the agency she told me I loved myself too much.

'Can you help me, please?'

'Don't sound pathetic, child.'

Before we hang up, she asks me a few questions. When I'm due. Who will take the baby if I go to work and how soon after the birth do I think that will be. Questions that are actually feelers for her helping me out. Kate hates everyone, but she's also always willing to help anyone. She is a horrible and helpful friend.

A FEW DAYS later I get an email from her.

> Accept the Logie nomination. If you want to work in any part
> of the industry, accolades help.

MY CLOTHES DON'T FIT, AND I need something to wear to Annie's thirty-under-thirty award ceremony. I ask Sarah if I can borrow the black dress I wore to her work party. She says yes then turns up at my apartment wearing it.

'I'm going to borrow something of yours,' she says. 'Do you still have that gold dress?' She takes my old pre-pregnancy clothes from the wardrobe. Tries things on and we remember times I wore them. Nights we got particularly drunk or high. I make us cups of tea and she asks if I have any gin.

'You took all the booze in the move,' I remind her.

She settles on a pair of bright blue, high-waisted silk pants and a white shirt. It was an outfit I wore to auditions because it was sophisticated and flattering, feminine but not overly. It was something of a uniform so it's weird seeing it on Sarah. Like I assume she's going to act differently now that she's in my clothes.

We meet Annie and James and James's parents at a restaurant in Carlton. Annie looks beautiful. She's had her make-up professionally done and she's wearing a shiny black coat that's long and angular like her. I didn't want to ask Annie if her parents were coming down from Queensland for this, but I'm not surprised to find they're not here. Most likely she didn't want to deal with the awkwardness of having her mum and dad here together – an awkwardness I imagine would be heightened around Ian and Maureen, who are intimidating in their competence as a family. I wouldn't put it past Annie to have kept the news of her award from her parents. Her determination to remain modest is deranged at times.

Ian and Maureen greet me excitedly. Maureen touches my big belly as she kisses my cheek. James introduces Sarah.

I'm using the bathroom when they order pizza for the table. Nobody remembers the pregnancy food rules, which is fine, as tonight isn't about me and we're all tired of my condition anyway, me most of all. I enjoy eating pizza with layers of salty prosciutto and big wads of milky mozzarella. Everyone else drinks wine, and when the bottle is empty Sarah orders a second one. Annie looks at her watch.

'Don't worry, we'll scull it,' Sarah tells her.

'Do you know any of the other people receiving the award?' I ask Annie.

'I went to uni with one of them, but I haven't seen her in years.'

Annie's unenthusiasm puts me off asking any more about this friend's work.

The restaurant is busy. The walls and floor are stone and the space is echoey. It gets busier as we're eating and we keep having to repeat ourselves to be heard. James's mum asks me when I'm due and what hospital I'll be going to. 'Are you girls going to join her?' She looks from Sarah to Annie. The way she words it – *join her* – makes it sound like we're going on a holiday.

'Fuck yes!' Sarah shovels almost half a slice of pizza in her mouth. She keeps her wineglass in her hand, not bothering to put it down between sips, or gulps, I should really call them. Maureen asks her about her work and her life. Sarah answers and when Maureen runs out of questions, there's silence. Sarah doesn't ask her anything back. James's dad gently tosses his credit card on the small dish with the bill at the end of the meal. I offer to pay for myself, but he refuses.

We walk to the university campus after dinner. I spot a few tired-looking students leaving the library, vacant, stoned. Students who study like others party. Go hard and go long, don't go home.

The large function room where the ceremony is to be held is filled with rows of chairs and there are plinths in the corners of the room with tall vases of flowers. The decor is dull and unattractive, something between a ceremony and a conference. Annie leaves us to go sit with the other awardees. The rest of us file into a row and sit down.

'Where's the free piss?' says Sarah.

'I think that's afterwards,' I say.

'This looks boring.'

'You'll live.' Although I don't usually mind Sarah's social negligence, tonight I'm not in the mood to indulge her. Before the proceedings officially begin, she leaves to use the bathroom. As she's walking across the room I notice, already, a slight wobble to her. She probably drank a bottle of wine to herself at dinner. When she returns she plonks down in her chair. A few seconds later she sniffs deeply. I look at her and see she's rubbing her fingers over her nostrils.

'You have *got* to be fucking kidding me.'

'What?' She glares at me then turns her focus to the stage, where a suit has just started speaking.

There are two speeches. I zone out in both, but gather the broader talking points: the importance of the legal system; the rapid changes in society that our system is unable to keep up with; how working to change a system from within is braver and more difficult than cynically walking away. There's a general acceptance of the faults or flaws in the legal system, but also an inherent respect for it.

I don't want Sarah to see me checking the time, so I glance at the woman next to me out of the corner of my eye, waiting for her to turn her wrist so I can glimpse her watch. Eventually they begin reading names and the people in the front row walk onto the stage. Our group claps loudly as Annie shakes hands with the presenters. Once all the awardees are on stage they stand there smiling awkwardly. It reminds me of a school prize day.

After the official proceedings, a partition on one side of the room is removed, opening up the space. There are tables covered with glasses of wine and platters with large wedges of industrial-looking cheese and greasy cured meats. Sarah disappears and returns with a glass of champagne. Maureen tells me they won't hang around long as they're driving back to Mount Martha, but they'll wait to say goodbye to Annie, who's off having photos taken. We mill around. James and his father are talking. Maureen and I have run out of fodder, but I'm comfortable in the silence. Sarah is texting and not looking at any of us. Eventually she puts her phone away and looks across the room to where Annie is nodding politely as two older men speak with her.

'Come on.'

'Why don't you just leave?' I say to her. 'You're acting like a child.'

'It's not just me. Everyone is finding this annoying.' She gestures to Maureen, who's watching Annie too. I suspect, though, this is partly to remove herself from our snapping at one another.

When Annie eventually joins us, James hugs her first and then the two of us cling on, with the same kind of genuine, yet hyperbolised congratulations my friends always gave me after a performance.

Despite having waited so long, James's parents are quick with their congratulations and goodbyes. They hug Annie and James, but only wave at Sarah and me. 'And good luck with everything!' Maureen gives my arm an extra squeeze before she leaves.

'What do you want to do now?' James asks us.

'I just want to go home,' says Annie. 'I'm exhausted and I have to work in the morning. Tomorrow's Friday – we can get a drink then, if you want.'

She doesn't have bags under her eyes but there is a despondence about her. Her shoulders are slumped.

'I'm working from home tomorrow,' says Sarah. 'I'm going to meet Renee now.' Sarah doesn't invite me out with them. Of course, she knows I wouldn't come but, still, she usually invites me. She hugs Annie goodbye but not James or me. This is pointed, I know, but it doesn't worry me. I know I was picking at her. She's irritated with me now and we'll get past this, as we always do.

IT'S FOUR DAYS AFTER THE award ceremony that I find out what happened that night. Annie rings me at lunchtime the following Monday. 'Are you home? I'm coming to get you.'

Sarah had forgotten when she planned to work from home on Friday that she had a meeting that day. When she messaged her boss in the morning to say she wouldn't be coming in, her boss rang to remind her of it. Instead of saying she was sick, Sarah went to work straight from having been out and *smelling like a strip club* – the words her boss used when she sacked her. She didn't do it on the spot. She sent her home on Friday. It was only when Sarah went to work this morning, planning on apologising, that she was told she needn't bother. I feel slightly jealous that she rang Annie for support and not me; I don't have a job, so obviously I'd be free. But then I figure I'd probably call Annie too. Although, of course, I would never end up in this situation.

Annie is silent on the drive to Clarke Street. She keeps opening her mouth as though she's about to speak, but instead she exhales. She exhales again, loudly, when we stop at a traffic light, and again when we arrive and park out the front. Sometimes I wonder if maybe

248

Annie's annoyance with Sarah is partly driven by jealousy. Annie is successful, but she's worked hard for everything she's ever achieved, colouring inside the lines. Opportunities land in Sarah's lap and she neglects them. Like every great person who's fallen in love with her who she's cheated on.

We sit with Sarah in her room. I make a pot of tea that Annie sips compulsively but Sarah doesn't touch. She's pacing back and forth, wondering what she'll tell her parents. She's not planning to tell them the truth; rather, she's wondering how she can skirt around it. She's going to start applying for jobs and hope she gets one soon enough that she doesn't have to lie for long about not working.

'They'll get over it,' I say. 'The thing about your parents is that they have to love you no matter what you do.'

'It's possible to love someone and hate them at the same time.' She runs her hands through her hair as she says this. Watching her despair, I imagine for a moment that it's my own child who's in their late twenties. Who's partied too hard and lost their job. I think I would probably feel a lot like I do now. I'm exasperated, angry at Sarah for being so stupid. But also, it's impossible not to feel sorry for her.

Annie tries to think of ways she might be able to spin having been fired. Wonders if she can speak to Sarah's boss, see if she might agree to give her a good reference, at least, despite this incident. She asks Sarah about her usual work ethic and what her boss thought of her before now. But Sarah is fixated on the night with Renee, unwilling to reflect on anything else.

'We should've gone home instead of going to Smith Street.'

'What happened to Renee?' I ask. 'Did she have work?'

'She never works Fridays – that's why we were going out.'

I begin to feel intensely irritated with Sarah. Not the Sarah in front of me, stricken, staring at her bedroom floor, but the version of her I can envisage months from now, after having been spotted rent by her parents, laughing this off. This has the makings of a well-worn anecdote. An amusing story to endear her to people, or to denigrate her old boss. It's impossible to picture this without picturing Annie too, firm and disapproving. I force myself to be present again and see my two friends, both looking as irritated as I feel. I'm conscious of the afternoon creeping along, and I want to protect Sarah from her housemates arriving home from work, exhausted and employed. 'Let's go out for an early dinner,' I say.

Annie tells Sarah to shower and we go to the kitchen to rinse the teapot and cups. While we're doing this Renee gets home. We tell her what's happened.

'I feel so guilty,' she says. 'I was the one who bought the bag on Smith Street. We should've gone straight home.'

'Sarah is nobody else's responsibility.' Annie is frowning as she scoops soggy tea-leaves from the pot and tosses them in the rubbish. Her sternness is jarring, compared with her compassion just moments ago. I know that Annie is good at being a good friend. Putting a positive spin on a poor decision. Suddenly I'm aware just how good she is at it and I begin to wonder what Annie actually thinks of my behaviour. I put my hand on my stomach and rub the baby.

Renee notices me rubbing my belly and changes the subject. 'I guess there are bigger things to worry about, though, aren't there?' She looks at me. 'I'm so sorry – I didn't realise Pat was the father. I just assumed it was a random guy. That's so tragic.'

I think I almost fall over. I stare at Renee and see when her face turns. Out the corner of my eye I can see Annie stop what she's doing. She braces herself with both hands on the sink and drops her head down.

I drive myself home in Annie's car. Annie stays to speak to Sarah once she is out of the shower. I scream the whole drive. 'You can't just behave like this!' I yell at the traffic through the windscreen. 'Thinking that you can do whatever you want and there's no fallout!' I grip the steering wheel hard, lifting myself up in the driver's seat.

It's a good thing I don't have alcohol in the house. If I did, I'd probably drink it. I put the kettle on then pace around my apartment and refine my argument with Sarah, articulating her failings. A poor person, a shit friend. It becomes a monologue I'm rehearsing. It was four days ago that Sarah and Renee went out. I look at Travis's Facebook account, knowing I'll find nothing there – it's not like if he knows he's going to post a status about this – but being disappointed still when there is nothing. As usual, it hasn't been updated. No photos, no posts. I reread the message I sent him back in January. It's still there, unchanged, unanswered. Vague sentiment scattered with clichés.

I've heard stories of women near the end of their pregnancy becoming so stressed they go into labour. I imagine this happening now. I'm seething at Sarah, but I will this not to happen so that I don't have to go into labour without her. 'Let me have my moment,' I say to my round belly. 'It'll be your turn soon.'

Annie arrives and lets herself in. I'm standing in the lounge. She talks to me from my front door.

'She doesn't remember telling her. She actually swears she couldn't have.'

'Then how did Renee find out?'

'I know.' Annie holds both her hands up, trying to settle me before I launch into a rant. 'Renee said Sarah told her.'

'She thinks she can do whatever she wants and everyone will just forgive her.'

'She knows she's fucked up.' Annie pauses. I can see she's gearing herself up for whatever she's about to say. She looks resigned. 'Renee said that when she told Matthew –'

'She told Matthew?' I interrupt.

'He already knew,' Annie finishes. 'He found out from someone else.'

'So, how many people has Sarah told?'

'She says she hasn't told anybody else.'

'She said she didn't tell Renee.'

Annie is still; not calm but rigid.

'Have you told anybody?' I ask.

'No, I haven't. But, Eva' – she pauses, a sad, strained look on her face – 'why aren't you telling people?'

'Are you defending her?' I demand.

'I'm here and not there, and she lost her job today.'

I sit down on the couch, for the first time since I got home. Annie hasn't moved from the doorway. I'm worried she's planning on leaving once we finish talking and I don't want to be alone right now.

I think of my life as it's been lately, with people knowing half the truth. I always liked standing in the dark corners on stage. *Step into the light, Eva*, directors would have to remind me.

'I think I've been worried that if I told people, it would make me regret my decision to have the baby,' I confess.

'Aren't you worried that if you never tell anybody you'll regret that too?'

I nod.

Annie joins me on the couch. We're both silent for a bit, staring at my coffee table. One of the plants Annie gave me is there; it's not dead yet, but it's deflated and saggy. In other circumstances, Annie would water it.

'Every day.' Annie pauses before she continues; she's staring at the coffee table, not at me. 'Every day, there are people who are living with decisions that they regret.' She nods slightly, agreeing with herself.

'Is that meant to make me feel better?'

She shrugs, turns to look at me now. 'It's not meant to make you feel any worse.'

She's not emotional and neither am I. She looks tired. Pale. Suddenly I'm reminded of when we used to take advantage of Annie in primary school. I wonder if we've ever stopped. Sarah and I careen around, making impulsive decisions, while Annie hovers around us, trying to block the worst of the consequences landing in the goal ring.

Annie and I spend the night on the couch watching *Friends*. I try to imagine what's happened today happening to Phoebe and Monica and Rachel, but I can't. It's a storyline more suited to a soap opera.

'I wonder if there's an app to order booze,' Annie says at one point.

'You need new friends,' I tell her.

She gets a bottle delivered. An easy-drinking shiraz that costs her a lot more than it's worth.

I really want to phone Travis and hear his voice calling out to nothing, but I can't with Annie beside me. Also, I'm worried he might suspect that the calls are from me. If he knows about the baby – as everyone else seems to – then who else would he think it is?

Annie leaves about six the next morning. I hear the door click behind her and I get up to pee. It only occurs to me now that she must've taken the day off yesterday. For a moment I wonder how it is she's going to go do her job today, and then I think maybe I envy her having other people's problems to deal with. I make a cup of tea and crawl back to bed, but I don't sleep. I heave myself to one side and then the other. Never comfortable. Unable to move easily. Periodically my legs cramp and my hips ache from the weight of me. I get out of bed earlier than I have been lately and waddle through Thornbury. I go to a cafe where people are working on laptops. Other women with babies are drinking tea and chatting. I stare at people I don't know and make up lives for them in my head. Horrible lives, full of affairs and death and jealousy. I wonder if Travis knows and, if he does know, how he feels about it. Has he not contacted me because he's mad at me? Or does he, like me, just have no idea what to say?

I message Fergus.

Can we hang out?

He hasn't replied by the time I'm leaving, so I message him again.

Things aren't great and I could use a friend.

I start to walk home but as soon as I reach the driveway I turn and walk away. I can't stand the thought of sitting inside all day with nothing to do. I walk back to High Street and jump on an 86 tram heading south. As I'm approaching Westgarth, I see the cinema in the distance and I remember that they have cheap films on Tuesdays. I've already spent five dollars on tea at a cafe and the film will blow out my budget for the day, but if I'm not going home I need something to do.

I watch Olivia Colman play a dominating, closeted lesbian queen. I recognise that I would enjoy this on any other day. I keep feeling for my phone, which sits cold and still in my pocket.

At the end of the film I text Fergus again.

Is everything ok?

This time he writes back almost immediately.

> Sorry. Everything is fine, I'm just at work. Won't be home until
> late tonight. I can ring you tomorrow.

I buy a tin of soup on my way home, heat it up for lunch, some
wilted greens that are only just edible on the side. I'd been planning
on doing the shopping yesterday. I start watching several things, but
don't finish any of them. Read the same page of my book ten times.

Early in the evening I go out and catch the tram south again. I feel
most content on the tram. Watching the world glide past through
the window is easier than trying to follow a narrative.

I get off at Smith and Johnston and from there I walk all the
way to Fergus's house. It's a long walk, but I have time. The summer
light is dimming slowly and the night turns amber before it becomes
dark. I wonder if what I am doing is sexy and romantic, or predatory.
Also, I wonder what undies I'm wearing. It's possible I knew I would
end up here when I left the house, but I wasn't honest enough with
myself to wear nice underwear. If he's at work, though, I can just
crawl into his bed naked. I'm not sure how I'm going to get into his
place – maybe his housemates will be home. I can work it out when
I get there. I tell myself this isn't what I'm doing but just something
I'm flirting with doing. I'm moving – walking one block and then
another towards his house. I'm moving slowly, my belly is a boulder.
I'll find out what I'm doing when I get there.

I reach his house and knock on the door. There's no light spilling
from the windows and I can't hear any movement inside. I feel
relieved when nobody answers the door, but I knock again. I look
under the doormat, then check the pots beside the letterbox, fondling
the soil. When I find the key, I place it in the door, but I don't unlock
it right away. I listen, expecting or hoping to hear someone coming.

I stay holding the key in the door, waiting for myself. Eventually I step into Fergus's hallway. I breathe out, relieved. I flick the light switch on.

I'm moving slowly, waiting to be caught each time I turn a light on or open a door. His room – like last time I was here – is immaculate. The bed is made, he even has a top sheet, its colour complementing the doona. I'd assumed last time that he'd presented it especially for me, but it appears not. I graze a finger over a few of his things, lightly, as though I'm afraid to wake them. He has a polished wooden desk on which is a small vintage-looking console, the type theatre technicians operate from. A framed Talking Heads poster on the wall and one fern, marginally less well off than those in the rest of the house, but still doing better than my plants. Maybe since I was here last his other plants have wilted. I don't want to check, afraid to roam the rest of the house, in case one of his housemates is actually home. I take my shoes off but keep the remainder of my clothes on when I climb into his bed. I don't want to surprise him naked. Or maybe I will, but I'll work my way up to that. I lie down and think about what I'm going to do if I need to pee. What if one of his housemates comes home before Fergus and I go to use the bathroom and they want to know what I'm doing here?

AT FIRST I'M baffled, wondering where I am. I hardly glimpse the woman whose scream awoke me before she runs out of the room. Then I remember where I am and I realise how bad it is that a woman is screaming.

'Eva, what the fuck are you doing?' Fergus is in the room now. He's wearing a clean blue shirt and cream slacks. The outfit is very unlike him and it's definitely not something he'd wear to work.

'I'm sorry. Sorry, sorry, sorry.' I pull my shoes on as quickly as I can and look around the floor for my jacket.

'What are you doing?' he repeats.

'I was going to surprise you. I'm sorry, I thought you were at work. I'll leave now, I'm sorry.'

I try hard not to look at him as I make my way to the door. I walk as fast as I can towards Johnston Street, where I order an Uber.

The driver turns to me as I climb into the back seat. 'Are you going into labour?'

'Please just get me home.'

As I start to calm down – breathing in for three and out for three – I see the funny side of what happened. He told me he was at work. I wasn't to know he was bringing a woman home. At some point, I'll be able to laugh about this.

Back at my flat I suddenly miss Sarah strongly. I'd slept quite soundly in Fergus's bed, which I don't manage to do for the rest of the night at home.

I WAKE IN THE MORNING with messages from Fergus and Sarah. The message from Fergus had come through last night, but I purposely ignored it and went to bed.

I will call you tomorrow.

I'm not sure who is going to make me feel better or worse, but I know Sarah is more important to me, so I decide I'll wait to read her message until I've gotten this talk with Fergus out of the way. He calls at ten and I answer with my eyes closed.

'I'm thinking about coming over there to have this conversation,' he says.

'Don't speak to me like I'm a child,' I retort.

He returns to these words several times during the ensuing fight.

I say I think it's unfair he's yelling at me this much.

'You set the tone of this conversation,' he responds.

'You said you were working. I wanted to surprise you when you got home from work. I didn't think anybody went on dates on Tuesdays.'

'You said you didn't want to do this anymore.'

'I was feeling bad and I wanted a friend.'

'Why didn't you ring your friends?'

'I wanted to have sex with you.'

'You said you didn't want to do this anymore,' he repeats.

I know that Fergus is right to be mad, and yet I'm defending myself. I should just admit to using him and try to plead my case for why I've been such an arsehole, but I can't help but argue back when someone is yelling at me. The argument is long and boring and doesn't go anywhere until suddenly we are somewhere very ugly.

'I just don't understand why you're so focused on controlling something that you don't want,' he says.

'I don't want to control you.'

'You're obsessed with my admiration.'

'I'm not obsessed.'

There's silence on the line for a bit.

'I'm sorry,' I say. More silence; I hope it's a sign he's softened.

'You know, I used to defend you when people in the industry called you a bitch. I won't anymore.' He hangs up.

My first impulse is to call Sarah and Annie. I know I'm too fragile to deal with more criticism – which I'm afraid Sarah's message might contain – but I also know I can't reach out to my friends for help until I've read it.

> I'm sorry. I want to make that very clear. I feel for you and I take responsibility for causing some of the pain you're experiencing now. I say that straight up because I know you, and I know you are going to interpret this message as defensive. It's not meant as a defence, but as a way to make you see the situation from another perspective. You can't entirely blame me for telling Renee what happened. If you weren't concealing this huge truth from people, then there

wouldn't have been anything for me to spill when I was high. Remember when I first started sleeping with women and I told you guys, but not anybody else? Eventually Annie said to me, 'You're not out of the closet – you've just dragged us in there with you.' I think you've sort of done the same thing with this pregnancy. The other night when Annie was talking to me about my behaviour she said I needed to start thinking about consequences before I act. And while I admit I do stupid things and I make mistakes a lot, at least I see my consequences through, like I'm doing right now, having lost my job. But you seem to be trying to avoid any consequences. It's like you see yourself as a character you're trying to get into and you can leave behind things that happen in your life like they belong to a show you've finished. I don't know why you're not telling people Pat is the father because we haven't discussed it, which in itself is telling. If we had, I would've said – and I think Annie would agree with me – that you should contact Pat's family and tell Travis too. I'm not sure why you haven't done this already. I don't know if you're scared or if you feel like you've done something wrong. But you haven't. Being pregnant isn't a crime. You didn't know Pat was going to die and you didn't plan to have his baby. It's just a fucked-up thing that happened. But what is wrong is having kept this big secret from everyone. Carrying on like you're the only person involved when you're not. I hope this doesn't make you angrier with me than you already are. I do honestly feel terrible for being such a shit mate. I'm so bloody excited for this baby and I really want to take care of it with you. Sometimes I think it might be the best thing that's happened to us. The thought that maybe

you're so angry at me that we can't be friends anymore hurts
me a lot and I hope that we can talk it out, properly, and
figure everything out together. Thanks for coming over the
other day when I was fired. I deserved to be fired and I don't
deserve to have such good friends. I love you.

FOR HOURS AFTER READING SARAH'S message I sit on the couch staring at the wall and thinking of an old wives' tale I heard: that what a woman sees or feels during pregnancy could impact on the development of the baby. Pat too many animals, your baby is born hairy. Eat lots of Pink Lady apples, it will be born with a red birthmark. Stare at the moon – lunatic. If this is true, I think, my baby will be born a mute. Like the crazed child in the horror movie who stares more than she talks.

He probably already knows.

He's probably angry at me.

Eventually I ring Travis. He doesn't answer and I realise I'm still on private caller mode. I change modes so he can see the caller ID, but he still doesn't answer, so I text him.

Hey, can you ring me?
Please.

I wait impatiently for him to reply. Impatient because I want to speak to him before I speak to Sarah. Impatient because I really want to speak to Sarah. I shower several times just to force myself to leave the phone. I go for a walk without it and then hurry home, anxious for his reply. But the vacant screen taunts me all day.

I google 'how to know if someone has blocked you', 'how to know if texts aren't coming through', 'will someone be mad if you are having their dead friend's baby'.

In the evening, before I go to bed, I message him.

> *I understand why you don't want to speak to me. You're not the only person who is angry at me right now. I'm sorry that I kept this from you. What's happened is so overwhelming and hard and I've been trying to deal with it as best I can. Anyway, I want to see you and speak to you about this in person. You were his best friend and if you want to be a part of his child's life then I want that too. I just want to do what's best for everybody – especially, obviously, the baby.*

I stare at the message after I send it. I wonder how long he's known. When I sent him the message from Mount Martha, offering to be there for him, was he already angry at me then? When I went to label the wines, was he hoping I would tell him?

By the time I go to bed he still hasn't written back – and I haven't replied to Sarah. I imagine her in bed, like me, only skating across the surface of sleep.

AT SIX I GET UP to pee, but I don't bother checking my phone. When I wake again at seven thirty, it's buzzing on the bedside table. So much so that I assume someone is calling. When I pick it up, I see that Travis has sent me several messages. He called me an hour ago, three times in quick succession, and now he is texting. New messages are pouring in quicker than I can read them.

> Answer your phone.

> I'm trying to call you.

> Are you saying that Pat is the father of your baby?

> I can't believe you told me this over text.

> Ok sorry I just reread your message and I guess you thought I already knew. You tried to call me but I've been camping in the Grampians. I only just got reception.

> I'm on my way to Melbourne now. Please let me know where I can meet you today. I'm reeling.

> What the fuck?

INITIALLY WE MAKE plans to have coffee in the afternoon, but we don't end up meeting until the evening. Travis needs a little more time to process things, he says. I'm pacing back and forth down my hallway when he tells me this and at first I'm relieved and then I start pacing quicker. I assure him there's no rush, and can wait until whenever he is ready, when I know I won't last more than one night in this state of suspense. I try to make a list of questions to ask him, like I did before I went to Kangaroo Ground, but I can't think of anything. I've spent months wanting to get closer to Travis, and I realise now that maybe all I wanted was the comfort of being around someone who knew Pat.

I count my breaths as I leave the house, like we learned in the birthing class. Stay present, stay calm. Breathe through each moment and remember it will be over eventually.

The baby keeps kicking, a lot.

WE MEET AT Joe's on High Street at eight thirty. Travis is already sitting in a booth, with what I think at first is an empty glass until I notice the skinny brown puddle at its bottom. He looks stricken and I feel terrible for having done this to him. All day I kept going over Sarah's words – *It's just a fucked-up thing that happened* – telling myself that this situation is just what a life is. Seeing Travis now soaks me in guilt. It's not just *a* fucked-up thing. It's *my* fucked-up thing.

I try to slide gently into the booth opposite him, like back at the party in Coburg, me moving carefully near him. The problem being that now I'm huge and nothing I do is graceful. 'How are you?'

He stands. 'I'm getting another drink.'

I wait while he orders at the bar. He returns with another glass, almost half filled with amber liquid. He must have asked for a double shot. Maybe the bartender took one look at Travis and free-poured. He sits across from me and doesn't say anything. My quick, shallow breaths fill the space between us.

'Are you okay?' he asks. 'Like, can you breathe?'

'I walked some of the way here. It tired me out. The baby is squashing my lungs.' I feel calm for a second – we're talking, the baby has been mentioned – then I don't. 'I'm really sorry, Travis.' To elaborate would take too long, so I keep it simple. 'If there's anything you want to ask me, feel free.'

Travis stares at his drink and doesn't say anything. The silence is maddening and I want desperately to leave. The fact that I can't only makes the situation worse. I grow impatient, then furious. I look across the bar, as though I'm hoping to see someone who can save me from this. I create a little fantasy in my head where we run into Renee and she sits down and then everything is easy and chatty. I turn back to Travis at the sound of him sniffing snottily. He wipes the back of his hand over his nose and then pulls the cuff of his shirt over his hand. I see his lips are folded in over each other. He's red and quivering with shiny, wet cheeks.

I've spent so much time hoping to catch a glimpse of this sorrow and now that I have I realise how naive I've been. Like seeing the fires burning on the front of the paper and thinking maybe they would be a spectacular sight, then getting dumped in the middle of it and realising that, actually, it's hell.

I try to strike a balance between showing enough concern and not staring at him as he cries. I look around the bar again but nobody is watching us; although I guess if they have noticed what's happening they've probably assumed we're in the middle of a break-up.

When he finally speaks his words almost shock me out of my seat.

'I was so embarrassed.'

His voice is impressively steady, considering how much he's shaking. 'After he died, I was so humiliated to be around your friends.'

I've no idea where this is going. I don't understand what he's saying, but it feels close to something I've wanted for so long, the anticipation is burning under my skin. I want to bang my hands on the table, hurry him along.

'I figured you must have all thought I was a terrible friend.'

'Why would we have thought that?'

'Because I wasn't there for him.'

I think about it now, imagine how I would feel if I were Travis. If Annie or Sarah killed themselves, yes, I probably would feel responsible. It hadn't occurred to me that Travis might feel like this because all I've been thinking about is myself.

All this time that I've been afraid of telling Travis, I'd thought I was afraid he'd be angry. I realise now that what I was afraid of was feeling my own shame and that I was right to want to avoid it. Shame is filling me now. Touching my mouth, the back of my throat, all the way down my oesophagus to my stomach, hot and prickly like drinking a whisky. Unlike drinking whisky, though, nothing is getting softer or melting at the edges. I'm excruciatingly present. I'm reminded of the horrible prospect of having a caesarean, of having to be awake while someone is cutting you open.

'Travis, it's nobody's fault. It's not your fault.'

I reach across the table and take his hand. He doesn't pull away, but he doesn't squeeze my hand back either.

'When I invited you to my parents' place, a part of me wanted to impress you. Show you how helpful and nice I was.'

I didn't care about you that day.

All I was thinking about was him.

Did a part of you suspect that maybe this was his baby?

I can't form the sentences. My mouth sits useless on my face.

Travis becomes still. He takes a deep breath in. His cheeks are still wet, but he's no longer crying. He takes his hand from mine and lifts his glass to his mouth.

'Do you know . . .' I stumble on the word 'why'. 'Do you know what it was?' I wish I had a drink to stare into. Instead I stare at my hand, which is still on the table between us.

'No.'

I look up. Travis is wiping his cheeks with his sleeve.

'Nobody ever knows, Eva. Even if there is a note. You can't explain something like that. There are no answers.'

He stands again with his empty glass.

When he returns from the bar his expression is severe and filled with dislike, which I don't mind. I'm more comfortable seeing this loathing directed at me than feeling it within me. I let myself return to anger too. A moment ago, Travis was talking about his sense of responsibility and guilt. If there are no simple answers, then what does he have to feel sorry for? I seize on the frustration.

'Why didn't you reply to my message?'

My words sound sulky and my anger diminishes quickly. I feel embarrassed, like a child.

'What message?'

'The one I sent at Christmas.'

Travis takes his phone from his pocket. I assume he is checking to reread the old message, which maybe he does, but he also punches out a text, his thumbs moving fast. I want to know who he is texting. Does somebody know he is here? Did he tell someone what he knows? When he puts his phone back in his pocket and looks back to me, his face is blank. I watch his expression as he catches himself back up, remembers where we were up to.

'Do you know how many of those messages I get? I never reply.'

'I'm sorry.' I'm not sure what this apology is for. 'I'm going to order a drink.'

I ask the bartender to make me something alcohol-free. He nods and starts muddling fruit. It's not busy here tonight, but not empty either. Mostly there are couples, probably people on dates. I imagine the kinds of conversations they're having – asking about each other's jobs and their plans for the weekend. Where they went to high school. Nobody's life is without drama but on a first date you pretend it is.

The bartender places a tall, pink-tinged drink in front of me.

'How much?'

'Don't worry about it.'

I wonder if he's been watching me and Travis.

Back at the table I feel more relaxed with something to fiddle with. I regret not getting a drink as soon as I arrived.

'So, do other people know?' Travis asks.

'I told Sarah and Annie. Sarah got drunk and told someone. I'm sorry I sent you that in a message. I thought you must have heard.' It sounds like an excuse. I think back to my anxiety yesterday, how I was convinced that he knew. I wonder now what I would've done if I'd known he didn't. I wonder if we'd be here now. In a way, I'm glad I didn't have to make that decision.

'Why didn't you tell me?' he asks.

'That's a good question.' This is media training. If an interviewer asks you something you either don't know or don't want to answer, you say it's a good question, not a tough question.

Travis's glass is empty already and he is batting it between his fingers, sliding it back and forth across the table. Why didn't I tell Travis? Because I was embarrassed? Because I didn't want him to pity me? Because I found the idea of a relationship with Pat's family awkward or too hard? Is it what I said to Annie, that I'm terrified of regret, is that the truth? All of these things feel real but not. They're not false exactly, but they're not the whole story.

'I think I was in shock myself, at my decision.' This will do. This is true.

I'm sitting in front of Travis and he knows now and I have nothing to say. Like when you're starving for hours and hours and then you're presented with a meal and are full after only two bites.

'I guess I did know.' He stops fiddling. 'I knew it was a possibility. He was so excited after he slept with you.'

Tears are screaming behind my eyes. Every fibre of me tries to push them away. 'I was excited too.' My voice chokes and Travis looks up. He stares at me, crying across from him, and he doesn't offer condolences, but I think I see him soften.

'We talked about it once.'

I think Travis is talking about me and Pat and am disappointed when I realise what he means.

'Once, years ago, I was feeling really weird. I'd had a lot of drugs and I was still coming down, although it was days later. I was having this out-of-body experience; like, dissociative. It's the only time I've ever thought about doing it myself. I can't describe what it was like.

'Anyway, I rang Pat. He said, "What I always think is: if you kill yourself, then you'll never be able to watch *Breaking Bad* again."'

I laugh. It is utterly inappropriate, and I can see that Travis is offended, but I can't stop laughing. The reference to *Breaking Bad* made me think of Sarah. She told me once her measure for knowing if a guy is too hetero for her to date is if he likes *Breaking Bad*. My affection for Sarah rushes through me like relief, but I can't dwell on that because of the look on Travis's face.

'Sorry,' I say. 'I just didn't expect that.'

'He said it then.'

'What?'

'His words: *What I always think*. He said *always*. I never asked him about it.'

I watch Travis and feel caught out. My own stupidity and self-absorption reflected back at me. I think about when Pat said, 'The solution to climate change isn't to stop having children.' I attached such importance to those words. I took them to mean that he didn't fear a horrendous future on earth. When it was probably just a throwaway line. Something that meant nothing that I've let ring in my ears since he died. Even if Pat had been thinking about suicide for a long time, I doubt there was any meaning in the *Breaking Bad* comment. I want to tell Travis this but, also, I understand the feeling. Of clinging to words like talismans – how it can drive you mad and how, in some fucked up way, that is comforting.

We agree that Travis will tell Pat's parents and let me know how they take the news. It will come as a big shock, and they will probably need time to come to terms with it before meeting me. We consider the possibility that they won't want to meet me. But, without even knowing them, I find this hard to believe and I sense Travis does too.

I watch him as he stands from the booth, drunk and sad. He looks too fragile to walk home.

'You're allowed to be angry at me.' I'm looking up at him, not having stood up myself yet.

'I know.' He nods. 'But there's probably a few things more important than being angry right now.'

He offers to wait with me for my tram. I insist I'm fine. I'm actually more worried about him getting home safely, but since I've said I can get home by myself I don't feel like I can offer to accompany him. I stumble on my words. It's either ironic that the most mundane part of our interaction has become the most awkward, or it's fitting since we've settled into our mess.

I watch him cross the street to the southbound tram stop. I wave at him when he turns around and he raises his hand. The same wave he gave me in almost the exact same spot months back, when I first told him I was pregnant. The tram rolls down the street from the north and Travis is hidden and then, with the tram, he is gone.

I DON'T GO home after, but walk straight to Clarke Street. It's ten thirty and initially I'm wondering how I will make my entrance, not wanting to ring the doorbell this late on a weeknight. I remember that Sarah doesn't have a job and I wonder what she's been doing these past few days. A moment ago, I wouldn't have thought it possible for me to feel any sadder but suddenly I do, imagining Sarah as listless as I've been lately.

Her bedroom window faces the street and I can see light seeping out between the curtains. I open the front gate slowly, making it creak louder than normal, then I sneak across the garden to stand beneath her window. There's the muffled noise of canned laughter and then nothing; she's snapped her laptop shut, listening. I rap gently on the glass. 'Sarah? It's me – Eva.'

The curtains fling open and there she is. Alarmed and then smiling. She puts her palms flat against the glass and slides the window up. She leans her body out and gives me a hug.

'I'm so glad you're here.' She kisses the side of my face.

'I'm sorry it's late.'

'Who cares? Come in.'

She lifts her window even higher and beckons for me to climb through, which is impossible with my belly. I walk around to the front door and she meets me there. She takes my hand in hers and leads me on tiptoe through the entrance hall to her room. This strikes me as uncharacteristically respectful. When she lived with me, she had no problem clomping around and slamming doors at any hour. Maybe her new housemates said something.

In her room we wrap our arms around each other and sway from side to side, hugging like people who're celebrating, or who haven't seen each other in years. This feels like both of these things.

'I've been desperate to call you.' She takes me by the hands and leads me to her bed, where we both sit cross-legged. 'Annie told me to leave you be.'

'I've missed you too.'

I tell Sarah about my drink with Travis.

She shakes her head, covers her face with her hands. 'I don't even know if what I said was right.'

'I feel better for having done it.' I'm unsure if this is true. I certainly feel better right now, but that may just be because I'm no longer in that bar, no longer sitting across from Travis. I describe to her the image I have of Pat lying on his back, his hands laced over his chest. 'The solution to climate change isn't to stop having children.'

'It just felt like a sign or something.'

'You realise that doesn't mean he was anti-abortion, Eva?'

'I know. It's just that he seemed so sure of himself. So certain. Content.' The word lands flat. Hangs in the air between us. 'But I realised tonight it was just an offhand thing he said. It probably meant nothing.'

'No, I think you're right.' I'm surprised to see that Sarah is nodding at me. 'He was a really good person. So much saner than Travis.'

I shake my head. I don't want to laugh about Travis. I don't want to think an unkind thought about him ever again.

'I think it's a good thing you're having his baby, Eva.'

We curl up together and watch *Friends*. Sarah falls asleep quickly – she told me she has hardly slept since Monday – but I don't. *He was so excited after he slept with you.* If I'd been told that months ago, I would've wallpapered it over my skull. It feels useless to me now, though. I'm not sure if this is moving on, acceptance. Or if I'm still too stricken from witnessing Travis, so utterly unenthused, to properly process anything he said.

I can't get settled and when I need to shift position I wake Sarah. I apologise. 'I can go home.'

'Don't go.' She turns to face me and goes back to sleep, her arm flung lazily across my stomach.

TRAVIS TELLS PAT'S PARENTS ABOUT me.

'You guys should meet,' he says when he rings. 'But they need time.'

I note the wording: he doesn't say they *want* to meet me, but that we *should* meet.

'Did they ask anything about me?'

'Once the shock wore off they did. But they're still pretty stunned. This will take some time.'

Travis's words haunt me after we hang up: *This will take some time.* It's like I can suddenly see every year, every month, every week, every day that I have to live through piled in front of me. Can't go over it, can't go under it. I feel relieved that he knows now and that Pat's parents know too, but it's not an uncomplicated relief, like taking a heavy pack off after a day of hiking. I feel lighter, but also tender, blistered.

I distract myself with final preparations. Annie refers to them as the 'finishing touches', which makes it sound like my life is about to end. I find a rocking chair from a second-hand furniture store, which we fit with a new cushion. I clean the apartment. I cook and cook and cook. Afternoons are spent on the phone to Mum as I reduce tomatoes and layer lasagne sheets. The cooking is my excuse for why I'm distracted during our calls. I'll have to tell her soon about Pat, but I can't bring myself to do it yet. She's arriving one week after the due date. When she booked her flights she said to me, 'If you want me there, I promise I will come, but I'm going to tell you now, I don't think I can cope witnessing my own baby in so much pain.' I wasn't sure how touched or terrified to be.

It strikes me that if Pat's parents want to meet the baby, then they're going to have to meet Mum too. I tell Annie how hesitant I am to tell Mum about Pat and I'm thankful she doesn't ask me to explain my reluctance.

'She'll probably just feel so desperately sad for you, she'll try to help.'

'Why do you say that?'

She shrugs. 'It's what I did.'

I don't have enough room in my own freezer for all the meals I'm preparing, so Annie and Sarah both offer room in their freezers. They've gifted me a car seat for the baby. I know Annie paid for most of it. I offer to reimburse her some of the cost, but she refuses.

'I got a stupid amount of cash with that award,' she says.

The girls help me with the birth plan, a process I find infuriatingly pointless. Choose from a list of options, but also know that everything can change and ultimately the choice is not yours. Sarah begins reading from a list suggested by the hospital. 'Who, if anybody, would you like present besides your partner?' It's over after the first question – we can't take this seriously.

'Will you want to have a bath or shower while you're in labour?'

'I've no idea – ask me when I'm in labour.'

'What about the lighting?'

'I don't care about lighting.'

'Dimmed,' Sarah decides, noting it down.

'What if the doctors can't see what they're doing?'

'Well, I guess they'll turn the lights on.' She laughs at me as I shake my head. 'Delayed cord clamping?'

'What is that?'

She turns to the very back of *What to Expect*.

'I'll just do whatever you think,' I tell her.

Other points are more important to me, but I don't agonise over the answers. Drugs? Yes, please.

'Nobody comes around with a medal if you don't have them,' Sarah says as she writes down my answer.

'Placenta?' Both my friends look at me, expectant.

'Bin it.'

Annie nods at Sarah, who ticks a box on the list.

My baby hasn't turned yet. I have weekly appointments at the hospital now, which I begin to dread, knowing myself that it hasn't happened. The first time a midwife mentions the possibility of a caesarean I collapse a little in my heart. I'm not like other women, I want to assure her. Not like those women with unrealistic expectations of themselves or weird hierarchies of different births. It's just my particular circumstance and that I've attached such symbolism to the labour. I realise, of course, a moment after the thought, that thinking you're different or unique is one way in which we are all the same.

We go on the tour of the birthing suite, which includes classes. In one we learn how the baby comes out and in the other we learn what to do with it when it does. We wrap dolls in blankets as if they were burritos. Even when they're born the babies are still referred to as food. I leave the hospital overwhelmed and nervous.

I manage to relax, or maybe I'm just exhausted enough to think I'm relaxed, for an hour or so in the evenings. The girls and I eat takeaway souvlakis and fish and chips on my couch. I'm so tired from cooking all day that I order takeaway almost every night. Then I go to bed a nervous wreck. I cry cathartic sobs before I sleep. I'm not even sure why I'm crying. Fear of meeting Pat's parents. Anxiety over not having told Mum about them. I run my hands over my large stomach and say aloud: 'It's okay. Everything is going to be okay.'

THERE'S A BIG DISCUSSION, OF which I am not a part, about where we will go to meet Pat's family. Initially Travis tells me he and I will go to them, which means driving to Warrnambool. We agree on a time, but then a few days later Pat's mother contacts Travis, who in turn contacts me, to tell me she and her husband have decided to come to Thornbury.

'She doesn't want you to have to travel so far. It will be too uncomfortable for you.'

I'm not sure if she means the physical discomfort of being in the car for hours or the emotional discomfort of going to Pat's family home. Either way, I'm grateful. 'That's sweet of her.'

My voice wavers, thick with tears, which Travis ignores. I offer to have them at my flat. He says he will run it by them. He texts me later in the evening.

> Maybe let's just meet at a cafe. They're pretty overwhelmed about this whole thing and I think they just want to have a chat. Eventually, they will want to get to know you better, but that might be a bit much to begin with.

WHEN THE DAY arrives, Travis comes by to pick me up. I'm wearing a linen sack dress that, while it is loose, somehow emphasises my giant stomach more than something tight would. But I don't feel comfortable wearing a tight dress to meet them. It will seem that I'm trying to make a point. I blow-wave my hair and apply pale pink blush and lipstick for the first time in I don't even know how long. I examine myself in the mirror and wonder suddenly if I look immature. I'm saved from an outfit change by Travis knocking on the door.

'You look nice.' He doesn't hug me. 'Are you ready to go?'

I grab a handbag with almost nothing in it – holding my phone and wallet in my hands seems too flippant for such a serious situation – and follow him out the door.

'They're really nice people,' he says. 'Once the shock wears off, they'll be great. I know it.'

'Baby steps.' My voice sounds small, maybe because of my nerves but possibly because I'm out of breath. Travis is walking too fast for me and I don't want to ask him to slow down. He looks nervous too.

I've seen a photo of Pat's mum on Facebook. She's standing with Pat outside a church. It looks like they're at a wedding. She's wearing a blue chiffon dress and a navy jacket. She has dark blonde hair and looks only slightly shorter than Pat, although she's probably wearing heels. She's staring at the camera. A closed-lip smile. She looks delighted – smug, even. Pat is looking at her intently; he isn't ready for the photo.

When Travis and I arrive at the cafe I look around and am certain we must be here first. When Travis announces they're the couple sitting up against the wall I am so stunned I stay rooted in place as he goes over to them. The woman who stands to hug Travis looks far older than the happy woman who stood by her son's side in the photo. Her hair is completely grey and frayed. Her face is sucked dry, covered in lots of tiny lines. When Travis hugs her I'm worried she might collapse beneath him. She's waif-like, a moment from fading away. Pat's father looks more solid. Also grey, but a soft, mousy tint. I can tell from his complexion that he had red hair, like Pat's. He looks less brittle than his wife, but he's certainly not animated. He's blank when Travis shakes his hand, not scowling, but not smiling either.

'This is Eva.' Travis turns and holds his arm out, gesturing to me.

There are no hugs or handshakes. Pat's father looks stern and interested, as though this is very serious, not emotional.

'You're from television.' Pat's mother is staring at me, petrified and bleak.

'Yeah.' I force a smile. 'I'm Eva.'

'Eva, this is Carol and Jim,' says Travis. 'Carol, I told you Eva was an actor.'

'I thought you meant she did amateur theatre or something.' Carol's voice is quiet, expressionless, her mouth downturned. I'm tempted to say that I don't act anymore, but then I don't want them to ask what I *am* doing. I wish we were at my flat – I don't want to go through another excruciating scene in front of waitstaff – but I'm also glad we're not. I couldn't have coped with them seeing my life, judging how small my home is or how worn my furniture.

Travis and I sit across from Pat's parents at the table.

Carol starts looking around for a waiter. 'What would you like to order?'

'I'll just have a water. Sparkling.' I add the last word too forcefully, awkwardly.

Pat's mother is shifting in her seat, trying to get the attention of a waiter. I guess her impatience is situational. That once we've ordered then perhaps she'll start asking me questions. Once the order is taken, however, a silence lands. Pat's mother is staring at me, while his father is looking between me and his wife. I look back at them both. At least nobody is crying.

'You're very beautiful,' Carol says at last.

'I don't feel like it right now.' Again, I'm worried I sound too forceful, that I'll shut her down when I only want to say that I'm uncomfortable.

'Pregnancy is the pits.'

I feel the tiniest bit of relief, a teardrop in this uncomfortable ocean – partly because of Carol's playful comment and partly because, I realise, she is the first woman to admit this to me. Most other older women have just been excited and gleeful about this physical prison. I smile at her, hoping for some camaraderie now, but she is still blank.

It's Jim who starts asking questions about the baby and, for once, I'm thankful for all the bland conversational fodder that pregnancy provides. Questions with yes or no answers. Dates and numbers. At one point he refers to one of Carol's pregnancies.

'You only had morning sickness with one of the boys, didn't you, Carol? Was it Pat?'

Carol blinks. The pause before she answers feels unusually long. 'No, that was Mark.'

'What do your other sons do?' I ask.

The word 'other' rings in the air for a few seconds before Carol replies that one is a teacher and the other a GP.

'We haven't told them,' Carol says. 'We just wanted to meet you first, to . . . to . . . We will tell them.'

I get the sense she stopped herself from saying that it was to check that I'm not insane, dangerous, awful. I don't blame her. 'Take as much time as you need,' I say.

Pat's parents exchange a look – the kind of look that is exchanged between me and Sarah or Annie, or between James's parents, Ian and Maureen. A look that's heavy with conversations I haven't been present for and is therefore impossible for me to interpret.

Carol lifts her tea and takes a sip. Jim smiles at me and the crow's-feet at his temples slope downwards. In that moment he looks exactly like Pat. I take a deep breath and remember the things I wrote out to say.

'I don't expect anything of you, or anything from you. I decided to have this baby because I want it. I have a lot of help around me, and any involvement from you is for your sake, not mine.' It comes out too quickly. I don't leave any space between my points. Travis smiles at me after I've said it, but Carol and Jim just nod. Carol's mouth is a small, clenched frown, like maybe she hasn't smiled ever. They don't respond and I'm unsure whether to go on or change the subject, though talking about anything else would be impossible. Any of the most obvious and easy conversations to grab at – what do you do for work? – seem wildly inappropriate. And we can't talk about the only thing we have in common, their dead son. I imagine asking them, *So where was Pat working when he died?* The thought makes me shudder. I'm too embarrassed even to ask Travis this. We sit in our silence like it's bad weather, our bodies all bound up tight, closed in on ourselves for protection.

When the waiter comes over to ask if we would like to eat, I'm relieved when Pat's parents say no. Carol looks like she hasn't eaten in some time. Her skin looks as heavy as a theatre curtain, hanging off her bones, and has a grey tinge, except under her eyes, where it is pink, almost translucent, rubbed raw. She asks the waiter to top up her teapot with more water. I use the interruption as an opportunity to go to the bathroom.

I look determinedly down at my hands as I wash them in the restroom – I'm afraid if I look at my face in the mirror, I'll see I look sweaty or dishevelled. My forearms look so meaty compared with Carol's bony body.

When I return Jim is asking Travis about his work. Carol is looking down at her lap, as though she's mentally drifted somewhere else, although the moment Travis finishes she lifts her head to look at me.

'What are you doing for work now, Eva? Have you continued acting?'

I tell her about Kate. I make it sound like I actually have a job in casting.

'I didn't know this.' Travis has turned to face me. His upbeat interest clashes like an out-of-tune key change. Carol looks perplexedly at Travis for a moment, as though she's worried that her informant isn't good enough.

I explain that my mum is moving down from Queensland. They ask about growing up there and I mention Sarah and Annie. I don't mention my father and they don't ask. The interaction reminds me of meeting a new boyfriend's parents. Trying to represent the shiniest, least blemished angle of my life. I will reassurance to flow out of my forced smile, but I realise as I'm talking that they don't seem to be taking much in. Or if they are, they don't really care; their expressions are opaque. I'm talking, but I'm disassociating. Thinking how poorly I was taught to act grief. The absurdity of all the wailing we did in drama school. But also, I realise, how necessary. Carol and Jim are as expressive as concrete pillars. Not entertaining for an audience.

Desperate for something to fill the air, I ask if they are still working. I mean the *still* to refer to their age and possible retirement, but as I say it I realise it sounds like maybe they can't work because of their grief. And I realise that maybe this really is the case.

'Jim is still working but I'm not.' Carol is stirring her tea even though she hasn't added milk or sugar.

It's the slowest cup of tea of my life. Eventually we're saved by the waiter arriving with the bill. Travis pays, which strikes me as strange, and suddenly I'm overcome by how strange it is that he sat through the entire event at all.

When we stand from the table there's a moment where I wonder if we will hug. I don't make any moves and neither do they. But on the street outside the cafe, before they leave, Carol touches my arm.

'I have some baby photos of Pat,' she says. 'I thought you might like to see them.'

'I'd love to.'

I smile at her and we still don't hug, but she leaves her hand on my arm. Her hand is cold. I imagine the blood no longer pumping around her body, her heart as inexpressive as she is. She looks me in the eye. 'You're about to become happier than you've ever been.' And finally, she smiles. A moment ago I would've thought a smile would look as absurd on her as a false moustache, but she looks beautiful. Her muscles realign and settle on her face. I feel the relief wash over me like a cool change. Maybe it's the relief of seeing her relax. Maybe it's because this is over now. Or maybe it's because someone has reaffirmed for me what I've wanted to be true for so long.

EVERYTHING IS SMEARED NOW. I played and replayed the same small interactions so often that, filtered through my memory, they took on the meaning I wanted them to have. It wasn't the truth, but it was a version of events I'd worn in. I'd written the script of our story and now I've gone and thrown all the pages in the air.

April

THREE DAYS BEFORE MY DUE date Annie arrives on my doorstep a howling mess. She's broken up with James. At first I think she's telling me that he broke up with her. When I realise it was her, I'm baffled, even irritated; I hadn't known she was going to do this.

Sarah has to move Annie's things out of the Collingwood house by herself – I'm simply too big to help. Instead I sit with Annie in my apartment. James has gone to his parents' place. The idea is to give Annie space, but she says she can't stay there. She shudders when she says it.

Annie's things, packed into boxes, gradually fill my lounge room. All the baby's things are moved to my room. She keeps saying sorry. Promises me she'll find somewhere else to live.

'I'll be the one saying sorry once the baby is born,' I reassure her.

I'm actually happy she's here, despite the state she's in. The only thing I mind is the extra obstacles for me to navigate. Every time I knock something over I'm worried it might be expensive, but she never seems to notice, let alone care. She spends days on my couch, staring into space. Not eating. She hardly talks and when she does, she repeats the same few statements she's said ever since she showed up.

'Four years pass, then five. You think, surely at some point I will want to be with someone else? And then one day I was talking to him about something going on at work and I realised I had no interest in hearing his opinion, and I was looking at him and I realised: Oh no, wait – *this* is what it's like when you don't want to be with the person you're with. All that time I spent wondering about it was such a waste. I should've been enjoying him while I still could.'

I think of the night she lingered here after dinner and the night of her award. I try to remember any time recently when she has expressed affection for or interest in James and I can't. I feel bad for not realising this sooner but, also, Annie rarely expresses much enthusiasm for anything. I feel uncomfortable, deep in my bones, at this realisation because, if Annie wasn't happy, what hope is there for any of us.

I don't say much. I make lots of cups of tea.

We spend our days waiting. Waiting for it to be evening, when Sarah will come over with takeaway and a bottle of wine, which Annie drinks quickly. Sarah stares at the wine glass longingly and occasionally remarks, 'I hope I don't miss you too much longer.' She hasn't had a drink since she got fired and is setting up a website to start working freelance as a social media consultant. Several of her old accounts have already told her they'll move wherever she does.

I have this image of my two friends waltzing across a ballroom. Sarah barrelling towards destruction and Annie with her shit together. Then they swap. As I picture them turning in circles again and again, the image grows bigger and bigger until the dance floor is infinite and this is what the rest of our lives are going to be – taking it in turns to fall apart.

'I feel awful,' says Annie.

'So do I,' I say.

She most likely thinks I'm referring to my physical discomfort, which would be truthful, but I'm thinking about Pat's parents. I tell Annie about meeting them, but she doesn't say anything; she just looks sad. It's the first time she's never had any advice to offer me.

'The shock has to wear off one day.' She says this out of the blue, hours after our conversation, and I'm not even sure what she's referring to. It's true of both of us.

We're waiting for me to go into labour. Waiting for one or, ideally, both of us to feel better. At least the baby has finally turned. The day after Annie arrived I had an appointment with an obstetrician at the hospital, who was pleasantly surprised. She told me a caesarean might not be so likely now. It's as though there wasn't enough room on my plate to worry about one more thing. Annie's misery nudged the baby in the right direction.

On my due date we wake up and eat breakfast together. My bag for the hospital is at the door. Once we've rinsed our dishes we look at each other, staring for a few moments, and then we're laughing, unsure what to do with ourselves.

We spend the day the same way we've spent the preceding days: sitting, staring, uncomfortable. I feel as if a small weight of sadness has lifted. Maybe replaced by anticipation.

I KEEP THINKING of what Annie said to me when she came to my flat the night Sarah got fired. That every day, there are people living with decisions they regret.

I've decided I won't tell our child that heaven exists and that you are there. I'll let it learn the nice stories, tell it things I know and show it photos. I'll let your parents do the same. But I'm not going to suggest that you are somewhere else, conscious. Because if you were, you'd be sitting with the regret that you should feel for having done what you did. And the truth is that everything you felt when you were alive didn't die with you: it has moved into those you left behind. Your parents. Travis. I haven't met your brothers but I'm sure it's in them too. If I go too far down this path, I envisage our child as a growing manifestation of your sorrow. I know it won't just be that, though. It will be an accumulation of your sadness and my sadness and my love and determination and whatever else I'm about to find out.

I know that I am being unfair when I think these things. That you would be horrified by what you have done to your parents and that to be able to do what you did requires a feeling, or a lack of feeling, that is unimaginable to me. I've given myself permission to feel angry at you, and also regret for that anger. Sadness and determination.

My different feelings are like outfits in a limited wardrobe. Each day I wear one, soil it, then put it aside in favour of another. It doesn't sound nice when I put it that way, but cyclical is better than where I was before: wearing down the one costume until it hardly resembled clothes. It's made bearable, too, because one of those outfits is hope. For me, for your parents and, most of all, for our child.

I HEARD A story recently that made me think of you. And like any time I think of you, this story made me both happy and sad. A man and woman meet overseas in South America, where they are both backpacking. They sleep together then go their separate ways. A few weeks later the woman finds out she's pregnant. She flies home to Sweden to get an abortion and, as a courtesy, she messages the man she'd slept with to tell him she is having the termination. He writes back, sympathetic, and offers to share the cost. Weeks go by and she's still pregnant. She decides she's going to keep the baby. She contacts the man again to tell him of her decision, assuring him that as this is a choice she has made herself and not something they planned, she does not expect him to be involved. His initial response is brief and noncommittal, but after a week he contacts her to say he's always wanted children, would like to be a part of his child's life and, while it is a bit forward of him, would she mind if he flew to Sweden to be there for the pregnancy and birth? They're both hesitant, but they also recognise that they each have a right to this child's life. He arrives in Sweden and they start seeing each other casually. Her belly swells as they gradually get to know one another. Late in the pregnancy, at seven months, she miscarries. It's sad, hard, horrible. They grieve together.

All of this happened five years ago and the couple are still together today, happily married. They have no children yet, but it's on the cards.

I THINK OF sealed envelopes and fresh sheets. Moist black earth patted down, dotted with green. Dabbing at chipped paint on a wall with a brush. Ice cubes falling into a clean glass. Threading the needle on a sewing machine.

There are so many ways a life can go.

I'VE TOLD TRAVIS I WILL let him know when the baby arrives. I wonder how much longer he will act as a conduit between Pat's parents and me. I wonder when they will come to meet the baby. He tells me that they're doing well. They're settling into the idea and have even bought the baby a few things.

When I'm three days overdue, he messages to ask if I'm okay. I say that I am. We're both overly polite. A couple of days ago, late at night, Travis sent me a long, rambling text about how terrible I've been, followed by a clipped apology the next morning.

> Sorry. I'm just so angry that he died and now I have someone
> to channel that anger into, but I know that's unfair.

I didn't reply. Not because I'm mad that Travis is mad at me, but because I don't feel I need to hold his hand through this. I can't help but be a little amused by how the tables have turned: Travis always texting me now, anxious about what I'm doing.

A GIFT ARRIVES one day, via the post, from James. A kookaburra hand puppet. There's no note, but I message him to say thanks. I don't say goodbye, although it feels a bit like what this is.

Good luck, mate. Lucky kid has three legends to raise it.

Later the same evening I'm dozing on the couch when Annie's voice wakes me.

'Maybe I made a mistake. Maybe if I'd waited, I would've circled back and loved him again.'

I turn around and see she has the kookaburra on her hand. She's not animating it or moving it, just holds it up still and proud. She looks completely clueless. How I imagine I would look if someone started explaining astrophysics to me.

The gift made me sad, too. I like James. I'll miss seeing him so much and I don't like to think of him heartbroken. But I'm also reminded of Sarah the night of her work Christmas party. How firmly I had to hold my hands on the shoulders of her stumbling and useless body. That's my job now, too. Annie is plastered with grief.

'You can't spend the rest of your life saying you'll get around to doing something you know will make you happy,' I say. 'You just have to do it.'

'But I'm not even happy.' Her response is crushingly immediate.

Later, though, she says, 'At least I can go to Finland now.' She's scrolling on her phone, the smallest microtone of positivity in her voice.

'Were you thinking of moving to Finland?'

'I only thought of it then.'

I feel abandoned already, just by the suggestion. I sit with the feeling for a moment and realise what I actually feel is jealousy. 'I can't move to Finland.'

'If I move to Finland, you can move to Finland.'

'I wonder if they have soap operas in Finland.' I too start scrolling.

'I thought you didn't want to act?'

'Maybe if I was in Finland I would want to act.'

I used to say that moving overseas was what people did if they didn't have any real interests. I think I said that, though, because I was afraid that's what I was – a person without a passion. But, as every man who's ever become prime minister, received a Logie or a Nobel prize has put it: 'It wouldn't mean anything to me without my wife.' And I have two wives. Maybe that's the more important part.

DAYS PASS AND I'm barely able to move. My feet are at their most tender. I'm swollen like a puffer fish and angry like one too. My baby is a bowling ball. It feels as heavy as two bowling balls. I can feel it inside me, weighed down. Sometimes I'm worried my insides – my bladder and intestines – will fall out the bottom of me. All the anxiety I've been carrying is eclipsed by desperation for this to be over, a bleak silver lining.

Annie plays Crowded House. 'You need to relax,' she says. 'That'll bring on labour.' Then one morning she blares Courtney Barnett.

'What are you doing?' I yell over the guitar and twangy vocals.

'Maybe we can blast the baby out of you!' She thrashes her head around and I laugh at her.

It doesn't work.

I lie on the couch, my good friend here, in an entirely different but equally real sort of pain.

I'M SIX DAYS overdue. If I reach ten my doctor will induce labour. I rub my hands up and down over my large stomach, comforted for a moment by my baby's instincts. If I was looking at this situation from outside, I'd be nervous to arrive, too. None of us know what will happen next.

Acknowledgements

THANK YOU, THANK YOU, THANK you. The entire team at Hachette. Vanessa Radnidge, you were handballed this book and you caught it with such kindness and handled it with such skill. Louise Sherwin-Stark, Fiona Hazard, Daniel Pilkington, Emma Harvey, Bella Lloyd and Layla Saadeldine, you're all brilliant. Ali Lavau and Bec Allen for your wise editorial brains (I realise it's clunky to use handballed and handled in the same sentence, thank you). Extra thanks to everyone at Hachette involved in the Richell Prize and the judges of the 2019 prize – Robert Watkins, Hannah Richell, Sarah Schmidt and Steve Sines – I am so honoured my book is one small part of such a special legacy. Robert Watkins, again, I will remember your encouragement and belief in me for a long time. Grace Heifetz, for being a great agent and great to be around in general, I can't wait to do it all again. Erin Sandiford, for the same reasons, you are my favourite thing about Australian publishing. Alissa Dinallo for the perfect cover. The fiction editors who published my stories and supported my career in its earliest days – Elizabeth Flux, Oliver Reeson, Khalid Warsame, Ash Hanson, Maxine Beneba Clarke, Amy Baillieu, Lachy McKenzie, Aviva Tuffield and Rebecca Starford. Morgan Rose for being a mentor – officially, then unofficially – and providing some very direct feedback that lead to the eventual publication of this book. Robyn, Laura, Dom and Brad for reading my stories and writing your own; extra thanks to Robyn for being one of the first people to read a part of this story. The judges of the 2020 Victorian Premier's Award for an Unpublished Manuscript – Ellen Cregan, Luke Horton and Natalie Kon-yu – and to The Wheeler Centre for administering the prize. My colleagues – you light up my life. My friends, old and new, thank you for being so intelligent and so weird and so keen to drink beers with me all the times I don't want to be writing. Mostly, thank you for being so understanding of all the times I can't be drinking beers with you while I'm at work. Life would be so tepid without you all. This book is a treatise to the life sustaining joy of female friendships, so extra thanks must go to Soph, Bec, Lauren, Jasmin, Thea, Jamaica and Erin (again) – without you I'd've crumpled to a sack of bones on the floor some point in my twenties. Fierce baby-catcher, Alice Pemberton, for some last-minute fact checking and for being a great new friend also. My family, you've been my cheerleaders since forever and I really hope you like the book. Failing that, I hope it's at least more entertaining than all the ballet concerts you sat through. Thanks also to my newer, second family, the O'Connors, for your support and your kindness. And finally to Scott, for reading all my stories and for being here with me, every single day.

This novel was written on the stolen land of the Wurundjeri People of the Kulin Nation. I pay my respects to Elders past, present and emerging.